more...

IN THE DARK

FORGET ME NOT

ALSO BY MARLISS MELTON

Forget Me Not
In the Dark
Time to Run
Next to Die
Don't Let Go
Too Far Gone

SHOW NO
FEAR

MARLISS
MELTON

FOREVER

NEW YORK   BOSTON

Copyright © 2009 by Marliss Arruda
All rights reserved. Except as permitted under the U.S. Copyright Act of 1976, no part of this publication may be reproduced, distributed, or transmitted in any form or by any means, or stored in a database or retrieval system, without the prior written permission of the publisher.

Book design by Giorgetta Bell McRee
Cover design by Christine Foltzer
Cover art by Franco Accornero

Forever
Hachette Book Group
237 Park Avenue
New York, NY 10017
Visit our Web site at www.HachetteBookGroup.com.

Forever is an imprint of Grand Central Publishing.
The Forever name and logo is a trademark of Hachette Book Group, Inc.

Printed in the United States of America

First Printing: September 2009

10 9 8 7 6 5 4 3 2 1

This story is written in honor of three American contractors, Marc Gonsalves, Keith Stansell, and Thomas Howes, who were held captive by Colombian rebels for five years and five months. While I was researching this story, you were all still hostages. It had been my intent to raise awareness of your plight, so that you wouldn't be forgotten. My prayers were answered when you were bravely rescued on July 2, 2008, in a combined effort involving the Colombian army and intelligence agents. Welcome home, gentlemen. You were never as alone as you must have felt you were. May you find peace with the past and fulfillment in the future.

ACKNOWLEDGMENTS

Lucy's story has been, by far, the toughest, most rewarding book to write in my entire Navy SEALs series. It took extensive research into the testimonials of those who've been held captive in Colombia, have aided the Colombian government in suppressing terrorism, or have interacted with the FARC in some personal way. My thanks goes to Glenn Heggstad, who described his captivity in Colombia in his testimonial *Two Wheels Through Terror*, giving me insight into that awful experience. My fullest respect and awe go to Russell Martin Stendal, author of *Rescue the Captors 2*, who, through his fearless missionary work, has converted hundreds of FARC rebels to the Christian faith, causing them to denounce violence and seek a peaceful resolution to the ongoing civil war.

Also, I could not have written such a realistic story without the advice of intelligence officers who cannot be named, as well as Navy SEAL commander Mark Divine. Special recognition must be given to retired Australian

Services Regiment sniper Chris Nally, for advising me on all matters military. You are my hero!

Lastly, I would be remiss were I not to thank Janie, who believed in my ability to craft a story even without her daily input. I'm afraid I have to agree with Lucy, Janie girl. Dodging bullets with a partner is way more fun.

"What happens in the jungle stays in the jungle."

—INGRID BETANCOURT,
FARC hostage for six years, four months, and nine days

SHOW NO
FEAR

PROLOGUE ══════════

Maiquetía, Venezuela

Lucy Donovan, top-notch case officer for the CIA, considered herself virtually fearless. But the Elite Guards' threat to blow up the warehouse, with her trapped inside it, made her skin feel too tight. She wasn't afraid to die, but thoughts of being blown to pieces touched on a memory so raw and painful that she came closer to panicking than she ever had in her life.

With a knife slipped in her hands at the last minute by a sympathetic Elite Guardsman, she had severed the flexicuffs that had kept her bound to a chair. The window through which a warm, sulfurous breeze wafted offered escape and certain survival. Only Lucy couldn't jump out yet. She had a job to finish—to find the CDs she'd been forced to hide when the Elite Guard first stormed the building.

Beaten and bleeding, with seconds draining away like sand through an hourglass, she slipped from the office to slink along the catwalk edging the outer wall.

The creaking of hinges one level below her made her freeze. *What now?* she wondered, uncertain whether the sound was real or just imagined. With no time to guess, she continued to search for the line of chalk marking the support beam behind which she'd hidden the CDs.

A scuffling sound confirmed that she was not alone in this vast, echoing warehouse. Footfalls, so stealthy they gave her pause, crept along the cement slab below.

Two people? Three?

Awash in a cold sweat, she wondered who they might be. *Damn it!* If they interfered with her exodus, they were all going to end up in little pieces!

Seeing the line of chalk, at last, she bent to retrieve the CDs from the aperture behind the beam. *Plop!* Blood dripped from her chin, landing loudly on the grooved metal flooring. At the same time, the stairs leading from the first floor to the second gave a groan.

Lucy held her breath. Someone was ascending the steps to the catwalks above. If he was equipped with night vision, he would discover her almost immediately. Her only option was to disappear.

Casting a desperate eye around her, she realized the metal supports for the catwalk offered possibilities.

Stuffing the CDs into the pocket of her cargo pants, she stepped onto the railing and reached for the horizontal bar high over her head. In a move called a roof assault, she pulled her feet, then her body, up and over the bar. The effort sent blood rushing past her eardrums, challenging her equilibrium. Had she imagined it, or had someone called her name?

The silhouette of a man edged cautiously into view. Friend or foe? she wondered, praying she'd climbed too high for him to see her. He wore night-vision gear, so it was impossible to see his face, to determine his affiliation. With a pack on his back, an assault rifle, and more gear strapped to his belt, he looked like a Navy SEAL, but she couldn't be certain.

She could tell that he was following her blood trail. With his gaze angled downward, he still hadn't noticed her, clinging to the support rod several feet over his head. She watched as he passed directly below her, crossing to the beam where she'd hidden the CDs.

The blood coursing down her face proved problematic. She tried to staunch the flow with her sleeve, but a droplet escaped, falling in slow motion to hit the metal riser with a musical *thunk*.

Lucy flinched. The commando shrank out of sight at the sound, hiding his broad-shouldered frame behind the slender beam. "Lucy!" he whispered from his hiding place.

At the sound of her name, Lucy's tense muscles went lax. Her body slid bonelessly off the bar. She hung by her sweaty fingertips for a second before dropping gracefully to her feet. "Here I am," she said, relieved beyond measure that she was being rescued and not hunted down.

He spun into view, lifting the visor of his night-vision gear, and Lucy's heart stopped.

It had to be the greasepaint that made him look exactly like her college boyfriend, James. The athletic body didn't jibe with her mental recollection. But as she took a curious step closer, his expression of horror confirmed her observation.

"James Atwater," she breathed, ignoring his concern over her ravaged face, amazed that her voice could sound so calm when her heart was trotting. "What the hell are you doing here?" But then her knees betrayed her, going suddenly weak.

As she started to sway, he leapt forward, catching her against him. "Lucy!"

"We need to get out of here," she warned him, grateful for the strength in the arm that kept her vertical. "The captain of the Elite Guard gave orders to blow up the building."

Thoughts shifted across his face, too quickly for her to gauge. "Let's go," he rasped. Anchoring her to his right side, he hustled her toward the stairs. "I found her, Vinny," he said into his mic. "Exit the building pronto. She needs medical attention."

"I'm fine," Lucy insisted. She could use a few stitches, but aside from that she was good to go.

He slanted her a frowning look, one that took in her battered appearance, the ponytail that hung askew, and the torn T-shirt hanging out of her pants. *Bullshit,* said his disapproving gaze.

A deafening explosion spilled them to their knees. With her heart in her throat, Lucy expected the building to incinerate. Only it didn't. She shared a look of relief with James, who hauled her to her feet. Together they raced for the nearest exit.

"This one's closer," she insisted, yanking him toward a door tucked out of sight.

They flew out of it, setting off an alarm, the wail of which was drowned out by the clatter of the nearby firefight. She could only assume the commandos had cut off the Elite Guard as they sought to escape with their cargo of weapons.

"Run!" James urged, impelling her across the expanse of sandy earth. Her legs felt strangely leaden, like she was running in a dream. But if all this was a dream, then she'd awaken to find that James was just a figment of her imagination, a composite of long-forgotten yearnings.

At last he pulled her to a stop, holding her fiercely to him as they caught their breath. Speaking into his mouthpiece, he tasked one of his men to call for a helicopter extract.

Listening to his voice—familiar, certainly, but deeper and more resonant—she wondered what circumstances had compelled him to become a Special Forces soldier. The last she'd heard from him, he was working on a master's in engineering at MIT, yet here he was, as hard-bodied as any action hero and, by all appearances, the officer in charge of his teammates. Who could have imagined?

When they got a moment to talk, she would assuage her curiosity.

"We'll be there in a sec," he said into his mic. But then he glanced sharply up at the sky. "No, we won't. Here come the Cobras. Get down!"

With that scant warning, he tackled Lucy to the ground, somehow managing not to crush her. Lying with her left cheek pressed into the sandy earth and blood pooling in her eye socket, Lucy drifted into memories of the past. She had broken things off with James after the tragic bombing many years ago. She'd never imagined they would meet again like this.

Boom, boom, boom, boom! The ground shook as gunships pounded the fleeing convoy. Secondary explosions followed the attack for minutes on end, frustrating her desire to connect the dots.

"Why didn't you answer me in the warehouse when I called for you?" he shouted, looking perplexed and frustrated.

"I think I blacked out for a minute," she explained, recalling how the blood had rushed past her eardrums during the roof assault.

He was astute enough not to ask any probing questions, though he could surely feel the CD cases in her pocket, gouging his thigh.

As silence descended at last over the dusty, foul-smelling air, Lucy went to ask a question of her own— *How on earth did you become a commando?*—but James hauled her to her feet, cutting her off before the words reached her lips. "Echo Platoon, rally up at the Hummer," he clipped. "Let's get out of here while we still can."

Their aerial attack would summon the entire populist army.

"Do you have your car key, by any chance?" he asked Lucy.

"Not anymore." It'd been seized by the Elite Guard. "But I keep a spare under the bumper," she told him.

"Excellent." He was all business, as was she. Obviously, this wasn't the time or the place for small talk. They weren't young people anymore with the freedom to explore their options. James Atwater had a job to do, and so did she.

The sooner these commandos whisked her to safety, the sooner she could deliver these CDs to headquarters.

James Atwater might have been the most promising fish she'd ever caught and released, but Lucy Donovan was way too busy to even consider reeling him back in.

CHAPTER 1 ═══════

Ten months later

Lucy Donovan loathed wearing pantyhose almost as much as she detested her three-inch stiletto heels. But stilettos, paired with a short skirt to show off her runner's legs, gave her an advantage very few men had: the power of distraction. And since she couldn't wear her favorite accessory—the Ruger she liked to keep strapped to her thigh—she had to arm herself in subtler ways.

The staccato of her heels as she headed for the clandestine CIA station in New York City helped to soothe the frisson of unease that tingled up and down her spine.

Following her extraction from Venezuela, the CIA's in-house psychologist had diagnosed her with post-traumatic stress disorder. She'd been prescribed mild sedatives, which she'd flushed down the toilet, and was benched in paperwork hell until they deemed her fully operative. Apparently she had passed her most recent evaluation with flying colors or she wouldn't be here.

Thank God. Her imposed R & R was finally over! She couldn't wait to get back into the game.

Swiping her CAC card by the engraving that read Department of the Treasury, Lucy shoved down a memory of the Elite Guardsman's fist slamming into her cheekbone. You didn't get to play with the big boys if you couldn't handle what they dished out. She'd known that when she'd signed up.

Crossing the marble foyer, she surrendered her briefcase for inspection while negotiating the retina scan and then the metal detector.

"Have a good day," murmured a security guard, his gaze sliding helplessly down her legs as he handed back her briefcase.

Sparing him a cool smile, she turned toward the elevators and, seeing one open, hurried to catch it, leaping into the soundproof space just as the doors began to close.

Oh, shit! It took all her training to conceal her astonishment at coming face-to-face with James again, though she really shouldn't have been surprised, having discovered that he was HUMINT, a sector of the military specially trained to support the CIA.

"Hello, James," she greeted him, managing to sound indifferent as she went to push the right button and found it already lit.

"Lucy," he said, looking stunned, a little perplexed. His brandy-colored eyes slid from her glossy ponytail to her high heels. "How are you?" he asked, his gaze centering on the tiny scar on her forehead.

She could tell he was picturing her as he'd last seen her, with a river of blood bisecting her face. "Good," she insisted, irritated by his frankly protective look. Hell, she wasn't made of porcelain.

The elevator rose almost imperceptibly, leaving her no choice but to breach the awkward chasm between them. As with their last encounter, this grown-up James threw her off-kilter. He'd had plans to become an architect. Yet even in a gray suit and white-collared dress shirt, he looked like an advertisement for the U.S. Special Forces. It hadn't just been the greasepaint that had made him look forbidding. Dressed as a civilian, he looked lean and powerful and downright dangerous to mess with.

"I'm sorry I didn't get to thank you," she began, having to clear her throat first. "I was flown off the carrier before I got the chance—"

"You're welcome," he said, cutting her off. His gaze jumped to the buttons lighting up over the door, an indication that either he wasn't interested in hearing her excuses or he didn't require her thanks.

Okay. Lucy squared her shoulders and looked away. This encounter had the feel of an awkward morning-after situation, only they definitely hadn't had sex the last time they'd been together. Too bad.

"What happened to becoming an architect?" She just had to ask him.

The gaze that swung her way reflected a stark emptiness. "Nine-eleven," he answered flatly. "My father died in one of the twin towers."

Lucy's stomach fell to her feet. Oh, no. His father had been the lead architect working for a banking firm. He and James had been as close as father and son could be. No doubt James had fed on that bond to motivate him through the toughest military training conceivable. She'd known he was smart enough. Devotion to his father's memory must have given him the mental toughness. "I'm so sorry," she murmured sincerely.

With a nod, he looked away. The elevator slowed and the doors slid open.

With too much to think about, Lucy stepped out before him, heading down the hall toward the designated meeting room. She sensed rather than heard James following right behind her, his footfalls silent on the sturdy carpet.

As she reached the meeting room, curiosity prompted her to glance back.

"We must be headed to the same meeting," he observed, coming to stand beside her.

Concealing her surprise and studying James from the corner of her eye, she gave a swift knock on the door. Why would they be summoned to the same meeting? Was this about the warehouse incident, or would they be working together on something new?

"Come!" boomed the familiar voice of SIS Gordon Banks, Lucy's supervisor. "Ah, good, you're both on time," said the black man, glancing at his watch as they stepped inside. "Close the door, would you, Lieutenant?"

Two men stood with Gordon, the trio backdropped by the dazzling architecture of the UN Plaza visible through the floor-to-ceiling windows. Gordon's companions were middle-aged, one stocky and bald, the other slim and dark.

"Lucy, Gus, thanks for coming. This is our Colombian branch chief, Louis Stokes," Gordon said, introducing the balding man first. "Louis, Lucy Donovan."

Stokes pumped her hand enthusiastically. "I've heard stories about you," he warned.

"All lies," she assured him, her heartbeat accelerating at the mention of Colombia, so close to Venezuela and the memories of violence that clamored within the locked box in her mind.

Gordon turned to James. "And this is Navy SEAL

Lieutenant James Augustus Atwater, otherwise known as
Gus."

Gus? mused Lucy. Apparently, he had reverted to his
middle name. It suited his transformation, she decided.

"Gus and Lucy, I want you to meet Carlos Santos,
director of human rights with the United Nations. At least,
that's his cover," Gordon amended. "He's with CESID,
the Spanish military intelligence service."

"Un placer," professed the Spaniard, bowing slightly
over Lucy's fingers. "I hear you studied in Valencia while
in college, *señorita,*" he said, turning back to Lucy after
shaking Gus's hand.

"Yes, I did." Her first experience with terror, a roadside bomb that'd killed three friends and dozens of others,
had persuaded her to join the CIA after graduation.

"I have family in the area. I myself am from Anda-
lucía," he added, unaware of the memories splintering her
thoughts.

"Carlos is going to be working with the two of you on
a special project," Gordon interrupted, recapturing Lucy's
attention and gesturing to the briefing table. "Let's all take
a seat. Did you want any coffee first, Lucy? Gus?"

They both demurred, facing off across the table as
the others took seats around them. Glancing at James's—
Gus's—expression, Lucy found it shuttered, unreadable.

"Lucy, I think I told you last year that the Navy lets us
borrow Gus from time to time," Gordon recollected, sliding an envelope marked top secret in front of her.

"Yes, sir," she affirmed. It was hard to get her mind
around it. James, who should have been an architect, had
become one of the most dangerous men on earth.

"You and he will be working on a common assignment," he continued, confirming her earlier guess. "I

assume the names Mike Howitz and Jay Barnes ring a bell?"

"Of course." Howitz and Barnes had been Lucy's colleagues, case officers like her who'd been assigned to Venezuela. In the coup last year, they'd been captured by Colombian terrorists, Las Fuerzas Armarias de Colombia, who'd come across the border at San Cristobal and abducted them.

The FARC, who called themselves advocates for the common man, processed and sold cocaine, terrorized villagers, and ransomed hostages to fund their forty-year-old rebellion against the Colombian government.

Lucy had assumed her colleagues were doomed.

The U.S. did not negotiate with terrorists. America had stubbornly ignored the FARC's demands to release Commander Gitano, one of their top political prisoners. Locked in a stalemate with the U.S. government, the FARC might hold Mike and Jay indefinitely, unless some neutral party like the Red Cross stepped in to mediate...

"The United Nations is sponsoring a team to spearhead negotiations for their release," Gordon announced, his words mirroring Lucy's thoughts. He nodded at the Spaniard. "Mr. Santos is one of the UN volunteers, along with a Frenchman, an Italian, a Turk, and two more Spaniards." He divided an enigmatic look between Lucy and Gus. "That's going to be your cover," he added.

Lucy glanced at Gus and found him frowning at her boss.

"Gus just completed Spanish-language school at the Farm. Lucy speaks fluent Spanish and is familiar with the culture," Gordon added. "We have a liaison agreement with the CESID, who are the only folks who'll know your true identity."

Lucy glanced at the dark-eyed Spaniard, who sent her an encouraging smile.

"Here's the cruncher," Gordon added, recapturing her attention. "We don't have much time to prepare. You'll need to fly into Bogotá on Monday," he announced.

Monday? Then she wouldn't have to step foot in paperwork hell ever again. She'd been hankering for an assignment for months now, so why wasn't she experiencing a powerful victory rush? Was she picking up on Gus's reticence to work with her? Or did she have doubts that she'd made a full recovery?

"Furthermore," Gordon continued, with a steady eye on Lucy, "given the humanitarian nature of your cover, you won't be able to carry any weapons or any overt communication devices of any kind," he added apologetically.

Her mind flashed back to the last time she'd had her gun taken away from her. *Oh, no.*

"The FARC are going to march you deep into the jungle," Gordon added, causing her to break into a sweat. "They're going to strip you of everything but your underwear and boots. Any weapons or cell phones you might try to conceal would be discovered," he explained.

Lucy's lips began to tingle. She could sense Gus's growing tension as he glared down at the table, refusing to meet her gaze.

"You don't have to take this assignment if you're not ready, Lucy," her supervisor added, no doubt aware of her diagnosis. "But Barnes and Howitz are your colleagues. I thought I'd give you first bite at this since you'd worked in-country with those two."

Lucy angled her chin at him. "Of course I'm ready," she scoffed, aware that Gus was finally looking straight at her. "Is that the reason Lieutenant Atwater is accompanying me?" she asked, with sudden insight. "For my protection?" If she was going to get her moxie back, she had to do this on her own without a freaking babysitter.

Her supervisor frowned. "As it happens, Lucy, a squad of SEALs from Gus's team has already deployed to Bogotá. They're assigned to the Joint Intelligence Center at the American embassy, where they've been gathering intel. Those SEALs are going to track your progress via microchips implanted under your skin. Your job is to discover, if you can, the coordinates to the camp where Howitz and Barnes are held, keeping in mind that the FARC tend to relocate every couple of weeks. When the UN negotiations fail— which we expect to be the case—the SEALs should have enough data to drop in and wrest our boys out by force."

"How can I pass on data if I can't carry a cell phone or radio?" Gus chimed in, his tone inscrutable.

"*We,*" Lucy corrected him, earning a piercing glance. She cocked an eyebrow at him.

"We'll cover that shortly," Gordon promised. "In addition to finding Barnes and Howitz, I want you to make a full report on the FARC's present circumstances. The Colombian army says they've cut off the rebels' supplies and killed off their leaders and it's just a matter of time before they disintegrate completely. We want to know if that's the case. Go ahead and open your envelopes," he added with a nod.

With an uncharacteristic tremor in her fingers, Lucy untied the flap and reached for the passport inside. As she cracked the cover, she assimilated her new identity with a shiver of excitement and a renewed sense of calm. This was a familiar process, the feelings of taking on a new identity, fraught with nuanced details, first internalized and then worn like a second skin.

The name beside her photograph was Luna Delgado de Aguiler, born in Valencia, Spain. The pages of her passport, heavily stamped, indicated extensive service to the United Nations. According to her bio, she was an associate human affairs officer working and living in New York City, married to Gustavo Aguiler, a human rights officer.

"You and Gus will be traveling as a married couple," Gordon added, confirming her sudden stab of suspicion.

Lucy's heart skipped a beat. She glanced across the table and found Gus scowling in concentration at his passport. Thankfully, there was no ring on his left hand, nor any telltale sign that he had ever worn one. At least she wouldn't be treading on another woman's turf, not that it would matter if she were.

They were professionals with a job to do. It wouldn't make a lick of difference if he was married or not.

Gordon turned and gestured to the Colombian branch chief. "Stokes, why don't you take over here?"

Hours later, her mind saturated with as much information as she could memorize, Lucy felt a renewed sense of certainty. The assimilation process had restored her accustomed self-confidence, reassuring her that her PTSD was a thing of the past. She could do this. The episode in Venezuela hadn't caused any lasting damage.

But first she and James needed to have a good heart-to-heart, which he seemed to be avoiding.

She hurried to catch up with him, trapping him as he stood waiting for the elevator. "James—Gus," she amended with a self-directed grimace. That was going to take a little getting used to.

He swung around slowly, his expression both guarded and disapproving.

"Would you like to go out for a drink?" she brazened, ignoring the invisible shield erected around him. It was obvious he wasn't feeling social. "We have a lot of catching up to do," she insisted. They weren't going to be able to proceed without airing their differences—whatever they were.

"We're going to dinner soon," he countered. Carlos had instructed them to meet him at a local restaurant, where they would practice their new roles as Mr. and Mrs. Gustavo de Aguiler. She sure hoped Gus's Spanish had improved.

Feeling rebuffed, she tried a different tactic. "Well, I can see you're just thrilled to be working with me," she quipped with sarcasm. "What's the matter? Never worked with a woman before?" she demanded archly.

He looked away, stuffing his hands into his pockets. "From what I recall, you were the one with issues about having me for a partner," he quietly reminded her.

Touché. Lucy's face turned hot. "I'm not used to working with anyone else," she explained. "I work alone. No offense intended."

His gaze slid back in her direction. This time he let her see the concern and dread warring in his eyes. "When's it going to end for you, Luce?" he asked her suddenly, ignoring the elevator as the door slid open. "When will you have had *enough?*"

"Oh, come on." She waved away his words with a quirk of her lips and a toss of her head. She got a sudden feeling that he knew more about her than she knew about him. Moreover, his concern was unwelcome; it undermined her self-confidence. "So I took a little beating on my last assignment, so what? I've taken worse and still landed on my feet," she assured him, giving him a not-so-playful push.

Beneath the linen-and-silk blend of his suit, he felt as solid as a tree.

Nor did he reciprocate her smile. His lips remained locked in a horizontal line as his eyes roamed her face, taking in every tiny trophy scar that gave testament to her words. "You mean like when you were stabbed by an asset in Madrid in '04?" he demanded quietly.

The breath disappeared from Lucy's lungs. He *did* know more than he was supposed to.

"Or maybe you're thinking of the car accident in Morocco that put you in traction for six months?"

"Who told you about that?" The elevator doors slid shut, giving up on them to heed summons from a higher floor.

"We work for the same people," he retorted. He took a sudden step toward her, causing her nerves to leap with awareness. Maybe he wasn't any taller, but his shoulders were certainly broader, his neck thicker, creating an illusion of immense height. His scent curled into her nostrils, so endearingly familiar that her heart clutched with remembered affection. "I want you to turn down this assignment, Lucy," he growled, his words cancelling out her tender feelings. "Go tell Gordon you've changed your mind, that you're not ready for this."

"The hell I'm not ready for it!" Lucy protested, her spine stiffening with affront. "Why wouldn't I be?" *Why, indeed?* asked a tiny voice inside her.

A ruddy color stained Gus's cheekbones. "Lucy, those guards beat the hell out of you," he grated with quiet force. "For all I know, they even raped you."

"They didn't," she retorted, tamping down memories

that sought to escape. "What's more, I didn't need your help," she added, heaping on false confidence to keep pressure on the lid. "I'd gotten what I came for, and I was on my way out."

"Congratulations," he said with a scathing look. "Just answer me this, Lucinda." He used her full name knowing she hated it. "When is it going to end for you? Or are you going to keep this up until you're good and dead?"

"I don't know," she answered him honestly, hating that he was feeding that tiny fear still lingering inside her. "I've never considered quitting. Have you?"

"I thought maybe it was over for you," he continued, ignoring her question. "You've been lying low for ten months now. Why can't you just keep doing that?"

"You've been spying on me?" she cried in disbelief.

"I told you. We work for the same people," he repeated. "Now, go tell Gordon you don't want this assignment," he repeated, crowding her with his larger body.

"No," she countered, giving him her most stubborn look.

In a gesture that she recognized from their college days, he turned away, jamming his fingers through his russet-brown, neatly trimmed hair. With a muttered curse, he punched the button for the elevator again.

His vehemence gave Lucy pause—that and the implication that he truly cared about her well-being. "Why does it matter to you so much, anyway?" she asked, remembering with a pang the tenderness he used to show her.

He swung slowly back around. "Because now I'm your partner," he articulated with a tremor in his voice. "And now it's my freaking job to keep you alive."

"I don't need you to keep me alive," she retorted. The

thought was ridiculous. She'd done fine on her own all these years.

His eyelashes came together as he glared at her with flashing eyes. "Is that right?" he countered softly. "How many ops have you done in the jungle, Lucy?"

She opened her mouth to shoot back an answer, then closed it with a snap. "None," she admitted, self-consciousness pinching her cheeks.

He raked her with another look, this one reflecting honest fear and concern. Then he turned and walked away.

"Where are you going?" she asked, frustrated by her inability to get a good read on him. Why was he so against her involvement?

Without a word, he pushed through the door marked EXIT.

She had the answer to her spoken question, but not the unspoken one. He was taking the stairs.

CHAPTER 2 ═══════

A thumping noise in the hotel room next door brought Gus's eyes wide open. He had just lain down, drained by their mentally exhausting dinner with Carlos, doomed to suffer dreams of Lucy imperiled in the jungle. It was 11:30 p.m., and by the sound of things she was still awake, doing jumping jacks.

He already knew she rarely slept. His sources claimed she liked to run at night, up to ten miles at a time. Maybe she was warming up for a run.

At night in New York City?

He sat up with a start, throwing off the covers. Surely she was smarter than that.

In the dark, he fumbled for his sweatpants, searched for his socks and sneakers. He was jamming his head through a T-shirt when her door thudded shut.

Shit!

Feeling a little like a stalker, he peeked outside his own door in time to see her turn the corner. She had changed out of a tiny black dress and into shorts, a jogging bra, and tennis shoes. She wouldn't thank him for trying to dissuade her from a run, any more than she'd thanked him for suggesting she turn down the assignment. Doing that had driven a wedge between them that even Carlos had detected, urging them to reconcile their differences before the outset of their trip.

There was no time like the present, thought Gus. With their plane departing in two days, they might as well strike a truce. As partners, they had to think and act as one.

Darting down the hallway, he turned the corner in time to see the elevator close with her inside it. Punching the button for a second elevator, he waited to see where she stopped—the mezzanine level, where the indoor gym was located. Of course, she wasn't so stupid as to go for a run outside.

By the time he joined her in the glass-enclosed fitness center, she was running like a mouse on a wheel, flying like the wind and getting nowhere.

The look of surprise on her face was worth losing sleep for. He was glad to see they had the place to themselves.

"What are you doing here?" she demanded, removing a pair of earbuds.

His gaze slid to the alluring expanse of her bare abdomen, which looked smooth and supple and perfectly feminine despite her level of fitness.

He stepped onto the treadmill next to hers and powered it up. "Might as well get used to it," he countered. "From now on, where you go, I go. That's how it works in the jungle."

For a moment they ran wordlessly, side by side. Worried that she might stick her earbuds back in, he said abruptly, "Carlos suggested we bury the hatchet. Maybe we should talk."

Her continued silence forced an apology from him

first. "Look, I'm sorry for my negative response this afternoon. If you were in my shoes, you'd have done the same thing," he assured her.

She flicked a considering glance at him but held her thoughts to herself, keeping aloof.

"Is there anything you wanted to ask me?" he offered in desperation. "You know, to even the playing field."

Another considering glance. "Okay," she relented. "How long have you been a SEAL?"

"Five years," he replied.

"But nine-eleven happened eight years ago," she pointed out, her expression not without sympathy.

Eight years later, his heart still cramped with grief whenever the subject came up. "My father would've expected me to finish school," he explained. "So I got my master's and then I went to Navy OCS. I needed the time to get in shape before I enrolled in BUDs." Officer Candidate School had been a walk in the park compared to BUDs.

"Did you make it the first time?" she asked, clearly cognizant of the rigors.

"Rolled out the first time with a strained Achilles tendon. I made it the second time, did two years of qualification training, and went to Afghanistan with SEAL Team Three," he added, recalling a hot, dry wind, the fear of never knowing where the enemy was.

"Is that what you wanted?"

"I wanted to understand the enemy. That's what drew me to intel in the first place. To understand them is to beat them, right?"

She grimaced, astute enough to understand that the question was rhetorical. "So, how long have you been loaned out to the agency?"

"Three years," he said, knowing what was coming next.

"Why didn't you just look me up instead of spying on me?"

Was that irritation in her voice, or had he hurt her feelings? "Keeping tabs isn't spying," he rationalized. "Besides, you wanted your space. You made that pretty clear eight years ago."

She'd explained in a final e-mail to him that she was joining the CIA, cutting ties with the past—for her own protection, allegedly. Her message, followed six months later by his father's death, had made 2001 the loneliest year of Gus's life.

"Why bother keeping tabs on me, then?" she demanded.

She'd been the love of his life, the one he'd wanted to stay with forever. "Just curious," he insisted, avoiding her gaze.

He hadn't been able to help himself. The first week the agency had acquired him, he'd made inquiries, only to be dissuaded by rumors of Lucy's fearlessness. Thoughts of rekindling a relationship recoiled in the face of reckless devotion to Uncle Sam. His own job was dangerous. He couldn't afford to extend his heart to a woman with an immortality complex.

"So when did you train in the jungle?" she wanted to know.

"Last year in Venezuela. A group of us went to train the Elite Guard so that the moderates had a fighting chance."

"And then they switched sides," she finished, visibly quelling a shudder.

"You should never have gone back to that warehouse," he scolded, glimpsing its lingering effect on her.

Jade green eyes flashed in his direction. "Look, it's over. Just drop it, will you?"

"Is it really?" he countered skeptically. "Can you tell me you don't think about it every time you close your eyes to sleep? Is that why you don't sleep, Luce?"

Without warning, she slammed the red button on the display before her, bringing her machine to a sudden halt. "What are you implying? That I have PTSD?" she demanded, breasts rising and falling as she turned to grip the handrail and to glare at him.

Powering down his own machine, he faced her squarely. He could smell her perfume, warmed by the heat of her body. Combined with the anger in her eyes and the flush in her cheeks, the scent was intoxicating. "Who wouldn't have PTSD after an experience like that?" he reasoned gently, wishing she'd just let him take her into his arms and tell her everything would be okay.

"Get out," she ordered, jerking her chin at the exit. "You're wasting your breath trying to talk me out of this assignment. Just go. Get some sleep. I'll see you on the plane to Bogotá." Turning her shoulder on him, she powered up her treadmill once again, cranking it to high as she stuck the earbuds back in and took off.

So much for trying to bury the hatchet. With a nod of defeat, Gus stepped off the treadmill and headed for the door. Sadly, the rumors regarding Lucy Donovan were true. She was a maniac, devoted to her career.

At the rate she was going she would run herself into the ground before her thirtieth birthday.

LUCY SHOOK TWO ADVIL TABLETS into her hand and regarded them in her palm, lit up by the bright sunlight shining through the airplane window. The 747's jet engines hummed serenely at an altitude of fifty thousand feet. The hour was fast approaching when over-the-counter pain medication would be a luxury she could only wish for, right up there with clean socks and a toothbrush.

Gus dropped into the seat beside her, startling her. It wasn't fair that men could pee so fast. "What's hurting?" he demanded in Spanish, spying the little pills in her hand.

She had discovered the other night that, yes, Gus now spoke fluent Spanish, but with a slight American accent that hopefully none of the European UN team members would detect. Carlos had suggested he tell everyone he had a Danish grandmother. That would also explain his height and coloration.

"I have a headache," she lied, tossing back the pills with the remainder of her Sprite. Truth was, the spot where her microchip was planted, on the back of her right hip, was throbbing.

Gus's protective hovering set her teeth on edge. Through prescription-free lenses, similar to the glasses he'd worn before the navy paid for corrective laser surgery, he studied her with grave concern. The glasses were part of his cover, meant to downplay his over-the-top physical condition and make him look more like a geek. Thanks to his intelligent demeanor, he managed to pull off the illusion.

Since taking off from Dulles on this nonstop trip to Bogotá, Colombia, he'd surprised her by showering her with the gentle affection of a new husband, treating her much the way he had when they were dating, not at all like the SEAL who'd tried scaring her off this assignment two days ago.

"Are you sure it's not your hip?" he murmured, annoying her with his acuity.

"Positive," she retorted, jiggling the ice chips in her cup.

"Can you look at me and say that?"

Turning her head, she sent him a hard glare, but lying straight to his face wasn't easy. "I'm positive," she repeated.

"You know, it's not too late to turn around, Luce," he mentioned quietly.

In Spanish, her shortened name came out as *luz,* meaning "light." Lucy sucked in a tight breath. "My parents are having marital problems, okay?" she hissed, bringing up a situation that had weighed on her thoughts since she'd limped into her apartment after her microchip procedure and discovered her mother had moved in with her.

His expression of dismay would've been comical if the subject wasn't so touchy. "Damn," he muttered. "Sorry to hear that."

Lucy popped an ice chip in her mouth and pulverized it between her teeth.

"How long have they been married?" he asked her quietly.

"Twenty-nine years," she replied, peering into her cup for another ice chip.

"They'll work it out," he reassured her. "It's probably just a bump in the road of life."

"I don't know." She sighed with worry. "My mother's living in my apartment."

"So that's what's bothering you," he said with a thoughtful nod.

"Yes," she retorted.

"You're sure you're being honest with yourself."

Lucy's temper simmered. "Yes," she repeated. "Would you drop it already? We've already been through this. *I am not backing out,*" she added in English.

Without warning, his mouth covered hers, muffling further words.

Lucy's breath caught in her throat at the feel of his smooth, warm lips against hers. Memories, unsettling for their blinding sweetness, caught her off guard.

The pressure eased. *"Cuidado,"* he whispered against her lips. *Careful.* They were supposed to remain a hundred percent faithful to their covers, speaking only in Spanish.

Did he think he could manipulate her at will? Offended by his heavyhandedness, she kissed him back, wresting the reins of control away. He stiffened as she slipped her tongue between his teeth. He met her stabbing tongue with a gentle, sensual parry of his own, and pleasure rippled through her.

Alarmed, she drew back. His taste and texture were still familiar, but his confidence bespoke sexual experience that sparked an immediate and powerful response. With the feeling she had unwittingly opened Pandora's box, she drew back.

For a moment they gazed warily into each other's eyes.

"Just curious," she whispered, explaining her impulse with a shrug, using the same explanation he had used the other night.

With a tight look, he straightened in his seat and sat back, thoughtfully quiet.

Lucy turned her warm face toward the window and peered down, dismissing her actions as an aberration.

Far below them, the coast of Venezuela drew a skirt of sand out of the tourmaline waters of the Gulf of Mexico. It was down there that she'd been stripped of her confidence in the first place.

She was coming back to reclaim it—not in Venezuela, exactly, but in neighboring Colombia. As tough as it was for her to admit, she couldn't do this without Gus. She would have to rely on him to cope with the jungle's rigors—that was no doubt true. But once this assignment was over, she'd be stronger and more self-reliant than ever. PTSD would be a thing of the past.

PERCHED ON A PLATEAU in the Andes Mountains, nine thousand feet above sea level, Bogotá sprawled as far as the eye could see. Seven million people living in one place had clustered into neighborhoods of differing wealth and ethnicity. To the north, a chain of mountains created a scenic backdrop for the wealthy.

The airplane floundered through the thin air, then bumped down on the runway at El Dorado International Airport. As the unique scent of South American soil stole through the open door, uneasiness roiled in Lucy's stomach, congealing into something approaching fear as she exited the plane. *I can do this,* she assured herself, stealing guilty reassurance from Gus's hand as they strode along the boarding platform into the terminal.

Bypassing baggage claim, they headed straight to customs with their backpacks, submitting them to a laughably lax inspection. Colombia wasn't big on catching smugglers, evidently.

"What is the nature of your visit?" inquired the bespectacled official at their next hurdle—immigration.

"Business," Gus answered for the two of them, and Lucy nudged his toe, reminding him to let her do the talking.

The man frowned down at their false passports. "You're with the UN?" he inquired.

"Yes," said Lucy, her stomach churning. Carlos had warned them during the in-briefing that the Colombian army would jump at the chance to follow a UN team into the rebels' hideout. Yet nothing was more guaranteed to get the hostages killed.

"Which areas of Colombia will you be visiting?" he asked.

"We're staying in Bogotá," Lucy lied. If rumors of an arriving UN team were circulating airport security, this man might report their arrival to the army.

"At which hotel?" he pressed.

Lucy shrugged. "We don't know yet. We don't have reservations."

Pursing his mouth with disbelief, he stamped their passports. His myopic gaze glinted watchfully as he slid them under the glass partition. "Enjoy your stay."

"Thank you," Lucy breathed.

Gus snatched up their passports and propelled her toward the exit. Shouldering her backpack, Lucy glanced casually back.

"He's making a phone call," she warned.

"Walk faster," Gus urged.

With a firm grip on her elbow, he drew her into the crowd thronging toward the glass doors. Together they scanned the crush of humanity for Carlos, who'd promised to pick them up.

Lucy spotted him first, lounging beside an advertisement for the TransMilieno rapid-transit system. At their approach, the Spaniard turned and marched ahead of them through the glass doors.

Humid air, choked with the smell of car exhaust,

enveloped them as they hurried after him. Carlos had waved down a taxi. He yanked open the rear door for Gus and Lucy. "Get in," he urged, his dark eyes snapping.

Lucy dove into the rear with Gus immediately behind her. "Hotel Hacienda Royal," said Carlos, jumping into the front.

"*Sí, señor.*" The driver peeled into traffic and immediately switched lanes, overtaking the taxi in front of it.

Lucy groped for a nonexistent seat belt. "Do we have company?" she asked, catching Carlos's eye as he peered over his shoulder to look behind them.

"I dare anyone to catch us," he replied as their driver veered into the oncoming lane, going head-to-head with a busload of passengers before lurching back onto the right side.

Dear God.

"How was your flight?" Carlos added as the taxi rumbled along boulevards of hand-laid brick.

"Good," said Gus, shaking off his backpack and digging out a small, oddly shaped cell phone. Lucy recognized it as the device he would hide inside his hiking boots. The heels of both boots were hollow, allowing him to stow his phone in one, a spare battery in the other. She watched him dial a lengthy number with quick thumb work. Leaning toward him, she hoped to overhear snatches of his conversation.

"*Buenas tardes,*" Gus casually greeted the man who answered. "We're here. Do you see us?" he asked in Spanish.

One of his buddies, already situated at the Joint Intelligence Center within the U.S. embassy, answered with an affirmative. Their microchips were working. Gus murmured that they'd arrived on time to make their appointment that afternoon. Then he dropped the phone into his shirt pocket.

Everything was going as planned. The knowledge eased Lucy's agitation, giving her assurance that she would soon regain her equilibrium. She would be exactly as she was before—composed and fearless.

The vision of the queen-sized bed as she entered their hotel room minutes later brought her up short. Considering Gus's broad shoulders, sleeping together on a bed, even that size, was going to resemble a contact sport. Remembering the spark that their kiss had ignited, she couldn't help but imagine that sex would be devastating. Only she would never get that carried away. Fraternization was discouraged by the CIA. Sexual involvement tended to dull awareness and cloud judgment.

"Nice room," said Gus, tossing his backpack on the luggage rack. He sent her a nonverbal cue to help him sweep it for bugs.

The methodical procedure focused Lucy's scattered thoughts. "Clear," she declared, sinking into the overstuffed chair by the window. The answering twinge in her right hip made her wince.

Gus saw her do it. He froze, his eyebrows sinking slowly together as he glared at her. "What was that?" he demanded in English.

"What was what?" she said, going with denial.

"Your incision is bothering you," he guessed, pitching his voice low in deference to the thin walls.

"It's fine," she insisted. "I'm a little sore, that's all."

"Maybe it's infected," he persisted, folding his arms across his chest.

"How can it be infected? I'm popping doxycycline. That's an antibiotic, right?"

He stepped over to her chair. "Stand up," he ordered. "Let me look."

"No!" The last thing she wanted was for him to force her off the assignment because of a little cut in her hip. She bolted out of the chair, dodging past him to race into the marbled bathroom, where she promptly locked the door.

With a calming breath, Lucy turned three quarters and peeled back the waistline of her European-style slacks to survey the damage.

Damn. Maybe she shouldn't have run again last night. The Band-Aid she'd stuck on her this morning was blood-soaked. She snatched it off to eye the small, gaping cut with foreboding. Yanking toilet paper from the roll, she dabbed at the wound, rolled her slacks over the tissue, and opened the door again, running straight into Gus.

"Do not," she warned, her temper flaring, "get in the habit of standing outside the bathroom door."

"No problem," he said easily. "There are no bathrooms in the jungle."

She pushed past him to get to her backpack.

"It's bleeding," he guessed as she upended her bag, shaking the contents onto the bed.

Band-Aids, check. She snatched one up, circling him as he stepped into her path, and headed back into the bathroom.

Flashing out a hand, he caught her back, his grip unbreakable. Lucy tugged uselessly, annoyed by the realization that he could overpower her with embarrassing ease. "Listen to me," he said, his gentle tone oddly menacing when paired with his steely grasp. "Even the smallest sore will fester in the jungle if it isn't treated. I can't let you proceed with this assignment."

"I'll be fine," Lucy insisted, tempted to stamp a foot. "What are you going to do, call Gordon and tell him I've got a little cut? I've also got a hangnail," she quipped, shoving a finger under his nose—her middle one. "Does that disqualify me, too?"

"I have a new word for your vocabulary," he continued, seeming to change the subject while tightening his grip as she struggled once again. "Teamwork," he articulated. "That's how Navy SEALs operate. That's why our casualty rate is as low as it is. We watch each other's backs. Now, I know you like to work alone. You made that pretty clear. But now we're partners, Luce. If you're going to wind up dead over an infection, then I have a right to know."

She had to admit his argument was reasonable. "Fine," she conceded, ceasing to struggle. "Whatever. I'll show you the cut and you'll see that it's nothing."

With a nod and a grimace of apology, he released her.

Lucy planted herself before the mirror, glanced quickly at her pink-cheeked reflection, then looked away, rolling her slacks down a scant inch for him to see.

As Gus stepped into the little room, the walls seemed to shrink inward. Their gazes briefly met, sparking heat and sexual awareness. With her heart pumping fast, she turned so he could see the slit. "See?" she said, "No big deal."

He bent over, depressing the soft skin around the incision as he inspected it. "You weren't supposed to run last night," he chided. "You tore the stitches open or rubbed them off or something."

How could he know she'd run last night, or was that just a good guess? "My bad," she apologized, every nerve in her body screaming in awareness of him.

"Do you have any antibacterial ointment?" he asked, all seriousness.

"No," she admitted, watching breathlessly as he ran a wash cloth under steaming water and pressed it to the wound.

She tried not to flinch as he pressed it to her hip. It would take more than an itty bitty cut to slow her down.

"Now," he said, dabbing her hip dry with a second cloth. "No more running. I want a good scab on this cut before you step foot in the jungle."

"Hooyah." She tossed off a mock salute, snatching the Band-Aid from his hand before he put it on her.

His touch was unsettling enough. She didn't need him coddling her. All that did was feed the little seed of doubt sprouting roots in her mind.

Lucy Donovan didn't do helpless. She could damn well put on her own Band-Aid. A knock at the door startled them both, making them realize they'd both been speaking English, and none too quietly, either.

Gus went to answer it while Lucy bandaged her hip and scrounged up her composure.

"Carlos, come in," Gus said in Spanish.

Adjusting her clothing, Lucy trailed them toward the window.

"I just checked the arrival times of the others," said the Spaniard, his gaze touching on her flushed face. "Fournier the Frenchman and Bellini, the Italian, will arrive this afternoon. The Turkish woman comes this evening," he added, looking back at Gus. "As long as you return from your meeting by six o'clock, no one will notice your absence. If someone shows up early, I'll tell them you're out sightseeing."

"Sounds good," said Gus.

"The safe house is ten blocks from here. I scoped it out this morning. You can either take a taxi or the Trans-Milieno," he added.

"We'll see how we feel," Gus replied with a shrug.

"Fournier will want all of us to dine together this evening, so don't get lost," cautioned Carlos. "Besides, you don't want to be out after dark in Bogotá," he added with a wink at Lucy. He headed toward the door. "Be safe."

Lucy couldn't help but reflect that *safe* was clearly a relative term. While she doubted harm would befall her with a Navy SEAL for protection, their chemistry was proving explosive enough to make any situation volatile.

CHAPTER 3 ═══════

It's about a three-mile walk," Gus pointed out as they stepped out of a fire-escape exit to avoid being noticed by the valets guarding the hotel's main entrance. "You want to take a taxi, or the TransMilieno like Carlos said?"

"And risk my life for nothing?" Lucy retorted, pulling up the hood over her waterproof jacket while sweeping a practiced eye up and down the tree-lined boulevard.

The falling temperatures and light drizzle left her feeling chilled. How much worse would it feel in the jungle without any type of real shelter?

"It might aggravate your incision to walk that far," Gus pointed out.

"Three miles isn't far," retorted Lucy. "Besides, I want to see the city. I've heard it's beautiful. Which way do we go?"

"North," he said, glancing at his watch. Realizing it had a compass on it, Lucy had to smile. James had always loved his gadgets. What a shame he would have to leave this one behind. "This way," he added, throwing a casual arm around her and steering down a brick-laid boulevard.

Awareness shot through Lucy as their hips collided. It was proving all too easy to play the role of Gus's bride. On an instinctive level, she was comfortable with him. Why wouldn't she be when, at one time, they'd been inseparable, two peas in a pod? But just as he had back in college, Gus knew how to push her buttons, how to infuriate her, how to arouse her. And when he did either, she lost focus. On an assignment as dangerous as theirs, that could be deadly.

Fortunately, things hadn't gotten dangerous yet. The only thing his hand at the small of her back distracted her from was a city that blended old-world charm with glittering skyscrapers. Caught up in Bogotá's allure, she led him away from the brick-lined avenues to the smaller streets to enjoy the capital's true flavor by mingling with the locals.

Many minutes later, she caught Gus glancing at his watch again.

"We're going to be late," she guessed, trying to gauge where they were.

"This way," he said. "There's the Museo de Oro."

The museum's golden dome was a landmark for the safe house. Once beyond its doors, they came to a residential neighborhood where middle-class houses hid behind walls topped with broken glass. "This is it," he added, pausing by a pedestrian gate at number 733. He depressed the intercom button.

"¿Sí?" asked a gruff male voice.

Gus announced them in Spanish, and the lock buzzed, allowing them to push their way inside. They crossed a pebbled courtyard to be greeted by a stern-faced American wearing a white Guayabera shirt. "John Whiteside, station chief," he introduced himself shortly. "Come in."

As they traversed a narrow hallway, Lucy realized Gus

wasn't touching her anymore. She felt suddenly wet and chilled.

They stepped into a tiled living space, stuffed with chairs and buff-looking men in civilian clothing. Lucy counted eight of them as they scrambled to their feet at her and Gus's entry. "Evening, sir!" chorused several of them, but all had eyes for just Lucy.

She was used to the attention; she would admit she even exploited it. When men made fools of themselves, that just made her own job easier.

Gus drew her front and center. "Guys, this is Lucy Donovan. Some of you helped extract her from a warehouse in Maiquetía, Venezuela, last year."

He just had to bring that up.

Lucy mustered a smile for the men she recognized, greeting them by name. "Vinny, how are you?" she said, extending a hand at the Al Pacino look-alike, a Special Operations medic. "Harley, right?" she added, turning to the blue-eyed chief who kept his head as shiny and bald as a billiard cue.

"Yes, ma'am," said Harley, looking impressed.

"And, Haiku?"

"Yes, ma'am," beamed the Japanese American, his dark eyes sparkling. He was obviously thrilled to be remembered.

"This is Lieutenant Lindstrom, the officer in charge," Gus added, turning her toward the SEAL who towered over the others and bore a striking resemblance to a former professional football player.

"Call me Luther," he said. His hand engulfed hers while dark blue eyes took stock of her.

"Did you used to play football?"

"Yes, I did," he admitted modestly.

And he'd given up all that money to become a Navy SEAL?

"This is Teddy Brewbaker, our explosives expert," Gus added, pulling her from her starstruck stare to introduce her to the only black man.

"My friends call me Bear," Teddy boomed, flashing the gap between his front teeth.

Gus introduced her to three more men: Gibbons, their spindly point man, Swanson, rear security, and finally the assistant OIC, Lieutenant Casey. By the time she'd shaken every man's hand, her knuckles ached.

"Let's get down to business," interrupted the station chief with an impatient nod at the OIC's laptop humming quietly on the coffee table.

There weren't enough seats for everyone. Five SEALs offered to surrender their chairs to Lucy, who accepted Vinny's offer since it gave her the clearest view of the laptop. Harley gave up his seat to Gus, who sat beside her.

"All set?" Luther asked, rousing his laptop with a deft touch. "This is where you're headed."

The top of Lucy's head tingled as she beheld a satellite photo of a snow-capped mountain.

"It's called La Montaña," the former football player continued. "The FARC have retreated onto this fourteen-thousand-foot monstrosity to recoup their losses. Due to heavy desertion, it's believed the number of rebels has fallen below ten thousand. The Colombian army has cut off their food and fuel supplies. They've burned their coca fields. Some say this is the end of the rebel movement.

"But up here on La Montaña, we don't know what the rebels are doing. The paths they've networked are completely invisible under the triple-canopy jungle. Our spy planes have yet to pinpoint significant populations or intercept communications. It's like they dropped off the map, only we know they haven't, because they're still holding two Americans hostage."

"Your job," inserted the station chief while fixing a stern eye on Gus and Lucy, "is to find Barnes and Howitz and discover what the FARC are up to on that goddamn mountain."

Lucy knew the objective, only she'd had no idea how big and formidable that mountain was. It made her think they'd be looking for a needle in a haystack.

"Any questions?" asked Lieutenant Lindstrom, drawing the briefing to a close an hour later. The legs of his chair creaked as he leaned back in it.

"Do we have an escape-and-evasion plan?" Lucy asked. "One that doesn't entail you coming to our rescue?" The lieutenant had just touched on all the things that could go wrong. Gus could run out of battery power for the cell phone. The rebels could suspect deceit and turn on them. Lucy didn't want to rely on SEALs coming to the rescue. She wanted to be able to save her own hide, the way she'd always done.

With a thoughtful look, the giant tapped a key and zoomed in on the mountain's peak. "Right here," he said.

Studying the satellite image, Lucy realized there were actually two snowy, jagged peaks on La Montaña, separated by a clear, pristine pool of water.

"The FARC have a radio station up here," he added, pointing out a structure built into a cave on the side of the mountain. "This is where they broadcast 'La Voz de la Resistencia.' Intel suggests it's minimally protected, so if you had to, you could subdue the unfriendlies and announce a mayday on their frequency. The NSA moni-

tors every word they broadcast and would alert us immediately. In theory, we can land a helo up there and pull you
out."

"It's not going to come to that," asserted the station
chief with confidence. "Just play your part as UN peacekeepers and nothing's going to happen to you. This
Fournier fellow is a damn good negotiator. Who knows,
he might get the FARC to let the hostages go and save us
the trouble of extracting them."

*Right, and then we'll all go home to Kansas and live
happily ever after.* Lately, Lucy didn't have much faith in
best-case scenarios.

"Anything else?" Luther asked.

The reality of their impending departure cut into her
consciousness like a razor. She concealed her sudden anxiety behind a cool shrug and glanced at Gus, who shook
his head.

"In that case," said Whiteside, who seemed eager to
wrap things up, "we'll call it a night. When does the UN
team get under way?"

"First thing in the morning, sir," Gus told him as he
and Lucy stood up. Eight more SEALs sprang politely to
their feet.

Whiteside turned to the OIC. "I want your night shift
in the embassy by midnight, Lieutenant."

"Yes, sir. We'll be there."

With the branch chief breathing down their necks and
the SEALs calling farewells and well-wishes, Gus and
Lucy left the safe house, stepped through the pedestrian
gate, and realized it was nearly dark. "Wow, what time is
it?" she asked, aware that Gus was touching her again.

He glanced at his watch. "Five-thirty. I think we'd better catch a taxi." It had stopped raining, but the mountain

chain flung its shadow over the city, making it feel later than it was.

Back on Jiménez de Quezada, they waited for a taxi to come along. One finally slowed before them. A cathedral bell tolled quarter till as they slipped into the back, giving directions to the hotel.

As Lucy settled on the plastic-wrapped seat, Gus pulled her against him, and her hand landed on his thigh. *Whoa.* His legs hadn't felt like *that* back in college, like they were hewn out of oak trees. Awareness tingled up her fingers, inspiring her imagination as she envisioned herself seated in his lap, her arms coiled around his shoulders, kissing him the way they'd kissed on the airplane...

"Hotel Hacienda Royal," he said to the driver, who took off with a squeal of his tires.

Jarred from her fantasies, Lucy brought her thoughts back to the present. Knowing Gus's teammates would be monitoring their every move from the JIC was oddly reassuring. "I think I see what you meant about having someone watch your back. It must be nice," she murmured.

Gus glanced at her sidelong. "Any one of those guys would give his life for you. Me included," he added, tightening his embrace.

Lucy's heart thudded unevenly. There was something highly disturbing about the thought of Gus giving up his life for her. "Don't say that," she muttered. "Nothing's going to happen to me—to us."

His answering silence reminded Lucy of his deep reluctance to partner with her on this assignment. She'd just have to prove to him that she was made of tougher stuff than he thought she was.

As the taxi gave a sudden turn, she glanced sharply out the window. The driver had just put them on a narrow, unlit side road. Maybe he was taking a short cut, she reasoned, meeting his darting gaze in the mirror. She elbowed Gus, who looked at the street they were shooting down and said to the driver, "This isn't the way to Hacienda Royal."

"My mistake," said the man. He slowed down, swinging the nose of the taxi into a dark alleyway as if to turn around. But then, twisting suddenly in his seat, he pointed a pistol at them. "Hand me your wallets!" he demanded fiercely, a desperate glitter in his dark eyes.

Lucy froze. Gus's warning squeeze told her he would handle it, which was well and good, because she felt paralyzed.

"Easy, easy, *señor*," he said, holding both hands up. "We don't carry much cash, but you are welcome to all of it." Keeping one hand in the air, he grubbed in his pocket with the other while Lucy swallowed convulsively, battling to bring her panic under control.

Greedy for Gus's cash, the driver held out a hand to take it. If Lucy had blinked, she would have missed what happened next. Under the guise of handing over his wallet, Gus broke the driver's nose and snatched his gun away. With a scream, the driver doubled over, blood gushing through his fingers. Removing the clip from the man's pistol, Gus dropped it on the floor of the car. He reached across Lucy to open her door, but she was already halfway out of it, adrenaline rocketing through her system, accompanied by the cowardly urge to run like hell.

Get a grip! she scolded herself as Gus grabbed her elbow and hustled her along the crumbling sidewalk. With a glance over his shoulder, he tossed the gun over a high wall.

"Damn it," he said, sounding only slightly irritated, "now we'll definitely be late."

"Not if we run," she urged, sounding shaken. What was wrong with her? A little show of hostility and she was falling apart. But the violence had been so startling, bringing back memories of being on the receiving end. Her heart was hammering. She was breathing too fast. She couldn't afford for Gus to notice, either, or he'd find a way to leave her behind.

"Running will tear your incision," he argued.

"We can't be late," she insisted. "Come on!" She urged him into a quick trot, and, almost immediately, her agitation subsided. Fueled by adrenaline, she flew along the sidewalk, scarcely hampered by the boots she would wear into the jungle.

Beside her, Gus easily kept pace as they raced in silence, down dark, deserted sidewalks, past storefronts whose doors and windows were barred by gates of steel. A light drizzle began to fall, dampening their clothing. At last, the lights of the hotel twinkled up ahead of them.

One block from the hotel, they slowed to a walk, catching their breath before pushing into the lobby through the revolving front doors.

Four middle-aged adults rose from the plush seats as they entered, flushed and damp. The silver-haired gentleman with patrician features glanced at his watch.

Carlos stepped forward to pull them over. "You're late," he scolded, tempering his impatience with concern. "I was beginning to worry."

"Our mistake," Lucy apologized, mindful of keeping Gus's Spanish to a minimum. "We took the TransMilieno and got off at the wrong stop," she added, smiling cautiously at the others.

"Well, you're here now," said Carlos. "Everyone, this is Luna de Aguiler and Gustavo, her husband. Luna works in my office in New York. Her husband is a human-rights officer also stationed in New York. Luna, Gustavo, this is Pierre Fournier, our lead negotiator."

"A pleasure," Fournier asserted, shaking Gus's hand first. He held Lucy's hand for an extra-long moment. "I was in New York last year. I don't remember you," he said, sounding puzzled.

Lucy's skin seemed to shrink. "I must have been out of the office," she agreed.

Carlos introduced Bellini next, an effusive Italian who bestowed three kisses on Lucy's cheek and apologized—ironically—to Gus for his wretched Spanish.

Şukruye Kemal, a Turkish woman in her midfifties, had worked for the Turkish Red Cross for twenty years before transferring to the UN. She was small and dark, with a compassionate gaze, and Lucy hoped the woman was tougher than she looked, or the rigors of the jungle would cripple her.

"Come," said Fournier, gesturing to the hotel's restaurant. "Let us dine in style tonight. Who knows when we may enjoy fine food again?"

Hours later, Lucy stood under a scalding shower, paralyzed by anxiety. Fournier had stared at her hard all evening. Visions of La Montaña loomed like a dark cloud in her mind. And her cowardly reaction to the taxi mugging filled her with self-doubt. What if her PTSD was here to stay?

She couldn't let Gus see her like this.

And yet Gus was part of the problem. He was the one who continuously fed her fear, implying that she was somehow on a quest to destroy herself. And then there was her shattering awareness of him. She would have to share a bed with him and, at the same time, maintain her professional edge, which was being called into question anyway.

Fed up with her anxiety and the realization that she was dawdling, Lucy shut off the shower and got out. Coiling her damp hair in a towel, she exited the bathroom in her boxer pajamas and found Gus inserting his cell phone in the sole of his boot, a sight that knotted her stomach all over again.

"Does it fit?" she asked, briskly rubbing her hair.

"Barely," he replied. He stood up to depress the heel fully into place. "A better question is, *Is it waterproof?*"

Lucy peered out from under the towel. "Would they give it to you if it wasn't?" she asked.

The anxious question had him glancing at her sharply. He sat back down and took the one boot off. "What's the matter?" he asked, watching her closely.

"Nothing." She tossed the towel over the back of the chair and picked up her hairbrush, dragging it through damp snarls. "Fournier seems a bit suspicious, that's all."

He stood up, coming to stand behind her. The sight of his broad shoulders filling the mirror did little to soothe her. "You can stay here tomorrow if you want to, Luce. I'll go by myself."

She whirled on him, holding up the hairbrush like a weapon. "Stop saying that!" she hissed. "I don't need your negativism undermining my self-confidence."

"It's not a question of self-confidence. You were traumatized at the warehouse. That's not going to go away just because you want it to."

"You see?" she said, menacing him with the brush.

"What are you going to do with that?" he asked, a hint of laughter in his eyes as he glanced at her weapon.

"Don't mock me," she warned. "I can have you doubled over and begging for mercy in five seconds."

"Go ahead," he offered, visibly bracing himself.

"Forget it." She shoved at his chest, needing space to clear her thoughts. Turning her back on him, she went back to brushing her hair.

For a nerve-racking minute, Gus just watched her. Awareness tightened Lucy's nipples, putting twin points on the front of her pajama top.

"A massage would help," Gus announced unexpectedly. "You're way too tense."

Startled, Lucy put the brush down. Oh, no. A massage wouldn't help anything. "Maybe you're projecting your anxiety onto me," she bluffed. "I am perfectly fine."

"You're right," Gus agreed with a nod. "I'm the one who's tense." He stripped off his T-shirt unexpectedly. "How about you massage me?" Suddenly he was standing in a pair of gray gym shorts and nothing else.

Lucy's gaze fastened helplessly on the expanse of naked chest. The lean youth she had loved in college had, in addition to widening his shoulders six inches, grown a six-pack and chest hair—lots of chest hair, the same russet brown as his head. It furred his upper chest before narrowing into a line that bisected his abs and arrowed into his gym shorts. "I suck at giving massages," she protested stonily.

"No, you don't. Come on, Luce. Don't be chicken." He sprawled gracefully across the coverlet, exposing a back that was all swells and ridges and thick, dense muscle. "It's just a massage."

Who was he calling chicken?

Resentment bolstered her courage. Seeing that he was watching her, she marched over to the bed and casually chopped his back, her hands bouncing off the resilient slabs of muscles. "There," she said, straightening.

"Not like that. Sit between my legs."

His legs were long and strong and bare, and dusted with light brown hair. Lucy swallowed hard.

Could she touch him and not get lost in the past? It would be a test of her professionalism, that much was certain.

Maybe he *was* testing her, in which case, she had better surpass his expectations.

With a careless-looking shrug, she kneeled between his slightly spread thighs and braced her hands on his smooth back. His clean skin exuded a familiar scent that made her head spin, made her insides melt with remembered pleasure.

With a tremor in her fingers, she dug in, instantly intrigued by the interplay of muscles and sinew.

Gus gave a low groan of pleasure, the sound of which seemed to vibrate inside her. The impulse to lower her lips to the expanse of bare back had her swimming in her desire.

Of their own will, her fingers trailed lower, drifting just under the elastic band of his shorts toward his firm buttocks. Even as his muscles loosened under her flexing fingers, a different tension invaded his body.

She could take this as far as she liked. The realization filled her with bittersweet triumph. She was still in control. She still had what it took to turn a potential recruit into an asset. Only Gus wasn't a recruit. He was her partner, the first she'd ever had, and probably the last.

Slapping his butt with a playful swat, Lucy jumped from the bed.

He cracked an eye. "Where are you going?"

"To brush my teeth." His groan of disappointment made her smile. She would have loved to have kept it up, enjoying reciprocal treatment in return. But even Gus knew better than to go that far.

People who fell in lust got stupid. Lucy was too smart to be stupid, especially now, when the stakes were so high.

CHAPTER 4

Lucy saw Gus glance at his watch, the only indication that this unforeseeable delay was getting to him. It sure as hell was getting to her.

In the rear seat of a stuffy little van chartered to drive them to the edge of civilization, they sat motionless on Highway 40, just one link in a chain of vehicles heading into the tunnel that burrowed through the side of a mountain.

Thanks to an avalanche of rock that had strewn debris across the road, the tunnel was blocked. Lucy could see highway workers under the vigilance of Colombia's equivalent of the National Guard scrambling to remove the obstruction.

If sitting in a stuffy van doing nothing could get her stomach churning, then how the hell was she supposed to come face-to-face with guerrillas and not embarrass herself?

Her slowly drawn breath caught Gus's attention. "*¿Estás bien?*" he asked her. *You okay?*

"*Claro.*" *Of course.* Why wouldn't she be?

She tried to focus on the scenery. To the east, Bogotá sprawled like a patchwork quilt, its lush green parks breaking up squares of steel and concrete. With the mountains looming protectively behind, the megalopolis looked downright picturesque, till one looked more closely and saw the shanties pushed up onto the sides of the mountains.

A high-pitched whistle snatched her attention forward. At last, the road was clear! Engines roared to life and their van inched toward the tunnel. But then a national guardsman waved them down.

Fournier swore under his breath, and a guard leaned into the passenger window demanding to see their passports.

One by one, the peacekeeping team was scrutinized. Lucy fought to hold the guardsman's gaze as he looked up from her passport to scrutinize her. Her heart sank as he stepped from the vehicle to confer with his companions, taking all the passports with him.

While a ripple of excitement seemed to pass through the ranks of the guards, Lucy sat in a cold sweat, wondering where her composure had flown.

"*Mon Dieu,*" Fournier muttered, looking as ill at ease as Lucy felt. Cars honked impatiently behind them. If they were detained much longer, they might miss their rendezvous with the FARC tomorrow.

At last, the guardsman returned with their passports. "Where are you headed?" he demanded inscrutably.

"To Villavicencio, to see how the peace is being kept," said Fournier, answering in a half-truth.

The man nodded. "You may proceed," he announced, handing back the passports and waving them on.

As the window closed, the entire UN team, Lucy included, heaved a sigh of relief.

With horns urging them to hurry, their driver lurched forward, eager to make up for lost time. They surged into the dark, unlit tunnel, and Gus pinned Lucy against the seat with his shoulder, bracing her with his arm in the absence of a seat belt.

Lucy snapped her eyes shut. *Please don't do that,* she wanted to tell him, recognizing his attempt to save her life in the event of a head-on collision.

The tunnel ended abruptly, spilling them onto lush, rolling plains called Los Llanos, where Gus's vigilance relaxed. Their first destination, Villavicencio, stood less than thirty miles away.

With a squeal of brakes, the van stopped for lunch. Seated at an outdoor café, the team enjoyed a midday meal under the watchful eye of soldiers patrolling the industrial city. Once terrorized by the FARC, Villavicencio was now occupied by the Colombian army.

"Eat well," Fournier murmured to them. "We have no way of knowing if the FARC will be able to feed us."

While Gus slipped away to place a call to the JIC, Lucy watched the soldier standing guard across the street. As they boarded their van to continue the journey, he spoke into his walkie-talkie. The suspicion that the army was tracking the team's movements congealed into certainty as a motorcycle, driven by two more soldiers, pulled out of an alleyway and started chasing them. Lucy met Gus's eye and he nodded toward the Frenchman.

"Monsieur Fournier," Lucy called up to him. "I believe we're being followed."

With a grimace, Fournier looked back at the motorcycle, then gave directions to their driver to outrun it. "The last thing we need," he grumbled, "is to lead the army to the FARC and start a war."

In the end, Mother Nature got rid of the soldiers for them. The sky darkened abruptly. Leaden clouds opened up and rain poured down. The motorcycle floundered. Soon it was just a speck behind them, eventually disappearing altogether.

The team members smiled at one another in relief. Their van slogged on, traveling over a highway that went from asphalt to gravel, to a muddy trail riddled with potholes of deceptive depth.

With every hundred meters, the road seemed to narrow until it was just wide enough for one car. Windshield wipers beat a frenzied tempo but never succeeded in clearing the fogged glass up front. The music on the radio crackled and faded into static. The driver turned it off.

A somber silence descended over the occupants of the van. Lucy dragged air into her tight lungs and wondered if the others were thinking what she was thinking: They'd come this far; now there was no going back.

Staring out a fogged window, all she could see were coca fields and banana groves. A swollen brown river ran parallel to the road for a while, then veered away. With every hundred meters, she felt their isolation deepening.

"There's La Montaña," Fournier finally announced.

Peering up the length of the van, Lucy felt her mouth go dry. The ominous-looking mountain had planted itself squarely before them, its twin peaks buried in rain clouds. Somewhere in the looming mass of vegetation, Howitz and Barnes remained hostages.

If she didn't screw her courage on tight, they might never make it home.

It was dusk when they arrived at the last outpost of civilization, Puerto Limón, a tiny pueblo at the foot of the mountain. In the single-story *ranchita* advertised as an inn, the UN team was warmly greeted by their indigenous hosts, offered bread and goat's cheese for supper, and dismissed to private bedrooms.

"Sleep well," called Fournier, instructing them to awaken early for another dawn departure.

Lying on a twin-sized mattress made of straw, Lucy realized that, while thoughts of sharing a queen-sized bed last night had unsettled her, she was looking forward to the feel of Gus's arms around her tonight, a circumstance that secretly worried her. She wasn't growing reliant on him, was she? Of course not. All she needed from him was his body heat.

Beneath the glow of a naked lightbulb, she could feel the mountain's looming proximity. Anxiety sat like a heavy weight on her chest. How was she supposed to throw it off?

Lucy Donovan operated alone. She was utterly self-reliant.

Or had the experience in Venezuela robbed her of her self-sufficiency? What then? It was her job to combat terrorists. She didn't know any other kind of life—didn't want to. She couldn't afford to be *afraid*.

The door groaned suddenly inward. Gus ducked into the room, his damp head nearly touching the ceiling. At the sight of her cowering in the bed with the blanket pulled to her chin, his jaw hardened. He whipped off his glasses, set them by the bed, and bent low to whisper, "You can't fight fire with fire, Luce."

"What is that supposed to mean?"

"It means you're trying to scare off your PTSD. That's not the way to cure yourself."

"I don't have PTSD," she insisted rigidly. "And I am not scared," she added.

"Jesus, Luce," he swore in disgust. Reaching for the string, he snapped off the light. "Make room," he warned her shortly.

Her senses clamored in anticipation of his touch. As he stretched out next to her she fitted her body to his, swallowing a sigh of relief as his warmth seeped into her limbs, his strong arms drove back the demons chasing her.

But then she imagined what tomorrow would bring. Soon she'd be sharing a campfire with guerrillas who blew up people in the name of *libertad* and exploited innocent children, forcing them to fight. A fresh wave of anxiety rolled through her.

"Relax, dear. I'm not going to let anything happen to you."

Lucy snorted at the macho assertion. At the same time, she hoped it was true.

She listened to him lapse into sleep, his soft snores deepening by degrees. With her head on his rising and falling chest, she waited for hours for sleep to claim her.

The FARC made them wait, choosing not to arrive in Puerto Limón until 10 a.m.

The UN team had been up since dawn, waiting tensely under the *ranchita's* covered porch, listening to the rain drum the red-tiled roof. For hours now they had stared up the muddy track that wound into the dense vegetation of La Montaña.

The mountain rose straight up. Lushly green, its glacial peaks remained hidden in rain clouds that moved sluggishly overhead, pushed by a wet, jasmine-scented breeze.

Nothing happened quickly in Colombia, Lucy reflected.

Seeing the jungle, smelling it, she envisioned how Howitz and Barnes had to feel, cut off from the world, chained like dogs, starved and humiliated. Ten months had to seem like a lifetime. God, she hoped she would never discover that for herself!

Gus's last communication with the JIC this morning had echoed that same sentiment. "Don't lose us out there, guys," he'd murmured into the sat phone. At his team-mate's reply, he'd raked his fingers through his hair. "Well, damn it, sir, we don't want to be caught in the middle of that," he'd hissed.

Sensing a problem, Lucy had leaned closer, hoping to overhear.

"Will do, sir. You, too, sir. Out." He'd severed the call.

"We don't want to be caught in the middle of what?" Lucy had questioned him once he hung up.

"Intel says a battalion of Colombian infantry are headed this way."

"Oh, hell," she'd breathed. "I thought we lost them yesterday."

"Evidently not. Our guys are busy working through the right channels to get them called off. Don't worry."

He'd powered down his cell phone and stowed it in his left boot. Later, he'd given his watch with the compass to the innkeepers' thirteen-year-old son. Lucy had felt a tug of pity for him. For a man used to relying on his gadgets, it couldn't be easy to let the watch go.

Other team members had left their belongings with the innkeepers for safekeeping, but Lucy clung tenaciously to her backpack, hopeful the FARC would let her keep a change of socks, her toothbrush, and her anti-malaria pills, at least.

"This isn't a camping trip," Gus had reminded her.

"Good. I hate camping."

Hours had passed since then. Lucy was considering the possibility that the FARC had stood them up when Gus looked up sharply.

"Here they come," he said, squinting up the road.

She had to look twice. Dressed from head to toe in camouflage, the guerrillas remained virtually invisible against the backdrop of the jungle till they were less than a hundred meters away.

"We should greet them," suggested Fournier, urging the team to step out into the middle of the street. "Come. Show them your hands," he urged, "palms facing out."

There they stood, growing soaked by the cold, steady drizzle, as rebels bristling with AK-47s, their chests criss-crossed with ammunition belts, trooped closer.

We come in peace. Lucy sought to convey that message in her expression, while battling the impulse to assume a fighting stance. A cold sweat made her shiver in her wet clothing. Dread made her scalp tingle. It in no way lessened when she noted that six out of the ten rebels were mere teenagers. Teens were notoriously unpredictable. They didn't think they could die, either.

Two leaders, older and burlier than the rest, with insignia on their shoulders, detached themselves from the group to approach them.

Fournier stepped forward and, in his accented Spanish, greeted the guerrillas with cautious courtesy.

One by one, they were waved forward and introduced.

Lucy suffered the scrutiny of two dark pairs of eyes, one cynical, the other hostile. The older man, a careworn-looking guerrilla whose beard was shot with silver, was Comandante Marquez. The younger man,

Buitre—Buzzard in English—was introduced as his deputy.

Bearing a scar that bisected his left cheek, Deputy Buitre struck Lucy as a dangerous entity. The crude, demoralizing look in his eyes brought back memories of another set of eyes that haunted her dreams. Dislike strangled her words of goodwill.

Gus brushed her arm reassuringly as he stepped alongside her. The commander's gaze sharpened as he took note of Gus's physique. "Remove your glasses," he ordered. "You may not wear them."

Tension rippled through the team members at this sudden show of hostility.

"*Por favor*," Gus murmured convincingly. "I'm blind without them."

Unmoved by his plea, the commander nodded at his deputy, who snatched the spectacles from Gus's eyes and tossed them to the ground, crushing the wire rims under his booted heel.

An uncomfortable silence ensued.

Then Marquez gestured up the path with his stainless-steel AK-47. "*Regresemos!*" he shouted, and his gaggle of armed teens did an about-face, slogging wordlessly up the trail they'd just traversed, looking bedraggled and depressed.

With that, the UN team began their march into the jungle, hastening to keep pace with the diminutive natives, who covered the ground swiftly, challenging them at once to keep up.

"Faster!" ordered Deputy Buitre.

With the mud sucking at her boots and the drizzle wetting her hair, Lucy cut a sidelong glance at Gus. She found his gaze alert, constantly moving, assessing their environment. Had she really thought she could do this without him? Heck, a part of being self-reliant was knowing how to use your assets, and Gus was definitely an asset she didn't want to lose.

Vegetation thickened and rose up, creating a tangled wall on either side. The path became an erratic corridor surrounded by hedges too lush to penetrate. Then, finally, it closed over their heads, swallowing them.

The trail grew steeper and narrower as it rose vertically up the mountain. Rainwater had carved out the middle of it, turning the trail into a V-shaped gulley, murder on Lucy's ankles, even in boots. She pushed herself, wondering how the others, those who didn't exercise as rigorously as she and Gus, would fare.

On the heels of that thought, Bellini and the Turkish woman began to flounder. Lucy, Carlos, and Gus stepped up to help. Gripping the Turkish woman's arm, Lucy was conscious of Deputy Buitre's dark stare as he prodded them up the slippery clay path, offering no assistance.

As Fournier had predicted, they weren't going to be afforded preferential treatment. This trek into the jungle might prove more arduous than any of them had bargained for.

They came abruptly upon a hacked-out clearing. Lucy breathed a sigh of relief to see five mules dozing in a circle around a mound of cloth sacks, hides quivering to keep the pestering insects off.

"Halt!" shouted the deputy. "Stand in a circle and remove all your clothing but your boots and undergarments."

Damn, Lucy thought, reluctantly shrugging off her backpack, while ignoring Gus's raised eyebrow.

"Throw your possessions into the center of the circle."

"Commander, sir," Fournier hedged respectfully, "could we keep our anti-malarial medication?"

"No." Marquez's reply was implacable.

Lucy was afraid of that. Now they would be at risk for contracting mosquito-borne malarial infection.

"Now your clothing," the commander added. "Strip to your underwear and your boots."

At least their intel had been right. They got to keep their boots. The FARC couldn't afford to shoe them all, especially not the men, whose feet were bigger than the average rebel's.

Lucy's relief didn't quite counter her self-consciousness at having to shrug off her sweater and pull down her pants. When Gus sidled over to block the men's view of her, he was jabbed in the ribs by a kid no more than fifteen years old.

Intentionally humiliated, each UN team member was made to stand for an uncertain moment in their underwear. That morning, Lucy had removed the Band-Aid stuck to her hip. It would have gone unnoticed, anyway, as she stood with her back to the trees.

In his near-naked splendor, Gus once again inspired the commander's suspicions. He circled Gus to examine his musculature. "You're strong, eh?" he asked, punching him lightly in the stomach.

Gus's abs flexed. "I lift weights at the gym," he explained.

"You know how to shoot a gun?" the man asked.

"No, no," Gus denied, lying. "I can't see the target."

Commander Marquez grunted. "I'll be watching you," he warned, his scruffy moustache twitching. Turning away, he barked orders that prompted soldiers to scuttle up with armloads of clothing. That was when Lucy realized two of them were girls.

Stepping into the stiff, itchy camouflage pants, she pulled them up to find them several inches too short. The green T-shirt she was given exuded a soapy smell that made her nose itch. Its soft fabric protected her from the chafing jacket that she buttoned up next. It would keep her warm in lieu of her sweater, which had been bagged, along with everyone else's clothing.

"Mount the mules," the commander ordered the minute they were dressed.

Assisted onto a burlap and leather saddle, Lucy groped for the horn as the mules swayed up the vertical path, their footing as uncertain as hers had been earlier. *Oh, God.* Maybe Gus had been right about fighting fire with fire. It wasn't working.

But then she saw that Gus had it even worse. With his feet too big to fit into the stirrups, his only option for staying mounted was to squeeze the mule's round belly between his knees and hold on tight.

Lucy's gaze dropped to the knee-high, needle-sharp bamboo spears that lined the path, the product of machetes cutting through the overgrowth. If Gus were to fall, any one of those spears could puncture his chest.

They had just reached the crest of a hill when a clatter of gunfire ripped through the tangled growth, startling their entourage.

Lucy's mule reared. With a stifled scream, she slipped sideways. Her foot tangled in the opposite stirrup, spilling her upside down. With her head just inches off the ground, she heard Gus shout her name—*in English.*

A barrage of gunfire drowned it out.

Marquez roared out an order, and his little army scattered.

Jerking her foot free, Lucy fell to the path, just avoiding the needle-sharp bamboo spikes. She scrambled from the mule as it pranced in terror. Her reaction to the danger, the sounds of gunfire, were automatic, instinctually ingrained.

All hell had broken loose. Bullets peppered the trees and thumped into the humus-covered earth around them. The FARC soldiers started firing back, putting the UN team members squarely in the middle of a firefight.

"Over here," Gus called, herding them toward a grove of bamboo just above the path.

Seeing Fournier down on his knees and struggling to rise, Lucy went to offer him a hand, ignoring Gus's shout to turn back. She had just pulled the Frenchman off the trail when the whistle of a mortar shell had her diving for cover. In the next instant, Gus landed on top of her, driving the air from her lungs as the ground shook and globs of mud and spongy lichen rained down on them.

"What's happening?" she wheezed in the shocked quiet that followed.

"Colombian army," he whispered in her ear.

Ah, shit. The bastards had tracked them down, after all. And despite the JIC's attempts to call them off, they were ruining the UN team's prospects for negotiating Howitz and Barnes's release.

Another barrage of gunfire echoed through the undergrowth, continuing for what seemed an eternity. Lucy closed her eyes tight, expecting at any minute to be blown into little pieces. But then she realized Gus was covering every inch of her body. If they were struck dead-on or hit with shrapnel, he'd be the one who died, not her.

Oh, God, no. There was no way in hell she was going to be a liability and cost Gus his life, just because he thought she couldn't handle the op.

She tried to roll over, to shake him off her, only she couldn't. Gus had her thoroughly pinned. "Hold still," he ordered, impatient with her struggles.

The gunfire intensified. Adolescent voices shouted back and forth. Someone screamed in pain. The mountain trembled under her ear.

There was no way ten FARC rebels, six of whom looked to be under the age of eighteen, could hold off an army battalion indefinitely. When their ammunition ran out, the army would swoop in and arrest the survivors. For the teens, who'd likely been coerced to join the FARC anyway, that could only be good news. For Gus and Lucy it would mean an end to the mission.

But then, as suddenly as the gunfire had started, it stopped.

The cautious twitter of birds and the screeching of howler monkeys seemed to indicate that the interlopers had fled. Either that or the FARC were all dead.

CHAPTER 5 ⟍⟍⟍⟍⟍⟍

"W ait," whispered Gus when she tried to move.
"I can't breathe," she gasped, causing him to
ease cautiously off her. He signaled to the other team
members to watch and listen.

Many minutes later, the FARC began to creep out of
hiding. Marquez's voice, like nails on chalkboard, shouted
orders for all to regroup so he could make an account of
the injured.

Fournier, shaken but still asserting his leadership,
urged the UN team to rejoin the group.

Deputy Buitre was the first to spy them, slithering
down from higher ground. "*¡Traidores!*" he screamed,
storming down the trail to confront them. "They led the
army straight to us!" He lunged for Fournier, pulling
him nose to nose. Hauling a handgun from his holster, he
thrust the barrel into the man's white hair, his black eyes
flashing with fury.

"*Cálmate,*" ordered his commander, and Deputy Buitre
restrained himself, breathing heavily. It was clear if it were
left to him, he'd have killed Fournier that very instant.

Lucy watched with pity as a wet stain bloomed on the crotch of Fournier's ill-fitting pants.

Marquez bore down on them. "Is this the thanks I get for having you as my guests?" he demanded with thunderous suspicion. "Is this how the UN means to treat the FARC, by betraying us to the enemy?"

Fournier, his voice quaking with fear, stuttered his reassurances. "We swear, we had no way of knowing we were being followed. Two soldiers on a motorcycle trailed us out of Villavicencio yesterday, but we left them far behind."

The accusations disgusted Lucy. "Why would we risk ourselves in the crossfire?" she interjected without thinking.

The commander and the deputy swiveled hostile glares at her. Gus touched her arm in warning. But it felt good to challenge the rebels, her fear overcome for the moment.

"We could have just as easily been killed as you," Gus pointed out mildly, his reasonableness diffusing their rage.

"Our only agenda is to find a peaceful resolution so the hostages may be freed," Fournier added. "We are not at war with you."

With mistrust still brimming in his eyes, the commander ordered Deputy Buitre to stow his gun. Then he and his assistant turned their attention to the soldiers who'd been wounded.

Lucy and the others sat on the muddy trail and waited. Dazed by the hostilities they had endured already, they consoled each other with murmured words of solidarity and encouragement.

"Things can only get easier from here out," Fournier assured them.

Lucy slid a wry glance at Gus's carefully blank expression. Could the man really be that naive?

Within an hour, the Turkish woman started vomiting—altitude sickness. They had climbed the mountain, relentlessly, for hours. Too weak to keep her seat on her mule, Şukruye was foisted off on Lucy, as the men's mules were already overloaded. Now Lucy was soaking wet, covered with mud, *and* had vomit on her right boot.

They journeyed on, relentlessly, crisscrossing trails, possibly even doubling back to confuse the UN team members.

Then they came to a river so swollen with rain it had carved a gorge of boiling, rushing water. Their only way to cross it was via a box, drawn by pulleys across a steel cable.

Hell, why not? Lucy thought, choking down the sudden, near hysterical urge to laugh as she met Gus's grave gaze. "Fire with fire," she said to him in Spanish, earning quizzical looks from the others.

By the time they stepped onto land on the other side, Şukruye had nearly fainted from fear, and even Lucy felt weak in the knees. Having left the mules behind, they were forced to walk again, into a jungle that grew increasingly dark.

Her stomach began to burn from hunger, yet they neither spoke nor stopped for food. The only sound besides the splashing and stamping of their feet was the incessant chatter of jungle creatures. Higher and higher they climbed, into the deepening gloom.

An exchange between the FARC leaders broke the silence. Suspending the march, they decided to make camp, right there in the thick of the jungle.

Let the bugfest begin, thought Lucy, scratching at half a dozen bug bites on her neck.

Gus scooped a glob of dirt off the trail and smeared it on his face. "Here," he said, offering some to Lucy. "It'll keep the bugs off."

She wrinkled her nose in distaste. "Mud? Are you kidding?"

"What's worse? A little mud, or malaria?"

He was right, of course. With a shudder, she accepted the glob of cold soil and applied it delicately to her face and neck.

The rebels, in the meantime, had hacked a clearing with their machetes. Lashing bamboo together with vines, they built platforms for their guests, stringing hammocks for themselves around the periphery of the camp. A fire was lit to boil the rice and quickly snuffed out.

Huddled on their platforms, each team member was offered a cup of rice to eat and a sweet beverage of boiled sugar cane called *panela*. With nightfall came the emergence of still more insects—buzzing, whirring, and screeching until Lucy longed to cover her ears.

They were ordered to relieve themselves and go to sleep.

Lying on their bamboo bed, shivering with cold, and soaking wet, Lucy felt nothing but relief when Gus pulled her on top of him. She shuddered silently against him, shamelessly absorbing his body heat.

"How's the hip?" he whispered in her ear, placing a gentle hand over the area in question.

"Fine." It had hurt until he touched it, his hand warm and soothing.

"Your feet?" he breathed. "Any blisters?"

Her feet were used to worse punishment than a hike.

"Nope," she assured him, cringing as a flurry of wings tickled her cheek. God, she hated camping! "Could you find your way back?" she heard herself whisper.

"It'd take me a while," he admitted. "It's too late to change your mind now, Luce," he added.

"I haven't," she assured him.

"Good. Try to sleep," he urged in a voice too quiet for anyone else to overhear. "Tomorrow I'll search you for leeches and jungle ticks."

Lucy's breath caught. "You're kidding right?"

"Sadly, no."

She grew conscious of every squirming, creeping thing around her. Wilderness stretched for miles in every direction. An ancient and instinctive fear rose up in her as she considered the possibility of a jaguar lurking close by.

Snapping her eyes shut, she tried to melt into the solid warmth of the man holding her. With her stomach still hungry, she doubted she would sleep any better tonight than she had the night before. Out here, there was nowhere to run.

Midmorning the following day, the trail ended abruptly, spilling the guerrillas and UN peacekeepers into a partial clearing.

A handful of buildings stood in a thin, wet mist. Chickens pecked aimlessly in the mud. What was probably once the farm of a *campesino* had been commandeered by the FARC's forty-eighth front and turned into an outpost, the perimeter of which was guarded by a fifty-caliber machine gun.

Soldiers at the camp, mostly bedraggled teens, meandered out of a lean-to to eye the gringos as they staggered with relief toward the burning campfire.

"Are the hostages kept here?" Şukruye whispered,

betraying her ignorance. Still suffering the effects of altitude sickness, she held her head in her hands.

"Probably not," Fournier replied, sweeping the area with a practiced eye.

Lucy met Gus's eye. She was certain they were not. The camp had an air of restfulness about it. With several targets standing on one end of the clearing, it appeared to be a training camp, only there was no training going on now.

"Who's that?" Carlos asked as a light-skinned gentleman ducked out of a leaf-covered bungalow to approach them. He wore the same camouflage as the rebels, but his fair complexion and hesitant demeanor set him apart. Nor was he armed with any weapon.

They all converged by the fire where Comandante Marquez made introductions. "This is Señor Álvarez," he explained, which told them nothing. "He was brought in to represent the FARC in this negotiation. You may begin the process at once." He gestured to a brick and clay structure with a screen door. "Step into the officers' quarters."

The clatter of a generator and the light shining inside made the hooch a welcoming sight. Lucy's confidence edged aside her misgivings. This was why she was here in this godforsaken jungle. Gus might have the advantage with his knowledge of the environment, but no one was better at reading people. She could interpret the smallest of nuances, the flicker of private thoughts, the flutter of eyelashes—details most people overlooked. It was a gift that couldn't be taught, inherited from her father, making her the best.

Once inside, Fournier insisted on more personal introductions. The thin, dapper Álvarez turned out to be an Argentine businessman with pipelines in northern Colombia. He explained that he was being forced to play middleman between the FARC and the UN or risk having his pipelines attacked.

Lucy'd had no idea a middleman was needed, but it made sense. The FARC's front commander, Rojas, wouldn't want to show his face to outsiders.

As they helped themselves to mismatched chairs around a worn table, she and Gus took stock of the single room, seeking items that might offer clues as to Barnes and Howitz's location.

The only other furnishings besides the table were a desk and a set of bunk beds. Stacked on the desk were several books of Marxist leanings, a worn notebook, and a pen. A shortwave radio had been left on the windowsill. Catching Gus's eye, Lucy made certain he'd seen it.

With tact and consideration for Álvarez's unwilling involvement, Fournier got the meeting under way. "Have you seen the hostages?" he inquired.

"No, no," said the Argentine. "I arrived here only last night. Before that I was at my home in Buenos Aires."

"Then please take our request for proof of life to the FARC leader—I believe his name is Rojas? When will you see him?"

"Soon, I suppose," said Álvarez.

Lucy slid a casual glance at Gus. This business of negotiations could take weeks, even months to accomplish. They had to find Howitz and Barnes before the batteries for their phone ran out—before Howitz and Barnes succumbed to the cruelty of their captors.

"We cannot proceed, you understand," Fournier insisted, "until we have proof of life."

"I understand," said Álvarez, looking gloomily overwhelmed.

With nothing else to accomplish, they basked in the

luxury of electricity until Marquez leaned into the doorway, suspending conversation. "I will take you to Rojas," he said to Álvarez.

"How long will that take?" Fournier dared to ask.

Marquez didn't answer. As the screen door banged shut, the UN team members stood uncertainly, trailing Álvarez out. "Deputy Buitre will assume command till my return," Marquez announced as he swung a pack onto his back. "In the meantime, you will sleep there." He pointed to the bamboo-and-thatch bungalow from which Álvarez had emerged earlier.

Leaving Buitre with last-minute instructions, Marquez marched off with the Argentine, plus a small detachment of soldiers, back the way the UN team had just come.

Had they passed Rojas's camp on the way here? Lucy wondered. What about the hostages? Maybe they'd walked right by them without even realizing.

Buitre swaggered toward them, suspending her thoughts. A ripple of unease ran through the team members as he hitched his trousers in a gesture of self-importance.

"*Oigan,*" he commanded. *Listen up.* "If any of you cause mischief, I will lock you in there." He pointed to a shed standing some distance from the camp. It appeared so rotten and dilapidated that it might collapse at any moment. "It is filled with hornets and rats. Stay out of my way," he added. With a dark look, he turned and stamped into the building they'd just evacuated to enjoy his electricity and, presumably, to rest.

The UN team members looked at one another.

"What shall we do?" the Italian asked.

"Let us have a look at our accommodations," Fournier suggested, leading Şukruye by the arm. Bellini followed them, but the three Spaniards—Carlos, Luna, and Gustavo—

remained outside, braving the drizzle to confer out of range of anyone's hearing.

"Where do you think we are?" Carlos murmured.

"The eastern side of La Montaña," Gus replied, "at an altitude of maybe ten thousand feet?" He lifted his gaze to peer through the thinned trees. The mountain's twin peaks were just discernable in the drifting mist. Somewhere up there was the radio station broadcasting the Voice of the Resistance.

"I agree," said Carlos.

"Why don't we ask the kids?" Lucy suggested, nodding to the handful of youth wandering toward a small field, passing a soccer ball between them. While the female rebels stayed busy cleaning utensils and toting firewood, the boys had broken away to play Latin American *fútbol*.

Carlos sent them each a measuring look. "How are your soccer skills?" he asked.

Gus gestured to Lucy. "She can play. I have two left feet."

"Let's suggest a game," said the Spaniard with a twinkle in his eyes. "Two against five. You think they'll go for those odds?"

"You'd better be good," Lucy countered, gesturing for him to lead the way.

"I'm not bad," he said with a modest shrug.

GUS WATCHED CARLOS AND LUCY walk toward the field. The ball rolled to a stop as the four teens noted their approach. As Carlos issued the invitation to a match, they glanced in unison at Buitre's brick hooch.

The deputy was evidently resting. Regarding one another, they shrugged. Sure, why not?

"Come on, Gustavo. We need another player," Carlos called, waving him over.

Gesturing that he couldn't see to play, Gus put his back to the trunk of an orange tree and waited to see what a soccer game could accomplish in the way of recruiting young informants.

The goals were marked by Russian-made AK-47s placed on either end of the flattest terrain. Lucy opted to defend the backfield and play goalie. Carlos played forward. With a nod, the game began.

Gus frowned in bemusement as the Spaniard let the ball slip away from him. It was up to Lucy to defend against three fleet-footed youths.

Then he couldn't help but smile a little. PTSD or no PTSD, she was proving an uncomplaining and resourceful partner. With her long legs and quick feet, she held her own against the practiced youths, stealing the ball out from beneath a young man's feet and passing it up to Carlos, who immediately let it go again.

Gus chuckled at her look of pure annoyance. Her temper, as daunting as it had been eight years ago, intrigued him as much as her cutting awareness. Regardless of his extensive training, no matter how hard he paid attention to what was going on around him, he tended to overlook the details, to lose himself in abstractions. Lucy, on the other hand, was a pro. He may have thought he could handle this op alone, but he couldn't. He was glad she'd insisted on accompanying him, despite the risk to his heart.

Stealing the ball away a second time, she yelled at Carlos to hang on to it. In that same moment, the door of

Buitre's quarters creaked open, and there stood the disagreeable deputy, glaring at them from his porch stoop.

Damn, thought Gus, wondering if the man would interfere.

Back in the game, three rebels swarmed the Spaniard. All at once, Carlos went into high gear, dribbling past all three astonished defenders as he worked his way up field. He then sent the ball straight between the goalie's planted feet.

From the corner of his eye, Gus saw Buitre hang his keys on a nail, hitch his trousers, and step off his stoop. Was he going to break up the game? Gus wondered as he strode onto the field. But then he saw the players take their places. No, he was going to join it.

Suddenly, Gus didn't want Lucy playing anymore.

With Carlos outnumbered by four defenders, the rebels took possession. Buitre kept the ball for himself, dribbling toward Lucy, who attacked him warily.

Wedging a foot between his, she managed to steal the ball, kicking it back to Carlos, who once more weaved through his opponents to storm the goal.

The score was Spaniards two, Colombians zero.

Carlos sent Lucy a surreptitious signal to let their opponents score. No need to make the rebels unhappy.

Once more, Buitre brought the ball up field, circumventing Carlos. Even with two men open, he kept it for himself, bearing down on Lucy, who put up a half-hearted defense as Buitre deliberately teased her, showing off his dribbling skills.

Suddenly, and without any forewarning, he slipped in the mud. Lucy watched in surprise as he landed hard on his back. His four teammates guffawed. Marshaling her own smile, Lucy nudged Gus's respect to a whole new level by offering Buitre a hand.

Maybe you could fight fire with fire, he marveled.

But then Buitre viciously slapped her hand away.

Biting her lip, she stepped back, squared her shoulders, and raised her chin.

Gus saw red. He found himself stalking onto the field, battling down the illogical impulse to bludgeon Buitre's ugly face.

Carlos headed him off. "Easy, easy," he said with a firm hand on Gus's shoulder. "It's just a game," he added.

It took Buitre several more minutes to roll to his feet. He sent Lucy a murderous look, as if she were the reason he had fallen. *Shit,* thought Gus. This was just what they didn't need—an enemy in the rebel ranks.

Turning his back on his team, Buitre limped toward his hooch to nurse his injured pride.

Back on the field, the rebels shyly approached their opponents. By humiliating Buitre, the Spaniards had unwittingly won them over. One youth trotted off, returning minutes later with hard-boiled eggs for the winners.

Lucy accepted her egg with relish, peeling off the shell with hands that shook. As she stuffed it in her mouth in one bite, she swung a guilty look at Gus, who hadn't been given an egg.

"Go ahead," he told her, ignoring the rumble in his stomach. "You're the one with a runaway metabolism."

He spent a second memorizing the names of the young rebels: Julian, Estéban, Manuel, and David, all of whom were eager to tell their tale of woe. Two had been kidnapped by the FARC and forced into service. Manuel had been sold by his family for three bags of rice. David, who wore the insignia of a squad commander, admitted that he had dropped out of college to join the rebel cause. His father had been a white anthropologist, his mother an Arhuacan Indian.

Gus held his intelligent brown eyes a moment, reading both caution and youthful idealism in their depths. As the product of disparate social classes, he had chosen to identify with his mother's people, the downtrodden indigenous, whom the FARC allegedly represented.

Lucy startled Gus by throwing out the million-dollar question. "Do you know where the American hostages are kept?"

The younger boys shook their heads with credible ignorance. Manuel joked that he didn't even know where his own home was. As an illiterate *campesino,* that likely was the sad case. David merely shrugged and said, obliquely, "*¿Quién sabe?*"

Who knows?

And Gus realized Lucy was a step ahead of him. She'd already ferreted out their best informant. Question was, would the kid confide in them, or would he hold out?

Just then, Buitre burst from his shelter, disrupting the congenial conversation.

He stalked toward Manuel, who'd been the one to dole out eggs. "Why do you waste our food on these strangers?" he raged. Seizing the youth by his collar, he shook him forcefully. "Our own people are starving. We have no medicines, no way of looking after ourselves. Do you think they are here to help us? They are friends of the American spies." He began pulling Manuel toward the dreaded shed, the keychain on his belt loop jingling.

Lucy shook off Gus's arm as she trailed after them. "Excuse me, Deputy Buitre," she called out, her voice surprisingly strong. The guerrilla leader stopped and turned, eyeing her incredulously. "I'm the one who made you fall," she added, taking the blame for his slip, "Perhaps you should take your anger out on me, *chamo*."

She snapped her mouth abruptly shut, and Gus's antennae for danger went straight into the air. What had she just called him? *Chamo*. What was that? Even Carlos looked perplexed.

Buitre cocked his head to one side. "*Chamo?*" he repeated. "You talk like a Venezuelan bitch."

Lucy's face struck Gus as suddenly pale, the confidence she'd displayed only moments ago all but gone. She gave an awkward shrug.

Buitre released Manuel abruptly. "You wish to take his place?" he threatened, marching up to her even as Lucy bravely stood her ground.

Gus stepped between them, pushing Lucy behind him. "Careful," he warned, staring the man down. "The eyes of the world are upon the FARC at this moment," he reminded him quietly.

Buitre sneered, pretending Gus's gentle reminder made no difference to him. But then he spat on the ground at Gus's feet and stalked off, slamming into his quarters seconds later. The rest of the rebels drifted away.

Gus turned toward Lucy, including Carlos in his questioning look. "What does *chamo* mean?" he asked her as he led her toward the low burning fire in the fire pit.

"Buddy, pal," she translated into English. "It's Venezuelan slang. Sorry," she added, rubbing her forehead with obvious self-recrimination. "I forgot where I was."

"Don't worry about it," Gus said, putting a reassuring hand on her shoulder. "No damage done. Come on, let's check out the sleeping accommodations."

They all faltered at the sight of Fournier standing at

the bungalow door, looking harried. "Is there a problem?" he asked.

"No, no," Carlos assured him. "Buitre's a sore loser, that's all."

"Ah," said Fournier, but his troubled gray eyes remained locked on Lucy.

CHAPTER 6

"We'll sleep here," Gus decided, choosing the cubicle at the far end of the building, adjacent to a rear exit.

The long, leaf-covered bungalow consisted of cubbies divided by bamboo blinds. The alcove Gus had chosen had probably been passed over by the others because it brushed up against the jungle.

"Then I'll take this one," said Carlos, disappearing into the cubicle beside them.

Lucy noted the sparse accommodations without reservation. Each team member had been given a thin mat, a blanket, and mosquito netting. She'd slept in worse conditions in urban settings, and with Gus to keep her warm at night she had nothing to complain about.

Dragging her gaze up from the mat, she found him watching her with a hint of amusement. "Take your clothes off," he told her in Spanish as he unbuttoned his own jacket. "Jungle ticks," he reminded her, zapping any erotic images before they had a chance to fully form. "Leeches. We need to search each other daily, when there's plenty of light to see by."

"Oh." She fumbled to release the buttons on her jacket, sneaking a peek at him as his T-shirt came off. Light slipped through the leafy ceiling to dapple his bare chest. All that chest hair and rippling muscle must have made him irresistible to women. She wondered how many there had been, whether he'd ever been as close to any of them as he'd been to her.

"Boots, too?" she asked as he bent over to scrabble at his laces.

"Everything," he said.

Everything? She complied, watching curiously from the corner of her eye to see if he would remove his boxer briefs. She wasn't sure if she was relieved or disappointed when he didn't.

"Okay, pay attention," he said, inspecting their cubicle. "Set your boots over here where you can find them, even in the dark. Never put them on without turning them upside-down and shaking them first."

She wasn't sure she really wanted to know, but... "Snakes?" she guessed.

"Bats. Rodents. Beetles. Could be anything."

"Of course." She shouldn't have asked.

"There are several venomous snakes in the jungle, but you'll probably never see one. Different story with the other creatures."

As she placed her boots in the corner, he pointed to her clothing. "Never leave your clothes on the floor," he instructed. "Hang them up. Right there." He pointed to a hook hammered into the crossbeam.

She followed his directions to the letter, her awareness notching several degrees as they brushed against each other while hanging up their clothing.

"Step over here," he instructed, drawing her into a

patch of sunlight. "Hold your arms up," he added, running an all-seeing gaze over her torso.

Lucy's breath caught as he hooked a finger behind each panel of her bra and peeked inside. "Do you mind?" she sputtered. "I think I'd know if a tick or a leech was in there."

"Check the undersides of your breasts every day," he said, ignoring her and spinning her around.

"Don't—"

But it was too late. He'd already pulled her panties from the small of her back to peek at her bottom. Catching sight of her incision, he paused to inspect it and she glanced back, distracted.

"It's red," he said, sounding none too pleased.

"It's just chafed from the walk. I had to take off the bandage."

"Does this hurt?" he asked prodding the skin around the wound.

It did, but she didn't want him worrying. "No," she assured him.

He sent her a hard look. "Keep it covered and clean," he ordered grimly. "Damn it, Luce," he added quietly, "if it gets infected, then we're both in trouble."

"It won't," she assured him, hoping she was right.

He squatted abruptly, sweeping a hand down, then up the length of her legs. "No hair," he commented, oblivious to the awareness fizzing inside her. "How do you do that?" He stood up with a frown.

"It's called waxing. A man couldn't handle it."

His eyebrows rose at the challenge. "Is that right?"

"Trust me," she assured him with a smirk.

"Check your crotch every morning," he continued, deliberately crude. "Centipedes like to crawl into warm, moist places at night."

"Eww!" Lucy exclaimed in a very American-sounding protest. She quickly followed up with a "¡*Qué asco!*" and an apologetic grimace at Gus, who, with a shake of his head, spread his arms wide. "Now you check me. Ticks like to hide in hair, obviously, so if you don't mind, comb your fingers through my chest hair and my... armpits," he added, groping for the Spanish word.

Lucy just looked at him in disbelief. "Why can't you do that yourself?"

He cast his eyes upward. "I can't see as well as you, obviously. We're married now," he reminded her. "We look out for each other." *Teamwork,* he mouthed in English.

Lucy huffed out a breath but relented. Stepping closer, she sifted through his surprisingly soft, cinnamon-brown chest hair, relieved to find it parasite-free. The fuzzy trail that disappeared into his boxers was tempting to trace. Giving his armpits a cursory inspection, she hauled him around the way he'd done to her and checked his back, snapping the elastic of his boxers as she stole a peek at his smooth, gorgeously honed buttocks.

Was it hot in here, or...? "What now?" she demanded, aware that the Colombian army could be striking the rebel camp and she'd never even know it.

"Feet," he said, turning around to point down at the sturdy double-layered socks she'd bought with hiking in mind. "Take those off."

He'd already taken off his own socks. "We wash them when we can, but not if they won't dry. Wet feet cause jungle rot, and that's the last thing you want. Hang up your socks every night, upside down unless you want to invite something inside them. Any blisters? Cuts?" He frowned down at her pale, narrow feet.

"No."

"Good. If you get them, you do whatever it takes to keep them clean and covered."

"Got it. Can we get dressed now?" she asked, painfully aware of how vulnerable she felt on so many levels. Once upon a time, she and Gus had known each other's bodies as well as their own. This quasi-intimacy brought it all back, the pleasure, the playfulness, only the emotional bond they'd once shared needed to stay in the past. There wasn't any place for it now.

"Sure. Do I make you nervous?" he asked her mildly.

"No, why would you?" she retorted, suppressing a shiver of longing as she recalled their kiss on the plane.

His brandy-colored eyes gleamed with mockery. "Just checking."

Lucy caught a whiff of boiling rice. With her stomach growling, she stuffed her feet back in her socks. "Come on. I think they're cooking lunch, and I'm starving!"

As she reached for her clothing, she was conscious of Gus's thoughtful gaze sliding down her rib cage. "What?" she prompted, sensing his disapproval.

"You should have fattened up before making this trip," he scolded.

"I did. I ate like a pig."

"And then you ran every night."

"I did not." Did he just assume that or had he been spying on her again?

"Do you ever ask yourself what you're running from?" he persisted, that same probing light in his eyes.

Memories of the bombing in Valencia ripped through Lucy's thoughts, causing her to flinch and draw back. "I don't know what you're talking about," she muttered, turning away from his astute gaze. What was he implying— that she'd been emotionally damaged by the bombing, too? Hell, no. The CIA's psych staff would have caught that years ago.

To her relief, he dropped the subject and concentrated on getting dressed.

Lacing her boots up tightly, Lucy left their cubby without a backward glance.

God, she was hungry!

"Luna!" Hours later, Gus found her squatting in the drizzle behind the bungalow trying to coax one of the fat chickens out from under the building.

"What?" Their midday meal of rice and *panela* had scarcely taken the edge off her hunger. Low blood sugar made her cranky. He was better off leaving her alone. "Here, chickie." She made kissing sounds that caused the bird to cock its head. She had to know if it was hiding an egg under its fluffed-up feathers.

Between Gus's suggestion that she was running from something and the Venezuelan slang word that had popped out of her mouth earlier, she was feeling like a failure. And failure in any way, shape, or form was not an option.

Gus pulled her to her feet. "Come on," he urged. "We'll find you something to eat in the jungle."

How could he tell she was ravenous? "We can't just leave, can we?" She cast an anxious glance toward the camp.

"Fournier's napping, and Buitre's busy," Gus reasoned.

It was anti-American hour on the radio. The deputy sat in his quarters with the radio blaring out of his window so the younger rebels could listen to a ranting Cuban speak of matters few of them understood. "I want to call the JIC," he added in her ear. "Come on. Let's go."

She responded at once to the call for action. With her

fingers linked in his, she let him lead her into a steeply descending forest. Vegetation swallowed them. The patter of light rain drummed the canopy, drowning out the radio. Within minutes it felt like they were miles from the camp, when they couldn't be more than a hundred feet away.

"Are you sure you can find your way back?" she asked, disguising her rising anxiety.

"I've been marking our path," he assured her. "Like this," he said, bending a low-lying branch as they passed it. "Every time you go into the woods I want you to do the same thing," he urged.

Lucy cast her gaze upward into the spiraling trees. She could feel dozens of pairs of eyes on them, monkeys, no doubt, hunkered in the branches overhead, subdued by the rain.

Putting his back to a tree, Gus reached for his left boot. With a twist and a click, he opened the hidden compartment and pulled out the sat phone. Lucy kept a sharp lookout as he dialed the JIC.

"You should tell me the number," she whispered, "in case something happens to you."

"Nothing's going to happen to me," he insisted ultra seriously. "I put them on speed dial, number seven."

Lucky number seven, she thought as a droplet of water coursed down her spine, giving rise to a shudder. Her stomach rumbled. Where out here was he going to find any food?

His soft swearword had her glancing at him sharply. He was scowling up at the leafy dome overhead. "This is a dead zone," he explained, putting the phone away. "Come on." He led her deeper into the forest.

Some distance later, he stopped and tried the phone again.

"Anything?" she asked, her stomach churning.

"*Nada*," he retorted. "Maybe the canopy is too thick for the sound waves to penetrate."

"That's not good," said Lucy.

"No, it's not," he agreed as he grimly put the phone away. "Let's find something for your hip." He drew her toward a thick vine dangling from an immense height and plucked a leaf off it. Tearing it in half, he squeezed a clear liquid from it. "Rub this on your incision," he said, handing it to her.

He watched as she lifted her jacket and tugged her T-shirt from her pants.

"What is this?" she asked, smearing the leaf's juice over her incision, only to suck in a sharp breath.

"Wild grape. It has antiseptic properties."

"No shit," she breathed, wincing as it stung the open wound.

"Memorize the shape of the leaf," he said, snapping off another for her inspection. "See how distinctive it is? It grows all over the place. Do this every time you take a potty break, and the wound should heal."

"Got it," she said, growing annoyed with his detailed instructions. Her stomach growled again. "Can we find something to eat now?" she pleaded.

He swept a discerning eye around them, pulled her toward some rotting fruit on the ground, then pointed up into the branches of a tree, where whitish globes dangled among dark leaves. "There."

"Are they edible?" Lucy asked, her mouth watering already.

"Yes. Search the ground. You may find some you can eat."

Lucy snatched up a spiked ball and turned it over in

her hands, looking for bugs. "It looks like lychee," she commented.

"Same fruit family. It's called garcinia."

As she pried off the prickly skin and popped the white globule into her mouth, Gus struggled to climb the tree, but the branches were too high and the trunk too slippery to get a firm grasp. Enjoying the fruit's pulpy aromatic taste, Lucy hunted the ground for more, but there weren't any.

"I'm not going to be able to climb this," Gus apologized, giving up.

"I'll stand on your shoulders," she offered, unwilling to take no for an answer.

"No. You could fall."

"So, if I fall you'll catch me, right?" she reasoned. "Please, Gus. I'm starving. Now, give me a hand up."

With an unhappy grimace, he planted his feet apart and held up his hands. Lucy wiped her sticky fingers on her jacket, grabbed his hands, and stepped from his thigh onto his shoulders.

From there she managed to reach a higher branch and pull herself onto the lowest bough. Fruit dangled enticingly overhead.

"Careful," he cautioned as she groped for them.

The slickness of the bark beneath her feet was daunting. But hunger compelled her to lunge for a branch just out of reach. She caught it, shaking it furiously to dislodge several garcinias.

Thump, thump, thump. Even as they hit the loamy soil, Lucy lost her footing. Swallowing a scream, she fell backward, crashing into Gus, who rushed to catch her.

Together they hit the earth with a squishy *thud*. Gravity lassoed them, pulling them down a near-vertical slope, over a slick layer of rotting vegetation.

"Hold on!" he cried as they crashed through the under-growth together. A sapling flashed by, and he seized it, bringing them to a jarring halt.

Lucy dug her toes into the loam to keep them there.

For a minute, neither of them moved. She heard Gus drag air back in his lungs. She bent her right leg to make certain her kneecap, which had struck a root, wasn't shattered. Then she slowly sat up and realized she was straddling him. If she tried to clamber off him, she'd slip.

Catching Gus's eye, she found him regarding her intensely. His hands flexed on her thighs. "You okay?" he rasped.

"Fine."

She hadn't straddled him like this since she was twenty years old and Gus was her playground. Remembered pleasures made her inner muscles clench with sudden longing. The realization that he was growing hard against her crotch prompted a rush of liquid heat. Suddenly, she wanted more than anything to feel him buried deep inside her.

No! Lucy Donovan didn't need that distraction. She couldn't let the promise of pleasure sweep her astray.

Summoning all her willpower, she dragged herself off him, only to start sliding again. He caught her wrist just in time to keep her from sliding out of sight and sound.

"Hold on!" he ordered harshly.

Keeping a firm grip on her and using the sapling as a crutch, he hauled himself off the ground. Then he pulled her firmly against him, banding her to his side with an arm around her waist. In spite of herself, Lucy luxuriated in his superior strength. "Don't do that again," he scolded. "Every decision you make out here, you check with me first. We're partners, got it?"

Partners. The word sounded symbiotic, summoning images of the way they used to be.

She'd been self-reliant for nearly a decade. Could she even operate that way with another human being? "Got it," she affirmed, dismayed by her desire to kiss and be kissed by him again.

"We'd better get back," he said, eyeing the slope they would have to climb. "This will take some coordination," he warned.

In the next ten minutes, Lucy discovered she could trust Gus to look to her safety. Of course, the reverse was also true. So long as safety was the result of partnership, she was all for it. She'd already admitted she needed him to make this assignment a success.

What she didn't need him for was to fulfill her deeply buried feminine yearnings. Those would have to go away on their own.

By the time they arrived at the garcinia tree, all the fruit was gone, stolen away by creatures unseen. Lucy didn't even want to know what they were. All she knew was she was still hungry, in every sense of the word.

A ROOSTER CROWED WELL before dawn, and Gus's eyes sprang open.

The ghostly shimmer of the mosquito netting reminded him where he was. Oh, yes, asleep in a bungalow, way up on La Montaña, a guest of the FARC.

Lucy's soft body pressed to his made up for the thinness of the mat. He could feel her shivering, but she was sleeping at last, given the steady rise and fall of her chest. He hadn't slept much himself, not with the dull ache in his groin.

Playing Luna's husband while remaining profession-
ally vigilant was even harder than he'd thought it might
be. Lucy's scent, her softness, the way she fit against him
like his long-lost other half were undermining his intent
to keep their relationship professional, to keep his heart
intact.

His weakness for her was one of the reasons he hadn't
wanted her on this assignment. Ironically, it was probably
also the reason he had given in. A number of women had
thrown themselves at him over the years—SEAL group-
ies, mostly—but he'd never found another Lucy. And
despite his common sense warning him of her danger to
his heart, his body and soul had a will of their own.

He wanted Lucy the way he'd had her eight years ago,
before she'd cut him from her life. Only Lucy didn't seem
the least bit interested in rekindling intimacies. She was
too obsessed with saving the world, regardless of the cost
to herself.

The groaning of Buitre's screen door interrupted Gus's
reflections. Curious, he parted the leafy wall by his head
and peered outside. With a clear view of camp from this
end of the bungalow and the sky a dull shade of pewter,
he could see Buitre stalking toward the head of the trail
with an AK-47 in one arm and a battery-powered lantern
in the other. The rebel paused by the fifty-caliber machine
gun to speak with the man on watch.

Where would the deputy be headed this early in the
morning? Gus wondered.

The promise of his departure brought Gus more fully
awake. He eased carefully from the mat, loath to waken
Lucy. Donning his socks and boots, he ducked out of their
cubby and slipped from the bungalow's rear exit, stepping
quietly off the platform onto the muddy ground.

By then Buitre had disappeared up the trail.

Studying Buitre's hooch, Gus weighed his odds of entering it unseen by the kid on watch. With the lean-to that housed the rebels blocking the guard's view, his chances of success looked good, providing he kept close to the building's shadows.

Counting on the wet earth to muffle his footfalls, he crept toward Buitre's quarters. The door yielded with a groan, and he slipped inside, shutting it softly. Letting his eyes adjust to the gloom, he waited for his fast-beating heart to find a steady tempo.

Predawn light shimmered in the window, but the radio that had been on the windowsill yesterday was gone. Buitre must have taken it with him.

The notebook, on the other hand, still lay on the desk. Crossing the room to pick it up, Gus cracked it open, deducing at once that it was a log, updated daily by the highest-ranking officer. Needing more light, he carried it to the window and flipped through the pages, skimming the contents. As he blundered into a hand-drawn map of La Montaña, his heart gave a leap of excitement.

This was just the kind of information the JIC desired from them. If there were time, he would snap off some digital photos with the camera built into his sat phone. But the sun was rising quickly. Instead, he would have to take the map and hope it wouldn't be missed.

Beneath his deft fingers, the page parted smoothly from the binding. Blowing stray bits of paper off the desk, he folded it and stuffed it in his pocket, returning the notebook to the desk.

The sky was already brighter.

He moved toward the bunk on the other side of the room and ran his hands along the headboard, encountering the haft of a small, sharp knife. *Yes!* He curled it into his palm, relieved to have a weapon, which he hoped Buitre would just assume he'd misplaced.

The sound of furtive footfalls caused Gus to freeze. Someone was creeping toward the door.

Flattening himself against the wall, he waited.

Crap! Now what? If a rebel stepped inside and saw him, he would have to subdue him without being seen, but killing him was out of the question. He dropped the knife into his thigh pocket and waited, resigned to using his bare hands.

The door creaked open, slowly, apprehensively.

A boot and a shoulder edged through the aperture. A pair of eyes rounded the corner, forcing him to react before the interloper spotted him. With a lunge, Gus clamped a hand over the individual's face, hauled him inside, and spun him around.

CHAPTER 7 ⸻

Lucy's muffled cry came just in time to keep Gus from suffocating her.

"Lucy!" His hoarse, spontaneous use of her name made him even angrier. *Jesus!* He whirled her around, put his nose to hers, and ground out, in Spanish, "Don't you ever sneak up on me like that!"

He could feel her heart hammering against his chest as fast as his own heart was racing. She shoved him with two hands, securing her freedom. "Why the hell did you sneak out without me?" she demanded.

"Because two of us would've been heard. We'll be lucky now if we're not caught," he answered furiously.

"Oh, yeah? So much for teamwork," she hissed.

"You were finally sleeping. What was I supposed to do, wake you up?"

"Of course."

Damn her, she was right. They were professionals first.

"Where'd Buitre go?" she added, peering around.

"I don't know. He headed up the trail alone with a rifle and a lantern."

"Did you find anything?"

"A map and a dagger," he confirmed, patting his thigh. "Come on. We need to leave." They'd stayed too long already. "I'll go first. When it's clear I'll give a whistle." Without thinking, he planted a distracted kiss on her lips. "Sorry," he muttered as her eyes widened in surprise.

With a self-directed grimace, he let himself out, slipping from the building into a distinctly brighter environment. The jungle quivered with birdsong and monkeys leaping through the branches. He crossed the compound casually, heading toward a clump of trees where the men were known to relieve themselves.

The coast looked clear. Giving a low whistle, he ducked behind a bush and watched as Lucy stepped from Buitre's hooch. At the same moment, a rebel rounded the long lean-to under which the soldiers slept. Shit! It was David. He spotted Lucy at the same time that she spied him. To her credit, she didn't stiffen or flee. Setting her shoulders, she bore right down on him.

When caught red-handed, go offensive. Lucy had acted on her father's advice more than once over the course of her career, and it had always paid off.

"Where is Buitre?" she demanded, stalking up to David while gesturing with annoyance at the empty hooch. "The Turkish woman has a fever, and I need the aspirin he took from my backpack. Where is it now?"

The suspicion that had creased David's brow eased. "Your goods belong to the people now. I'm sure your aspirin was handed over to one of our doctors, who will distribute it equitably," he said quietly.

"Equitably?" She propped her hands on her hips and sent him a dubious smile. "You mean everyone gets the same treatment?"

"Yes," he insisted. "We are all equals. No one person should have more than another."

"What about the hostages," she inquired sweetly. "Do they get aspirin, or are they not considered people?"

He opened his mouth to defend his ideals, realized she had found a flaw in them, and closed it.

Didn't think so. "So, there's no aspirin here."

"No," he said with a shrug.

"No medication of any kind."

"Sorry."

She heaved a long-suffering sigh. "All right, never mind." With that, she marched straight for the bungalow, hoping Gus had witnessed the encounter. Maybe it would erase any lingering doubts he still had about her.

Lucy Donovan could handle even the slipperiest situations.

"Hurry up," Lucy urged. "Show it to me," she added, casting a glance behind them as they slipped into the forest on a potty break. They weren't being followed. Both the rebels and the UN team were still finishing their breakfast. Gus and Lucy had a minute to themselves.

"Ten more yards," he answered, holding her tightly as they scrambled down the steep, wet slope. At last he pulled her behind a tree, withdrew a folded square of paper from his pocket, and handed it to her. While Lucy opened it, he fished the sat phone from his boot.

She eyed the crude ink drawing with puzzlement. "These must be the names of the camps," she determined, noting the words written over four X's. "*Ki-kirr-zikiz*," she pronounced slowly. "Do you think that's an Incan word?"

"Doubt it," said Gus. As he powered up the sat phone and waited, his look of hopefulness faded.

"No signal," Lucy guessed.

"No," he corroborated.

"So if it's not Incan, what is it? *Cecaot-Jicobo*," she added, making a face at her poor pronunciation of a second camp.

"I think it's an encryption," he said shortly.

She glanced at him sharply. "Really?" she asked, intrigued. Looking back at the names, she tried to see a pattern in the strange words but couldn't. "I wonder if that's the river we crossed," she mused, noting the drawing of a waterfall.

"You can't make that assumption. There's water all over this mountain," Gus refuted, angling the phone in the chance of getting a signal.

"How come this camp's not named?" she wondered, pointing to an X near the top of the mountain.

"I don't know," said Gus, giving up on getting a signal. "Maybe that's the radio station." He accessed the phone's internal camera. "Hold the map against the trunk so I can get some clear shots."

"How can we upload pictures without a signal?" she asked, holding the map against the tree.

"We can't. The pictures won't go anywhere till we can get coverage."

"Do you think they're worried that we haven't checked in?" she asked as he snapped off several close-ups. *She* was getting anxious. Their assignment wasn't exactly going according to plan.

"As long as they have us on radar and we're moving around, they won't worry," he assured her, stepping back. "Fold that up for me, will you?" he asked, bending to put the phone away.

SHOW NO FEAR 97

"When are you going to shred it?" she asked, folding it the way he had.

"Not until I know the JIC got the pictures. I may have to break the code myself."

Remembering how incredibly smart he was, Lucy gave him a nudge. "You can do it," she said with confidence.

"Thanks," he said, quirking her a smile as he struck the heel of his boot, shutting it. "We'd better get back before we're missed."

When a shout came out of the jungle hours later, Lucy's first reaction was relief. She hadn't agreed to this assignment just to sit around and wait for something to happen. The morning had been a lesson in boredom. At last, there came a distraction.

But the rebels responded with alarm. The youth manning the machine gun let loose a stream of bullets that sent leaves and bark flying. Lucy hit the dirt, just in case.

Buitre flew at the youth, shaking his fists in the air and roaring for him to stop.

One minute Gus was playing cards with Carlos and Bellini in the shade of the orange tree. The next he was hauling Lucy off the ground and pulling her behind the brick hooch, where he pinned her between the wall and his bigger body.

A taut quiet fell over the camp. Even the chickens seemed to listen. As Gus peered cautiously around the corner, Lucy eyed the pulse in his powerful neck. Having a partner wasn't all that bad, she reflected. This defensive positioning wasn't necessary in her opinion, but it was fun dodging bullets together.

"Who is it?" she asked, reading puzzlement in his golden-brown eyes.

"I don't know." He loosened his grip so she could see what he was looking at.

A band of men in solid green fatigues led four mules into the clearing.

"I hope that's food," said Lucy, eying the sacks on their backs.

"Check out their uniforms," urged Gus. "Those aren't FARC."

"Then who are they?"

"I don't know. ELN, maybe?" Colombia's National Liberation Army was a notorious rebel faction, smaller than the FARC but equally ruthless.

They watched as Buitre waved his own soldiers over to take the sacks and carry them to the kitchen lean-to that housed the cooking utensils.

"Why doesn't he just bring the mules over?" Lucy asked.

"Good question. Maybe he doesn't want us rubbing elbows with those guys. Let's see what happens when we wander closer," he proposed, grabbing her hand.

Together they walked toward the newcomers.

They hadn't made it past the fire pit when David stepped into their path. "Stay back," he warned as he lowered a sack marked *"Frijoles Negros"* onto the growing pile inside the lean-to. Black beans.

"Perhaps we can help," Gus inquired. "I can carry two at once."

Rebels ran back and forth, huffing and puffing under their fifty-pound sacks.

But David just shook his head. "No," he insisted. "Stay over here."

"Who are they?" Lucy called as David turned away. "Are they ELN?"

With a resolute set to his shoulders, the youth ignored her and plodded back to the mules.

In minutes, the foodstuffs were all unloaded and the little entourage turned and melted into the forest, leaving Gus and Lucy with more questions than answers.

That afternoon, Comandante Marquez returned with the Argentine.

As with the previous day, the UN team and the FARC's representative sequestered themselves in Buitre's quarters, where the droning generator muffled their conversation.

Occupying the same seats, they looked expectantly at the Argentine, who seemed to have aged overnight. He'd grown a prickly-looking moustache. Beads of sweat glimmered on his brow.

"Rojas's camp is a three-hour hike," he explained, wiping his brow with his sleeve.

Lucy slid a glance at Gus while wondering which camp on the map was three hours from this one.

"I have brought proof of life," Álvarez declared, withdrawing two wrinkled letters from his jacket and handing them to Fournier.

Bellini jumped up to snap on the tarnished brass lamp, which he positioned nearer to the table, and the Frenchman began examining the evidence.

"These appear to be authentic," he murmured with a frown, "but we will decide as a group." He passed one letter to his right, the other to his left.

When the letter from Jay Barnes fell into Lucy's hands, a dark, somber emotion smothered her. Given the water splotches and the smeared ink, it was obvious Jay had been suffering when he wrote it. It was addressed mainly to his bride, whom Lucy had met several times at embassy socials.

Jay's distress at being kept from her, deprived of human liberties, and cut off from civilization summoned oppressive feelings. Disguising her distress, she pointed out to Gus the phrases that offered references to time, and Gus nodded.

Barnes was hoping to be released by Independence Day, ten months and eight days from the day he was kidnapped.

When the second letter made its rounds, Lucy leaned on Gus's arm, struggling to decipher the poorly written message. The difference in Mike and Jay's tones was striking. Mike was less coherent, his letter an outpouring of grief and depression. He mentioned an illness, but he made no reference to time other than to lament having missed his son's ninth birthday.

"When was his son's birthday?" Gus asked, looking around. "Does anybody know?"

"December 8th," said Lucy, earning surprised glances. "I did my homework," she defended herself with a shrug.

"The date on this letter is May 15th," Gus noted.

"Would he still be dwelling on that six months later?" Şukruye asked.

"Can I see the letter?" Taking it from Gus, Lucy angled it toward the light. "Someone else wrote this date," she declared, handing the letter back to Fournier. "They didn't even use the same pen."

Fournier frowned at the letter. "It looks the same to me," he said, passing it to the others.

"I agree," said Şukruye.

"No, I think Luna's right," Carlos countered, looking up from the date. "The ink is different."

"I agree with Carlos and Luna," said Bellini. "Both the ink and the writing are different."

Fournier looked at Gus for his response. "What do you think?"

Gus slid the letter back to him. "My opinion doesn't matter. If there's any question, then the letter doesn't qualify as proof of life."

Fournier heaved a long sigh and nodded. "You're right." He turned to the Argentine. "I'm sorry, but we cannot accept this letter as proof of life for Mike Howitz."

The slim, dapper man seemed to shrink into his chair. Lucy felt sorry for him. As a pawn for the FARC, he was as much a hostage as Mike and Jay, despite the respect with which the rebels treated him.

"If we could only see them for ourselves," Carlos muttered, giving a push toward Lucy and Gus's objective.

"The FARC leaders would never allow it," said Fournier with certainty. "Would they?" he asked the Argentine.

The man shook his head. "No," he said. "Not even I may see them."

"What if we heard their voices?" Gus suggested.

All eyes focused with surprise on him.

"Buitre owns a shortwave radio," he continued, nodding toward the radio presently perched on the windowsill. "There's bound to be another one somewhere. We wouldn't have to see the hostages to determine who they are. Their accents would identify them."

Even better, thought Lucy, America's premier spy plane, the Predator, could snatch the radio waves out of the air and maybe pinpoint where they came from. Gus's suggestion was nothing short of brilliant, providing the FARC took him up on it.

Fournier shot a look at the Argentine. "What do you think?"

The middleman gave a weary shrug. "All I can do is ask," he replied. "Rojas told me to remind you of the FARC's demands. Commander Alfonso Gitano must be surrendered by the United States and delivered to La Montaña. Only then will the hostages be freed."

"We will not discuss any terms until we are certain the hostages are alive," Fournier quietly reminded him.

Álvarez ducked his head. "I understand," he answered.

"Then we're done for now," said Fournier, dismissing everyone. With heavy hearts, they pushed back their chairs, resigned to the soul-numbing task of waiting.

As they exited the building, the scent of simmering beans drew them toward the fire pit. Álvarez shared a word with Marquez, who gestured to the cauldron hanging over the pit. "First we eat," he declared.

Thanks to the mysterious delivery that morning, Lucy would get a decent meal, at last.

She had scarcely finished eating when Buitre shouted unexpectedly, "Get up! You're leaving."

The team members regarded each other in alarmed confusion.

"Where are we going?" Fournier dared to inquire.

"No questions. Follow the squad commander," the deputy replied, pointing to David and his three sidekicks, Estéban, Julian, and Manuel, all of whom clutched their AK-47s.

With the beans sitting heavily in her stomach, Lucy rose, suspicious of the FARC's intent. The rebels were notorious for relocating their hostages. Why would they treat the UN team any differently? She sent Gus a worried look. His alert expression only increased her apprehension. Were they being marched to a different camp? How long or arduous would the hike be?

"You," Buitre called to Bellini. "Carry the bucket."

Looking mystified, Bellini did as he was told. With a cautious peek inside the pail of hammered tin, he sent the others a sheepish grin. "Soap and towels," he explained.

Lucy sagged with relief. Hallelujah! They weren't being sent on another long march. They were being led somewhere to bathe!

As they entered a second path on the north side of the clearing, a watery sun slid from behind the clouds, further lifting their spirits. It sent feeble rays through the canopy, enhancing every pigment of green around them. The sound of rushing water grew from a hiss into a gushing enticement to hurry.

They burst upon a clearing with a chorus of appreciation. A twenty-foot cataract spilled with dizzy abandon over a cliff, thundered into a basin the size of a back-yard pool, then tumbled onward over a series of smaller rapids to disappear into the lush forest.

The waterfall drawn upon the map? Lucy wondered, catching Gus's eye.

Bellini dropped the bucket as he and Carlos raced to see who could undress the fastest. Shucking her boots, Lucy watched Gus to see what he would do. He had hidden the little dagger in the bungalow near their mat, but he still carried the map in his trousers, the phone in his boot. Surely he'd be nervous about parting with either.

Deciding her clothing needed a bath as much as she did, Lucy removed just her boots and socks before wading into the shallows. Shocked by the cold temperature, she hesitated a split second, then dove into the pool headfirst.

Bone-chilling water closed over her, numbing the itchy welts on her neck. Thunder roared in her ear, muffling the exclamations of Bellini and Carlos as they waded in the shallows. A current of frigid water threatened to wash her downstream. Fighting her way through it, she anchored herself on a large rock at the bottom and, ignoring her air-starved lungs, reveled in her momentary isolation.

A sudden disturbance had her looking around. A shadow flashed before her eyes. A powerful arm coiled abruptly around her midsection, and she was hauled to the surface with breathtaking speed.

"You all right?" Gus rasped, water spiking his eyes as he searched her with real concern.

Embarrassed that she'd alarmed him for no reason, Lucy felt her face heat. "Yeah, I'm fine." She'd forgotten that she was supposed to clear decisions with her partner first. "Sorry," she added.

His mouth firmed with disapproval. "You shouldn't dive into unfamiliar waters," he chastised, his kicks powerful enough to keep them both afloat. "I thought you hit your head on a rock."

"No, I just wanted some time to myself. Sorry," she repeated. Glancing self-consciously toward shore, she caught sight of Manuel picking up one of Gus's boots. At her soft gasp, Gus turned his head and frowned.

"Estéban," Manuel called, holding up the boot for his friend to see. "Look at the size of Gustavo's feet!" He tossed it at Estéban, who held it up and hooted.

They had the left boot, the one with the phone in it. "Put it down," said Gus, managing to keep his tone mild. Releas-

ng Lucy, he headed toward the shallows and was pushing
himself out of the water to get his point across.

"Hey, señora," Estéban called, ignoring him to grin at
Lucy. "Is it true what they say about a man's feet?"

Manuel pointed down at his friend's boots and collapsed onto a boulder, laughing.

With Gus bearing down on him and angered by his
friend's nonverbal insult, Estéban hurled the boot at Gus.
The heavy boot landed with a splash next to Carlos, who
snatched it up and swiftly upended it. Flicking Gus a
tense look, Carlos rounded on David, who'd been watching passively up to that point. "Who's in charge here?" he
demanded. "Do you want your guests to get jungle rot?"

Coming sharply to attention, David stalked toward his
friends to admonish them.

As Gus went to put the boot back with its mate, Lucy
realized he'd jumped in with his pants on. If the map was
still in the pocket as she suspected it was, it would be
nothing but a soggy wad of paper by now.

Oh, no. Surely he'd considered that.

But as he pulled his sagging pants up over the pale
strip of flesh beneath his tan line, he sent her a flat look
that said it all.

He'd opted to save her when she didn't even need saving, over keeping the map dry.

Terrific.

If the JIC never got the images they had taken, then all
was lost. They might as well not have stolen the map in
the first place.

CHAPTER 8

In the dusk's purplish light, Lucy could see Gus kneeling in the corner of their cubby, taking the sat phone out of his boot. *What are you doing?* she nearly asked, but the sharp question would have been overheard by the other team members as they settled down for the night.

Her incredulity mounted as he powered up the phone, hiding it inside his buttoned-up jacket. She realized he had to be testing whether it had been damaged when the boot was thrown into the water, but her heart thudded with concern that the phone's lit display might be noticed by the others.

Dropping to her knees beside him, she helped him shield its bluish glow. Clearly it still worked.

Set to mute, the phone didn't make a sound.

As he stared down inside his jacket, Lucy regarded its reflection in his eyes. He sent her a quick smile of relief and she realized that they were getting satellite coverage, at last, right here in the camp, where the canopy had been thinned.

With quick thumb work, he uploaded the images of the map to the JIC, waited several seconds to make certain the message was fully sent, then powered the phone down, putting it back in his boot.

Peering over her shoulder, Lucy strained her ears for any indication that the others might have noticed. Hearing nothing but sniffles and groans and low murmurs, she relaxed. Gus had taken a risk, yes, but he'd made headway on their objective.

"Ready for bed?" he asked, casually setting his boots aside.

"Sure." She reached for her own boots, tugging them off.

"If your clothes are still wet, you'd better take them off," he warned, stepping out of his pants.

She didn't even want to know what kind of strange jungle fungus she might contract if she didn't. Stripping down to just her bra and underwear, she shivered at the encroaching chill. Hanging her clothes up, she joined Gus under the mosquito netting, squirming into the warmth that awaited her under their common blanket.

Her senses leapt as her bare legs brushed his. This was the first time they'd gone to bed together nearly naked. The novelty jolted her nervous system. She wasn't sure she could even sleep this way. Keeping to the edge of the mat, she tried to warm herself without touching too much of Gus at once.

It wasn't easy, no more than it was easy to ignore the yearnings that ebbed and flowed in her like a warm tide.

"So what did you do with the map?" she whispered, wondering if the soggy thing was still in his hanging pants pocket.

"Buried it in the woods," he replied. Without warning, he turned onto his side, hooked an arm around her waist, and pulled her closer. The weight of his sex brushed against her thigh. She was positive she couldn't sleep this way.

"I don't understand why you jumped into the water with your clothes on," she commented, determined to ignore her body's awareness.

"No, I guess you wouldn't," he replied.

Lucy stiffened. "What is that supposed to mean?"

"Nothing. If you'd had the kind of training I've had, you wouldn't wonder why. That's all."

"So now my training is deficient?"

"That's not what I said."

Outside their bungalow, the rebel camp went suddenly dark. Water hissed over the campfire's embers. Buitre switched off his generator, making the hum of insects seem suddenly louder.

"Look, I'm not trying to fight with you, Luce. We're on the same side, you know. I'm not the enemy," he murmured in her ear.

Given the longing rippling from her neck to her toes, she wasn't so sure about that.

"We used to be best friends, remember?"

A vision of Gus driving from Rhode Island to Washington, D.C., in a blizzard so he could see her over Christmas break put pressure on Lucy's chest. "I remember," she conceded.

A long, reflective silence ensued as more memories sluiced through her mind, every one of them tinged with tenderness and love. Had her life really been that wonderful?

"What we had was pretty good," he commented, revealing that his thoughts ran parallel to hers.

"We were young," she reasoned. "Life wasn't complicated like it is now."

She gave a start at the feel of his finger running lightly from her forehead, over her cheekbone, and along the soft flesh of her lower lip. Desire looped through her, tightening its hold on her like a satin ribbon, matched by equal parts fear.

"Does this feel complicated?" he asked her.

Lucy's chest felt tight. For the past eight years, she'd focused exclusively on her career. There had been no place in her life for tenderness or honesty. Yet here was Gus, touching her the way he used to, sweetly, gently, summoning a softness she hadn't allowed herself to feel, let alone reveal the need for. "Yes," she breathed.

"Why?" His fingers moved lower, down the length of her neck, giving rise to a pleasant shiver, before sliding away to trace her delicate collarbones.

"Because."

"Because why?" His fingers drifted lower still, warming her as they traced the outline of her satin bra. With a crescendo of desire, her nipples peaked.

She grabbed his hand, her heart pounding. "We can't," she protested. But desire outmatched her reason, and instead of pushing him away, she pressed his palm to her aching breast.

Suddenly decisive, he pulled her under him, cupping her jaw and kissing her thoroughly as he settled between her thighs. Lucy clung to him, helplessly responsive, her thoughts spinning in confusion.

But the hum of desire as Gus's lips trailed fire down her neck quieted her fears.

They were consenting adults, they were *married,* at least according to their cover, and suddenly it didn't seem so dangerous, so threatening.

He edged her bra aside, and the rasp of his tongue over her stiff nipple silenced her reticence once and for all. She wrapped her arms and legs around him, reveling in his power and breadth, pleased by the way he'd transformed himself, heartbroken by the reason for it.

Oh, Gus. He must have been devastated when his father died. She wished he'd found a way to tell her, only she had severed communications with him just months before, fully focused on her upcoming career with the CIA. She hadn't wanted distractions to slow her down.

She refused to consider that her decision had been a mistake. Still, she would have wanted to comfort him.

As he suckled her nipples, she sank her fingernails into the thick muscles of his back, longing to pull him closer, closer, but he eluded her, nibbling and licking his way down her torso, swirling in and out of her navel.

Lucy gasped, her back arching off the mat as anticipation bathed her in moist heat. *Oh, please, yes.* The mountain air touched coldly on her naked breasts, but with the blanket around her knees and Gus's head between her thighs, she felt nothing but warmth and pleasure and heart-pounding anticipation as he tugged her panties down and stabbed his tongue against her pulsing flesh.

It had to be the danger, the threat of discovery heightening her pleasure. My God, she hadn't come with another person in the same room for longer than she could remember, and here she was on the verge of shattering already. But then, this was Gus—James, who used to know her, truly *know* her. She didn't have to fake it with him.

Adding his clever fingers, he coaxed her higher. Climax ripped through Lucy, so powerful and so endless that it seemed to wring her from the inside out. No sooner did it ebb than emotion ambushed her without warning.

As Gus covered her, nudged her slick opening, and sank implacably inside her, she held in the alarming urge to cry.

What is wrong with you? It's just sex. Get a grip.

But the gentle rhythm he set resembled lovemaking more than sex. It summoned memories of a simpler time—a time filled with pleasure and excitement, anticipation and optimism. Tears seeped between her tightly closed eyelids, sliding into her hair. He kissed her, and the sweet surge and retreat of his body combined with his tender kisses was just too much.

"Just fuck me," she ordered hoarsely, tearing her lips from his. Sinking her nails into the sleek muscles of his buttocks, she urged him faster, deeper before his tenderness undermined something she'd worked so hard to build.

His body stiffened in surprise. At the same time, his thumb encountered the moisture at her temple and he stopped moving.

"Why the tears, Luce?" he demanded with puzzlement.

"I'm just frustrated," she insisted. Her body was drawn as tight as a bow. She just needed release from this internal crisis, and she'd be fine. "Please." She rocked against him, making demands he was forced to answer.

He complied all too thoroughly, grinding his hips into hers the way she needed him to. Within seconds, Lucy shattered again, as intensely as the first time. With a groan against her neck, Gus buried himself deep inside her and followed suit.

For a long minute, neither of them moved. Lucy, whose uncharacteristic tears had dried, hoped he wouldn't bring them up again. She turned her face aside, feigning drowsiness as he raised his head to regard her in the darkness.

"I assume you've got a handle on birth control?" he asked on a neutral note as he pulled out.

"Mm-hmm," she hummed, searching for her panties. The Depo shot covered her for three months at a time.

As she settled back upon the mat, he gathered her against him, tucking the blanket carefully around her shoulders. They lay back to front, absolutely quiet, their bodies sated for the time being.

Lucy could sense that Gus's thoughts were churning. She hoped he wouldn't ask her any more questions.

A good case officer had to be tough, vigilant, hard-edged. Relationships were for one of two purposes only—to appease her basic appetites or to obtain information. There should never be emotional overtones.

So, maybe she hadn't had sex with Gus. Maybe she'd made love to him.

No! She couldn't do that. Times had changed. Al Qaeda had attacked the United States on American soil. Now battles were being waged in every corner of the world. Caught in the midst of it, a key player, Lucy held the line.

She couldn't afford to let her guard down, to be soft, to listen to the yearnings of her heart. She had a job to do.

She couldn't afford to fall in love again.

GUS SCRUBBED A HAND over his four-day beard and sighed. He'd broken the map's code. At least, he *believed* he'd broken the code, but only the JIC could confirm that by looking at a geodetic map, and the guys at the JIC might not have even considered that the camps' names were encrypted.

He had to get in touch with them. If they directed the Predator to the right coordinates, the spy plane would be able to pick up heat signatures, get a feel for the rebel population, maybe snatch up some radio communications. He needed to talk to his teammates, but the only place the phone got coverage was right here in camp.

Placing a discreet call in the bungalow was out of the question. By day, the female rebels raised the bamboo blinds and beat the mats and blankets to chase out the vermin before sweeping the floor.

There had to be someplace *else* in this camp that offered a modicum of privacy so he could make a quick call.

Sweeping his gaze over the clearing, he was distracted by the sight of Lucy chumming up to the female rebels at the fire pit. Just the sight of her tightened his gut and sent a wave of warmth to his groin.

She had been just as amazingly responsive as he remembered. He suddenly wasn't as upset about having her for a partner as he used to be. The experience had been close to perfect, even better than he'd imagined, except when Lucy had shed those private tears. For some reason, though, those tears gave him hope. Maybe she'd been remembering how rare and precious their relationship once was. Or was that him projecting his hopes onto her, setting himself up for a fall?

Catching himself off-task, he turned his thoughts back to finding a private place from which to call the JIC.

His gaze settled thoughtfully on the dreaded shed.

Well, why not? he asked himself. Sure, it was ostensibly filled with hornets, which in equatorial regions carried stingers with twice the venom as in North America. There were probably vampire bats in there, too, and maybe the roof would screw up his signal, but with the shed set off to one side of the camp, he'd have all the privacy he needed for a lengthy conversation.

It couldn't be any worse than Hell Week at SEAL/

BUDs training, he reasoned. Or the mock torture they'd put him through at the Farm.

With a deep breath, he pushed off the bungalow deck, resolved to do whatever it took to get thrown into the shed.

Lucy was going to be pissed at him for not consulting with her first. He hadn't exactly modeled the concept of teamwork lately, but then again, one of his jobs on La Montaña was to keep Lucy alive and out of trouble, not drag her down with him.

Crossing the camp, he ignored her curious regard as he passed through the muddy clearing toward the orange tree that edged the training field. One of the rebels had left his AK-47 propped against it in lieu of carrying it on his back during drills. Either Buitre hadn't noticed yet, or he didn't care.

Arriving at the tree, Gus paused to listen to the deputy's instructions on burying a landmine. Buitre was down on his hands and knees placing a dud in the wet soil, showing the younger rebels how to cover it up. If the FARC were disintegrating, as intelligence suggested, then this level of training wouldn't be necessary, would it? Gus wondered.

Picking up the abandoned rifle, he turned it over with the air of a man who'd never held a gun before. From the corner of his eye, he noted Lucy's tension as she watched him from the fire pit. He'd better move fast before she thought to interfere.

Hearing a rustling overhead, he looked up, making eye contact with a howler monkey. "I'd move if I were you," he advised. With a final glance at Buitre, who'd noticed him at last, Gus pointed the weapon up into the branches and fired, missing the monkey by a mile.

"*Crack-crack!*" Bullets splintered branches overhead, raining down splinters and leaves.

"*¡Estúpido!*" roared Buitre, drawing his handgun as he stormed toward Gus, wild-eyed, his face flushed. "Drop the weapon!"

Feigning startled surprise, Gus dropped the assault rifle instantly. Lucy and Fournier were racing toward him nearly as fast as Buitre, but the deputy got to him first. Pulling back his fist, he plowed it into Gus's jaw with a swing Gus could've sidestepped, only he didn't.

Ouch, that actually hurt. Clamping a hand to his swelling lip, he put on a face of wounded innocence. But it wasn't over yet. Buitre spun him around, shoved him against the tree trunk, and thrust the barrel of his handgun between his ribs. "You idiot!" he seethed. "What do you mean firing a weapon at my soldiers?"

"Sorry," Gus rushed to apologize. "I was pretending to shoot the monkey and the gun went off."

"He wasn't even aiming at your soldiers," Lucy jumped in, defending him. "Put your gun away," she ordered. "It was an accident."

"Accident?" Buitre rounded on her. "There is no allowance in this camp for accidents. He could have killed one of my soldiers with his carelessness. He must be punished."

"*Comandante,*" said Fournier, addressing the deputy by a title calculated to inspire dignity. "Please, excuse Gustavo. He knows nothing of weapons. His sight is poor. I'm sure he meant no harm."

"You are sure?" Buitre repeated. "I am not. I have watched these two." He nodded at Gus and Lucy accusingly. "They are not like the others."

His accusation struck Fournier dumb. The negotiator swung a troubled look between them.

"You're paranoid," Lucy accused Buitre. She seemed hell-bent on getting punished along with Gus.

"Let it go, Luna," Gus advised, sending her a meaningful look. "I made a mistake. I'll take the punishment. Just stay out of it."

"Stay out of it?" she repeated, displaying classic Spanish temper. "You're my husband. You want me to stay out of it?"

He could practically hear her saying, *What happened to teamwork, buddy?*

Fournier placed a settling hand on Lucy's shoulder. "I am sure when Commander Marquez arrives, he'll resolve the matter at once."

Buitre very deliberately released the safety on his shotgun, causing all three of them to fall silent. "You," he said to Lucy, who had stepped protectively between him and Gus, "step away from him."

Fournier took a cautionary step back, pulling her with him.

"And you," the deputy growled at Gus, "will have time in the shed to reflect on your stupidity. Now walk."

Gus marched obediently forward. With Buitre's gun gouging his right shoulder blade, he managed to look over his left shoulder and catch Lucy's eye, sending her a subtle wink.

Her expression did not alter one iota, save for a faint thinning of her lips. But he knew by her sudden silence that she'd gotten the message.

He was going to sacrifice his body for the cause.

Fucking hornets had stingers the size of hypodermic needles.

With a shout of agony, Gus slapped the insects stabbing at the back of his neck and focused his efforts on keeping the intermittent signal. As long as he stood below the hole in the tin roof, straddling a puddle of fetid water, the signal was strong enough.

Holding down number seven, he speed-dialed the JIC, keeping his fingers crossed.

The familiar voice of the platoon medic, Vinny DeInnocentis, came from what seemed a great distance. "This is Fred," he said in his strong Philadelphia accent. "Who's this?"

"This is Ethel," corroborated Gus. The pass phrase had been Vinny's idea. "Did you get the images I uploaded last night?" he inquired, getting straight to the point, afraid he'd lose his signal.

"Roger, sir," said Vinny, abruptly professional. "We've been lookin' at 'em all day."

"I think the place names are encrypted, and I think I know how," Gus advised, keeping an ear pricked for any sounds outside of the shed, hoping nobody was eavesdropping. "The GPS on this sat phone puts me at three degrees, five minutes, and 31.9 seconds latitude, right? Convert those numbers to letters and you get C for the first letter, E for the second. See a camp that starts with those letters? It's *Cecaot-Jicobo*."

"Gus, this is Luther," rumbled the lieutenant, either taking over the call or putting him on speaker phone. "We copy you loud and clear and will play with the rest of the numbers and see if we can't break the code. I'm thinking the O in *Cecaot* is a decimal."

"Agreed," said Gus.

"So we may have positions on four camps. Any word yet on where the hostages are located?"

"Not yet," Gus confirmed. "We're awaiting proof of

life for Howitz. Barnes appears to be living, but there's a question about Howitz's health. I'm trying to get the rebels to let us speak to them via shortwave radio."

"Excellent call. We'll alert the Predator."

"Ow! Shit!" Gus smashed a hornet against the side of his head. "Little bastard." He brushed it off and felt for the stinger, lodged somewhere in his hair.

"You all right, Gus?" Luther sounded bemused. "Where are you?"

"In a torture chamber, but I'll live. Listen, I need to keep this brief. You have the names. Try and break the code."

"Will do, Gus. How's the missus?"

The simple reference to Lucy sent a pleasant shiver up Gus's spine, beating back his sharp discomfort. "Still alive and kicking," he retorted shortly. Which was how he intended her to stay.

"Roger that," said the OIC. "Call when you can. If we break the code, we'll leave you a message."

"Thank you, sir. Over and out."

With the call complete, Gus put the phone back in his boot, then hunted for a place to stand where he wouldn't draw so much attention from the hornets. Moving to the far corner, he ran into a giant spiderweb and stepped back, nearly stepping on a rat that scurried under his heel. Jerking the collar of his jacket up to protect his neck and eyeing the vampire bats dangling unperturbed under the eaves, he waited for however long it would take to be released.

"LUNA, WAIT," FOURNIER COMMANDED, grabbing the back of Lucy's jacket as she made to push off the bungalow platform.

A shout had just come from the jungle, preceding Marquez and the Argentine, who'd finally made an appearance, hours later than expected. Lucy had been sitting on the narrow deck, sweating under a muggy sun, tormented by flesh-seeking flies. She wanted to be the first to speak to Marquez on Gus's behalf.

Gus was her partner. She couldn't tell how he was faring in the shed, but that didn't prevent her from imagining the very worst. Helpless to protect him, she simmered with agitation, swearing to herself that she would deck him when they found themselves alone. He had to be calling the JIC. He could've cleared that with her first, before putting his life on the line. *Teamwork, my ass.* He didn't know the meaning of the word!

She, on the other hand, was doing a very credible job playing Gustavo's distraught wife. Since Buitre might have aroused Fournier's latent suspicions with his assertion that she and Gus were different, she even forced herself to shed a few tears for Gus.

Fournier didn't need to know they were tears of frustration.

Gus had gone too far this time. What if those hornets in the shed were deadly? What if a few too many stings led to toxicity? He could actually die in there trying to make a stupid phone call, and what would she do then, huh? Had he thought of that?

Some of the anxiety she'd suffered at the outset of this assignment returned to her, making her wonder if her PTSD was here to stay. She had just begun to think she was getting a handle on it.

Holding herself back, per Fournier's recommendation, Lucy watched Buitre hurry over to Marquez. Gesturing at the shed and nodding toward the bungalow, his dark eyes smoldered with contempt.

Lucy's stomach cramped. God, she hated that look. But surely Marquez wouldn't believe Gus had intentionally shot at the rebels. He listened at length, then abruptly raised a hand. "Release the Spaniard," Lucy overheard him say.

She expelled the breath she was holding.

"I told you," said Fournier with a comforting pat on her back.

"But, Commander!" Buitre protested.

"I said release him." Lowering his voice, Marquez added something that put a cold, resigned look on Buitre's face. The deputy swiveled toward the shed, removing the keychain from his hip to unfasten the padlock that kept it closed.

Lucy couldn't wait a second longer. She leapt off the bungalow deck, sprinting to the shed to see how Gus had fared.

As he stumbled out, blinking against the harsh sunlight, the desire to deck him disintegrated. A lump on the side of his head disfigured the shape of his skull. Another puffed out just below his left eye. His neck was swollen and red.

"Oh, Gustavo," she exclaimed, her dismay perfectly genuine. "Someone get a wet cloth," she pleaded, touching fingertips to his swollen cheekbone and finding it hot to the touch.

"I'm okay," he gritted.

"Here, you should sit down," she said, dragging him toward a tree stump.

"I'm fine," he assured her, but then he swayed against

her, forcing her to catch him before he fell. She hoped to hell he was faking it.

Şukruye, who'd rushed to get a wet cloth from one of the female rebels, handed Lucy a cool rag. She pressed it to Gus's neck as the others converged around the Argentine.

"Rojas has agreed to let you speak with the hostages," Álvarez informed them tiredly.

As Gus turned his head in surprise, Lucy whispered, "Did you get through?"

He gave a discreet nod, regarding the others intently.

"When?" Fournier demanded. "When can we speak to them?"

"Now," said Marquez, approaching and waving them toward the hooch.

They were going to speak with the hostages via short-wave radio! With a look of shared victory, Gus let Lucy haul him to his feet. Together they trailed the others into Buitre's quarters, thrilled by the prospect of speaking to Lucy's colleagues. She couldn't help but hope freedom was just around the corner for Mike and Jay.

CHAPTER 9

For the third time, the negotiating team took their seats at the crude table, waiting tensely as Marquez worked the shortwave radio, scanning frequencies until he found the one he was looking for.

The radio ceased to crackle. A voice responded to Marquez's greeting, and they exchanged brief words. Marquez extended the radio to Fournier. "This is the *jefe,* the boss who guards the hostages," he imparted with a stern look all around. "You have two minutes to speak to the Americans." As Fournier took the radio, he left the building.

"Hello?" said the Frenchman cautiously.

"Yes, hello!"

Lucy's heart leapt at the familiar sound of Jay Barnes's voice. Relief sang through her veins. Soon he would get to go home. He would put this behind him and move on.

"Er, who is this?" Fournier replied in his heavily accented English.

"This is Jay Barnes, from St. Louis, Missouri."

"Mr. Barnes, good afternoon. My name is Pierre

Fournier. I am with a UN negotiating team. We are currently situated on La Montaña."

"Thank God," Jay exclaimed, his voice breaking with the force of his relief. "Please, I appreciate whatever you can do to seek my release."

"How is your health, Mr. Barnes?"

"Fine. I'm weak, but my health is . . . it's okay."

"You make no mention of your companion," Fournier pointed out.

"Oh, he's . . . he's here. He's not doing so well, though."

"Is he ill, Mr. Barnes?

"Yes, yes, he's terribly ill. Cranial malaria, I think."

Jesus. Lucy fought to keep her reaction from showing. The distress in Jay's voice made her chest tight, made her eyes sting. She longed to reassure him. *Jay, it's me. We're gonna get you out of there, I swear it.*

"Can Mr. Howitz speak?" Fournier inquired.

"Uh, yeah. I'll hold the radio for him."

"Hello? Mr. Howitz?"

An unintelligible grunt followed.

"Are you Mike Howitz?" Fournier asked as every team member strained to hear the man's reply.

"Yes," rasped a voice.

Lucy cocked her head, sending Gus a frown. It didn't sound like Mike.

"Mr. Howitz, my name is Pierre Fournier. I'm with the United Nations. Can you tell me where you're from?"

"Los Angeles," rasped Howitz.

With hope in his gray eyes Fournier nodded encouragingly. "Can you tell me the date of your son's birthday?"

A muffled whisper followed the question.

"Mr. Howitz?" Fournier repeated.

"Mikey," breathed the ill man on the other end.

"Yes, when is Mikey's birthday?" Fournier repeated.

A long pause ensued. Either the man was too ill to remember, or—"February 3rd," he wheezed at last.

Fournier cut Lucy a frown, meant to chastise her for getting the date wrong.

No. Lucy shook her head. Mikey's birthday was December 8th. She was certain of it.

Across from her the Argentine appeared to be meditating.

"Have any doctors tried to treat you, Mr. Howitz?" Fournier asked with grave concern.

"They gave me pills," the man corroborated.

Lucy closed her eyes to conceal her sudden dismay. Whoever was pretending to be Mike Howitz was not a native English speaker. He'd pronounced pills as *peels*. That meant Mike was either too sick to talk or he was dead.

But Fournier, who spoke with an accent himself, couldn't hear that subtlety. Carlos caught his eye and vehemently shook his head. "He is not American," he mouthed.

"Thank you, Mr. Howitz. May I speak, again, with Mr. Barnes?"

"*Basta*." growled the voice of the *jefe,* hostage boss. *Enough.* "Your time is up."

The radio in Fournier's hand emitted a low hiss. He lowered it to the table, swallowed hard, and looked up at the others with a sad, troubled gaze. "I'm afraid we may assume Mike Howitz is dead, or too ill to speak at all."

Shocked and horrified, Lucy slowly lowered her eyes to the radio. Mike had been so full of life, always grinning, full of jokes, up to any challenge. Apparently, being held against his will, in a jungle rife with disease, was just too much.

She thought about his eleven-year-old son, and his beautiful wife, and her throat constricted. Life—or was it death?—was so fucking unfair, stealing away the most precious people.

Lucy lifted an accusing gaze toward the Argentine. "Did you know anything about this?" she demanded, fighting to contain her runaway emotions.

"No," said the man tiredly. "They tell me nothing. I travel from one camp to the other bearing offers to Rojas and counteroffers to you, nothing more."

"Where are the hostages kept? Have you heard anything?" asked Carlos, ever mindful of Lucy and Gus's objective.

"I believe they are kept at a remote camp," Álvarez replied, darting a quick, frightened look toward the door. Leaning in, he pitched his voice lower to add, "I've heard rebels whispering of a place called *Arriba,* up there."

Remembering the place on the map marked with an X and nothing more, Lucy cut a glance at Gus.

"Sounds like it's near the mountaintop," he mused, ignoring her look.

Bellini sat forward. "How does the death of one of the hostages change our situation?" he asked in awkwardly phrased Spanish.

Fournier frowned. "It gives us the advantage, actually," he admitted, slowly. "Clearly they were hoping to pass some other hostage off as Mr. Howitz, only we are not fools, are we?"

He focused a compassionate eye on the Argentine. "Tell Commander Rojas that because we have no proof of life for Mike Howitz, we are unable to fulfill the FARC's demands. General Gitano will never be released in exchange for a single hostage and a dead man. If Rojas is wise, he will accept the Colombian government's offer to release ten FARC captives of midlevel authority instead."

Álvarez rubbed his closed eyes. "Ten guerrillas for one U.S. hostage," he mumbled. "Sounds fair to me."

Lucy dragged air into her pressured lungs. At this rate, negotiations would continue indefinitely. And Jay would be left suffering in the meantime, not knowing if he would be rescued or if he, like Mike, would sicken and die. "Plus the body of Mike Howitz," Lucy suggested thickly.

"Yes," the Frenchman concurred, sliding her a look. "We must bring him home, dead or alive."

Mike was dead. *Dead.* The realization loosed the lock that kept Lucy's older memories contained, and they spilled free, rushing through her mind in streaming video.

The friends who'd studied in Valencia with her, Amy, Melissa, and Dan, had been put in closed caskets, their bodies mutilated by the roadside bomb. She'd attended every one of their funerals, watching as family members and loved ones mourned their loss.

Since then, she'd done everything in her power to give their deaths meaning—befriending scum, risking her life for information. She was still at it, even here in Colombia. She did it for Mike and Jay's sakes. Only she was too late.

Mike was dead.

Suddenly, just sitting in this stiflingly humid little hole of a building, stuck under the watchful eye of fanatics like Buitre, was more than she could tolerate. Unwieldy emotion kept her in a chokehold. She could not escape it.

She could feel her poise slipping away like granules of sand through her fingers. PTSD was here to stay, apparently. Even Lucy Donovan had her limits. There was only so much of this hellish work that she could take.

*   *   *

SENSING TENSION IN THE woman next to him, Gus glanced over. Lucy's face was, as always, serene as a marble statue's. He slid his gaze to her lap and realized with an unpleasant start that she was digging her nails into her palms, leaving little purple crescents in her flesh.

Howitz's death was freaking her out. She needed to get away from these people before she lost it.

With Fournier still drawing negotiations to a close, Gus thrust back his seat, stood, and weaved uncertainly. Everyone gaped up at him.

"Gustavo!" Lucy cried, snatched from her self-absorption.

"I don't feel so well," he confessed. "Mr. Fournier, please excuse me and my wife."

"Of course." The Frenchman dismissed them with a frown of concern.

Şukruye rose to help.

"I've got him," Lucy reassured her.

Together they staggered from the building to find Buitre seated at a crude field table, erected in the shade of the orange tree, inspecting rebels' weapons. A growing pile of discarded rifles lay at his feet.

"We need to talk," Gus whispered.

"The bungalow?"

He spied Marquez sitting by a crackling fire, looking tired and grizzled. "Ask Marquez if you can take me to the waterfall," he suggested. It was a long shot, but the man had shown some compassion; perhaps he'd show some more.

As Lucy steered him toward the fire, the commander

looked up, his expression not without sympathy as it touched on Gus's ravaged face.

Lucy's voice sounded strained as she made her request. "The stinging is too much," she added, and Gus hung on her, showing every indication of a man suffering from an overdose of insect venom.

To Gus's surprise, Marquez conceded. He swung a thoughtful look toward the rebels, then waved David over. "Take these two to the *salto*," Marquez ordered him. "Do not let them out of your sight."

"*Sí, comandante,*" said the youth, shouldering his weapon and gesturing for them to precede him.

Giving Marquez no time to change his mind, Gus and Lucy hastened across the field toward the vertical path that disappeared into the jungle.

LUCY COULD TELL THAT Gus was on to her. Somehow, some way, he'd intuited her need to escape, to flee the rebel camp and every horrible, violent thing it represented. Her impulse was so *unprofessional*, showed such *weakness*, that she tackled the incline at a near-run, furious with herself.

Gus tugged her back, slowing her down.

From the corner of her eye, she could read his concern. The fact that he was worried about her at all was as unpalatable as this alien feeling that she might burst.

"Luce, I'm sorry about Mike," he apologized.

David had evidently fallen far enough behind that he felt safe speaking in English. English made his words seem all the more final, the more painful. Regret stabbed Lucy in the heart. "Fucking bastards," she choked out.

"Talk to me, Lucy," he demanded as they struggled up the hill.

"There's nothing to say. Mike's dead. People die." A recollection of the bombing in Valencia streaked through her mind.

Glancing back, she was alarmed to find David practically upon their heels. Shit! Why were they speaking in English?

"I'm just lightheaded," she added in Spanish. "Probably dehydrated." She increased her speed, pulling Gus with her.

The roar of the waterfall grew louder. They came upon the little slice of paradise abruptly. As Gus threw himself onto a log to remove his boots and socks, Lucy stared at the sheet of rushing water, soothed by its endless flow.

"You coming in?" he asked, approaching the water with his clothes on.

"No," she answered. She didn't want to talk to him, to explain what was wrong with her. She'd lost it. That was it.

"Join me," he urged, "I want to show you something." He flicked a look at David who stood with his back to the trees, hands in his pocket, looking distinctly uncomfortable.

"No, I'm fine," she insisted, afraid he would pull the only thread that kept her from unraveling. "Go in without me."

She should have guessed what he intended when he approached with his eyes averted. He snatched her up, tossed her over his shoulder, and ran into the water with her. Her startled screech of disapproval came too late.

They landed in the frigid water with a *splash!* The chill sobered Lucy from her daze. Furious that he'd physically coerced her, she went to strangle him.

But he easily deflected her hands. Seizing her wrists, he locked them behind her back and pulled her into what was no doubt meant to be a comforting embrace.

No! Lucy panicked. *Not tenderness! Not again.*

She screamed at him under the water, a hoarse, bubbly roar that earned her immediate freedom.

Pushing to the surface, she gulped down air while swallowing back a sob. Keeping her stricken face averted, she swam to shore to anchor herself on a rock.

Get it together, Luce! What the hell is wrong with you?

She heard Gus break the surface behind her. She could sense him treading water thoughtfully, keeping his distance.

The mineral scent of stone filled her nostrils. *Just breathe,* she told herself. This storm, like the occasional bouts of depression she'd suffered through the years, would pass. She would land on her feet. She would pull it together. She just needed more time.

"*Señor*," called David unexpectedly. "I am going downstream to look for a special tree bark that will help with the welts," he explained.

David must have sensed the tension between them. Despite Marquez's orders, he was leaving them to hash it out. *Oh, no. Not today.* Lucy started climbing out. She would rather just forget about it.

Gus caught her by the pant leg. "Wait, I want to show you something," he insisted, repeating what he'd said earlier.

Streaming water onto the rock, Lucy hesitated. Maybe he just wanted to update her on his call to the JIC. After all, it had been important enough for him to risk his life to make it. "Show me what?" she demanded, slipping back into the pool.

Grabbing her hand, he pulled her toward the wall of water dimpling the surface in front of them.

"Hold your breath," he cautioned as he hauled her through it.

Water pounded briefly on their heads. In the next instant, she was treading water in a tranquil shelter, a wall of water on one side, mossy granite on the other. Bluish light flickered on Gus's face as he awaited her reaction.

"I didn't know this was here," she admitted, her strained voice echoing in the natural enclosure.

Clasping a ledge with one hand, he pulled her slowly, cautiously against him.

She stiffened, marshalling the emotions swirling inside of her, overlaid by physical awareness as he slipped a leg between her thighs. Even with his head swollen and his face disfigured his eyes drew her. She clasped his shoulders, loving the rock-hard feel of them beneath her hands.

"I should kick your butt," she growled at him, clinging on to her anger to keep from dissolving into tears. "You know you could've died in that damn shed."

"I know. And trust me, I'm sorry. But I think I broke the code, and I wanted to tell the JIC."

She blinked. "You broke the code?"

"I think so." He explained that the letters in the names possibly spelled out the camps' global positioning.

"You're a freaking genius!" she praised him.

"Yeah, right. If I was that smart I would've figured it out yesterday, and the JIC would've had the Predator in position, analyzing today's transmission with the hostages."

"It was probably up there. Give yourself a break. We've only been here a few days," she reasoned.

He sent her a grave, searching look. "I'm not the one who's hard on myself, Luce," he countered gently.

Emotion gripped her by the throat. She cast her eyes about, but there was no getting out of this.

"What's on your mind?" he prompted patiently.

She drew a deep breath. "I hate it when people die before they're supposed to," she admitted quickly, managing to guard her composure.

With a sigh of understanding, he lowered his forehead to hers. "Yeah, me, too," he admitted sympathetically. "I wouldn't be a SEAL at all if it weren't for what happened to my father. I just couldn't understand how anyone, regardless of culture or religion, could target thousands of innocent people like that. It was just so warped."

The pain in his voice made her clutch him tighter. "I saw my friends die in Valencia," she heard herself admit.

He lifted his head abruptly, surprise fixing his gaze. "You saw them die?" he repeated in astonishment. "You were there? You never told me that." They'd still been in contact via e-mail.

"I was sitting in the outdoor café with them when the bomb went off."

"Jesus, Luce," he breathed. "How'd you keep from getting killed?"

"The wrought-iron table flipped over, pinning me under it."

He searched her rigidly held face with horror. She could feel his heart pounding through their wet clothing as he pulled her suddenly, fiercely to him. "God, no wonder," he rasped by her ear.

For a moment she let him hold her, and she absorbed the comfort of his heat, his honest and complete sympathy. "No wonder what?" she prompted after a while.

He set her slightly away from him, seeming to consider what he would say next. "No wonder you've taken so many risks all these years," he said steadily.

His assertion made her frown. "What are you talking about? Our jobs are dangerous. I don't take any unnecessary risks," she insisted.

He just looked at her. "Think back on your career, Luce, and be honest with yourself. Ten months ago, the agency told you to bury your intel gear and go on ice. Did you do that? No, you had to sneak into the warehouse to get those CDs. And don't try to deny it. I could feel them in your pocket."

She drew a sharp breath. "That was completely necessary," she insisted.

"And the car chase in Morocco? Was that necessary, too?"

"Of course."

He sighed and shook his head. "Haven't you ever considered that you feel guilty for not dying when your friends died?" he asked her gently.

A mix of emotions erupted in Lucy's chest. She fought to keep her tone light, incredulous, even. "Bravo, James," she exclaimed. "You should have majored in psychology. Like I said before, you're a freaking genius." With a mighty shove, she managed to secure her freedom, pushing off the wall of granite to dive beneath his arm, swimming out of the intimate enclosure where his words had opened a raw wound.

He thought she suffered from survivor's guilt. What a crock of shit.

As her eyes cleared the water, adrenaline dropkicked in her stomach. *Oh, no.* There sat David on a log not ten feet away, regarding her with puzzled wariness. There was no telling how long he'd been there or how much he might have overheard of their conversation. A single English word could have been enough to betray them.

She could sense Gus about to break the surface beside her. She tried kicking him underwater and missed. And all she could do was hope he would open his eyes before he opened his mouth first and got them both killed.

THE INSTANT HIS HEAD CLEARED THE WATER, Gus mentally kicked himself. *Stupid, stupid, stupid!* he raged, wrestling down his powerful dismay in order to send the stealthy Arhuacan a pleasant smile.

With a long side stroke, he shared quick eye contact with Lucy, who looked pale-faced but composed. Maybe all wasn't lost. It depended on how much, if anything, the youth had overheard.

"What do you have there?" he asked, nodding at the object in David's hands as he dragged himself from the water.

"Achoi tree bark," said David, showing him the bark's milky underside. "My mother's people have used it for years. You boil it in water to make a tea. It will stop the swelling." He flicked a glance at Lucy as she rose from the water.

Easing onto the rock next to David, Gus reached for his boots, practically under the rebel's feet. He made a point to sit parallel to him, keeping his body language friendly, nonconfrontational. Wringing the water from his T-shirt and then his pants, he breathed in sync with him as Lucy sat on the shore, presenting her profile and doing likewise. Second by second, Gus could sense David relaxing, reordering his suspicions.

Damn it, they should've been using this opportunity

to milk the kid for information. Instead he and Lucy had been too caught up in each other and their motives for doing what they did to even notice his return.

"Do you feel better?" David asked him with a searching look.

"I do, thank you," said Gus, patting him on the back.

His touch, like the other nonverbal cues, was a CIA tactic, employed to foster trust. Both he and Lucy had been trained to utilize such techniques. David, hopefully, didn't realize that. But given the grave expression on his face, he wasn't going to be the prime informant Gus had hoped he might be.

CHAPTER **10** ═══════════

The marvelous tea made from the bark of the Achoi tree didn't just reduce the welts on Gus's neck and head; it put him into a deep, peaceful slumber.

Lucy, fated to play his loving wife, sat cross-legged at the edge of their mat under the protection of the mosquito netting, watching over him. As shadows lengthened in their cubby, thoughts flowed through her mind like the endless rush of water at the *salto*.

Gus's insinuation that she fueled her efforts on survivor's guilt had left her simmering with resentment. What she felt about the bombing that had killed her friends wasn't guilt. It was anger.

She could still picture the perpetrator, a bearded stranger who had caught her eye as he walked against the tide of pedestrians marching along Calle de los Caballeros in a festival parade. With a wild glance back at the car parked along the narrow street, he'd groped under his jacket. Instinct alone had alerted Lucy to his intentions, only she'd had no time to warn her friends, who were seated with her at the outdoor café.

In the next instant, the force of the blast had ejected them from their seats. The wrought-iron table had slammed into Lucy, shielding her from the bomb's blast, then pinned her beneath it as they crashed to the ground together. By the time she'd regained consciousness and crawled out from under the table, the quaint artsy district called Barrio del Carmen had been filled with smoke and blood and dismembered bodies.

Of the four exchange students studying at Don Quijote Language School, she was the only one to escape alive, not a mark on her.

Wasn't that reason enough to be riddled with survivor's guilt?

Tears stabbed the backs of Lucy's eyes as she glared down at Gus's dozing countenance. She wished he were awake so she could hiss at him, *Damn you. I don't take unnecessary risks!*

Only that would make her a liar, wouldn't it?

If she was being honest with herself, the high-speed chase in Morocco two years before had been unnecessary. She could've just turned into an alleyway and waited quietly for her pursuers to roar by, only she'd wanted them to chase her and to die trying. She hadn't even considered that she might get hurt herself. And ten months ago, she could have boarded the rescue helicopter at the embassy in Caracas, Venezuela, like all the other staffers, and gotten the hell out of there. But she hadn't. And Gus had to be sent in to extract her.

Hell, it wasn't that much of a long shot to deduce she had a death wish.

Maybe Gus wasn't so far off the mark with his assertion.

But the incident at the warehouse in Maiquetía must

have been the turning point. The lieutenant who'd bru-
talized and nearly raped her had put her in touch with
her fear. She had gone from one extreme to another, her
recklessness replaced by reluctance, confidence ousted by
cowardliness.

Unacceptable. She needed to get her professional edge
back. She *had* to. Because once this assignment was over
and she and Gus parted ways, she would have no one to
bolster her courage, no one to look out for her.

Lucy swallowed hard. She didn't want to think about
that day. Not because she'd miss Gus. She'd done fine
these past years without him. She'd do fine again. But
what if she never shook her PTSD? What if it remained
with her forever? She'd be a wash-up, taking some quiet
assignment that did nothing to promote the security of her
country.

God forbid. She'd rather go out in a blaze of glory than
live forever as a sputtering flame.

A woman's tearful supplication jerked Lucy from a
light sleep.

"Easy," whispered Gus. The effects of the herbal tea
must have worn off. He sounded fully awake, his body
tense and coiled for action as he peeked through an opening he'd made in the leafy wall.

"What's going on?" she asked drowsily, shivering at
the draft he'd created by moving.

A wedge of golden light danced on his brow ridge, illumining his alert gaze. "Buitre's got three of the women
tied together," he whispered. "It looks like he plans on
taking them somewhere."

"Now?" She came more sharply awake. "In the middle
of the night?"

"That's probably why they're tied together. So they won't get lost."

Lucy squirmed higher, making her own little peephole to peer out. In the light of Buitre's electric lantern, she discerned three helpless, sleepy-eyed females roped together at the wrist—Petra, Maife, and Carmen. "Where's he taking them? To another camp?"

"I don't know." He sat up abruptly, reaching for his boots. "But I'm going to find out."

She tossed off the blanket. "Not without me, you're not."

Before she could roll off the mat, he body-checked her. "It's pitch-black outside," he informed her on a whisper.

"So?" She tried to push him aside. It was like trying to move a mountain.

"So you'll be a liability, Luce," he argued in her ear. "I'm used to moving in the jungle. You are not. Now stay *here*."

Why did he have to be so goddamn logical? It left her without an argument. "I thought we were partners," she hissed, giving him an angry shove.

He caught himself from spilling onto his backside. Rolling forward again, he reached for her. Lucy flinched, surprised when he pulled her lips to his, and kissed her hard. "We are," he reassured her.

Befuddled, frustrated, and only a little bit mollified, she watched him dress in his damp clothing, then slip out the back flap of the bungalow. She strained her ears to hear him, but all she could discern were leaves ruffling under a light breeze.

Peering outside again, she saw Buitre's lantern bob toward the trail, casting grotesque shadows on the trees. The poor females straggled behind him. Lucy had befriended several of them. No doubt Buitre was dragging them off to service some high-ranking FARC in a different camp.

Bastards. The girls here already did the brunt of the work—cooking, toting, cleaning, even fighting alongside the men. Having to pleasure them, also, seemed so grossly unfair.

Welcome to Oz, Luce. You wanted to be here, remember?

She watched until the light of Buitre's lantern disappeared abruptly, leaving the camp pitch-black. There was no sign of Gus at all, skulking along in his wake. Presuming he could keep up, how would he ever find his way back?

Squirming back beneath the blanket, she dropped her head on her forearm and squeezed her eyes shut.

She'd been sleeping just fine before the interruption. Now she knew she wouldn't sleep a wink till Gus got back. Having a partner could be downright excruciating.

THE JUNGLE WAS IMPOSSIBLY DARK—so dark, in fact, that the only way for Gus to know what the terrain under his feet was like was to memorize the dips and turns illumined by Buitre's lantern several yards up ahead of him.

Praying he wouldn't sprain an ankle or spear himself on one of the razor-sharp bamboo spikes hemming him in, he inched along after them.

Without night-vision goggles, this kind of surveillance wasn't just risky, it was virtually impossible. He tried to be quiet, but bumbling along like a blind man made that difficult. Thankfully, a stiff breeze caused the leaves to rustle and branches to creak, masking the sounds of his pursuit.

There was no going back now. Darkness dogged his footsteps, as impenetrable as tar. If Buitre didn't backtrack tonight with that lantern, Gus had no idea how he'd get back, only he couldn't leave Lucy by herself. Then again, after what he'd said to her yesterday, maybe she'd be glad if he didn't come back.

He shouldn't have laid his survivor's-guilt theory on her at a time like this. She had enough to contend with just coping with Mike Howitz's fate. They used to be colleagues, for Christ's sake. But her confession had made everything so startlingly clear to him that he'd felt compelled to share his realization.

No wonder Lucy had cut ties with him shortly after the bombing. She'd been driven by the need to honor her friends' memories, to avenge their deaths. Her own life, her own happiness didn't matter, and, by association, neither did Gus's, apparently.

Maybe if she understood her motives, she'd pace herself and live a little longer. A healthy bond with another human being might even supply impetus to live life for herself, not just for her dead friends. He'd be the first to volunteer for that position.

The realization of how susceptible his heart was had him stumbling over his own feet. He caught himself at the verge of falling off the trail into what he sensed was a ravine. *Focus, damn it, before you get yourself killed!*

He forcibly shut down his thoughts, concentrating to follow the lantern bobbing up ahead of him.

How far had they traveled already? It might have been several miles, or less than a mile. In the dark, he'd lost his sense of direction.

He was just beginning to regret following Buitre when

the sound of coarse laughter floated down from higher ground.

Gus crouched, his heart beating faster. Buitre's lantern broke right, pushing through branches up a sharp incline. Calls of welcome told him the deputy and the women were being received.

Pausing to smear mud on his face, Gus backed into the vegetation. The only safe way to move through the undergrowth was butt first, keeping his eyes peeled for a guard on watch.

The glow of Buitre's lantern illumined a makeshift camp consisting of hammocks strung between trees and an empty fire pit. Gus counted ten men, including Buitre, milling around, buttering up the women, swilling some intoxicating drink out of canteens.

These were the men who'd delivered beans the other day, Gus realized, recognizing their uniforms—plain green with no other markings whatsoever. He wondered who the hell they were.

He needed to get closer. Covering ground with excruciating care, he removed sticks before they crackled and betrayed him. He was practically on top of the man standing guard before he even saw him.

Shit! He froze, breaking into a cold sweat.

The watchman stood with his back to a tree, his shape blending into shadow, making him virtually invisible. The Russian assault rifle in his arms had been adorned with leaves, so that it resembled a tree branch. The brim of his hat hid the whites of his eyes. For a shocked moment, Gus thought he was looking at a Special Forces soldier.

He sure as hell wasn't a teenaged rebel with a gun.

Measuring his breathing, Gus kept perfectly still. The soldier, unable to resist peeking at the action in the camp,

urned profile to watch what was going on. And the insignia on his broad-brimmed hat caught Gus's eye.

Red shield, black star.

Jesus Christ, he had to be imagining it. These couldn't
be the Venezuelan Elite Guard, the same men U.S. Navy
SEALs had trained a year ago, the fuckers who'd mauled
Lucy in the warehouse.

Gus's scalp tightened. Gooseflesh rippled down his
back. What other army bore that insignia? No one else, so
far as he knew. Plus it made perfect sense to find the Elite
Guard here in the jungles of Colombia. The populists had
been arming the FARC for decades, backing the rebels in
secret while denouncing them to the rest of the world.

Wait until the CIA learned who was backing the
FARC now! Jesus, God, it curdled Gus's blood to think
what these soldiers could teach the rebels—techniques
taught to them by U.S. Navy SEALs. Tricks and tactics
that could turn the tide of this revolution in the FARC's
favor forever.

He had to inform the JIC as soon as possible. But
crashing out of there was just as risky as getting closer.
Besides, he wanted to be sure. Having trained the Elite
Guard himself, he might recognize a face.

With the man on watch distracted, Gus backed another
yard closer and then another, making no more noise than
a boa constrictor slithering toward its prey.

At last, peering through the fronds of a fernlike plant,
he glimpsed the orgy taking place around Buitre's lantern.
The poor females were outnumbered three to one. Jesus. He
jerked his gaze from their humiliation, appalled by what
they were being subjected to.

Thoughts of Lucy in a similar position made his blood
boil, made him sick to his stomach. *Keep it cool,* he

ordered himself, focusing on the faces of the men grimac-
ing with lust.

To his disappointment, none of them looked familiar
except perhaps the one with the thin moustache. Was that
the captain who'd taken such diligent notes in the class for
officers only? It was hard to tell a full year later, harder
still to ignore the guttural cries of pain tearing from the
young girl beneath him. If he'd had his semi-automatic
with him, he'd be so tempted to mow every man down.

If any one of these pricks had been in the warehouse
last year, that meant they might recognize Lucy if they
saw her.

Shit, shit, shit! This was exactly what he was afraid
might happen. He needed to get hold of his teammates.
Hopefully they'd insist on taking Lucy off the mountain.
Nothing would make Gus happier. Nothing would piss off
Lucy more, but a mad Lucy was better than a dead Lucy.

First, though, he needed to pull back before the Elite
Guards laid hands on him.

One by one, the men were finding their fulfillment,
further degrading the females by ejaculating on them.

"Hey, Ponce, cover for me here so I can get a turn,"
called the man on watch.

"Take the bitch with the breasts like papayas," urged
his companion, crunching over to take his place.

Now was Gus's chance to flee. As the men traded
places, he reversed direction, scuttling like a crab into the
dark void. He crashed into a bush, turned, and scurried
around it, slipping down the spongy ground on his butt.

"What was that?" he heard one of the men ask.

"Probably a *tigre*," joked his companion, using the
local word for jaguar. "Go on before the girl faints."

Their voices faded at the same time that the foliage abruptly cleared, and Gus found himself on the path.

Now what? he wondered, coming slowly to his feet.

It was so intensely dark he found it difficult to keep his balance. Sliding one foot forward, he inched into what he believed was the right direction only to bump into a tree. He modified and tried again, eventually hitting a wall of rock.

At last, when the sounds of the camp had faded, he sat on the path and removed the sat phone from his boot, powering it on. Faint blue light drove back the darkness. He replaced the heel and stood up, hoping for a signal.

Of course not. Apparently the only way to ping the satellite with this piece-of-shit technology was to stand in a clearing. He'd have to try again when he got back to camp, and the only way to get there was to use the phone as a flashlight, which would drain the battery.

But he still had a backup battery in the other boot.

Pointing the display in front of him, he started walking.

A crash of thunder made him jump. In the next minute, rain poured down on him like water coursing through a million drain pipes.

It was all he could do to keep the phone dry while using it to guide him back to camp.

FOR THE HUNDREDTH TIME, Lucy peeked outside for any sign of Gus's return. Lightning crackled, illumining the cluster of ugly buildings and the clearing by the trail. She realized David was manning the fifty-caliber machine gun tonight.

Crouched under a tarp, he did his best to ward off rain drops as they pelted the muddy ground around him.

What was taking Gus so long? How would he find his way back in this deluge? Worry knotted her intestines. He was probably hunkered down somewhere, she reasoned waiting the rain out. She forced herself to lie back down aware that she was giving herself a headache.

Damn it, no wonder she preferred to work alone.

Minutes later, she shot to her elbows. She hadn't heard or felt a thing, but she sensed Gus's approach. The leaf flap twitched, and a dark shadow crept into the bungalow easing under their blinds to stream water onto their cubby floor.

She could hear his teeth chattering. Shaking of the covers, she ducked under the mosquito net to help him peel off his sodden clothing—boots, socks, jacket T-shirt, pants, everything. She diligently hung them up as he huddled on the floor, shivering.

Then she drew him into their nest, tossing the blanket over them both as she wrapped her body around his speeding him to recovery.

Moment by moment, his shudders subsided but his tension did not. "Better?" she asked.

"I'm good."

"What did you find out?"

He hesitated, notching her concern higher. "You know those guys in the pea green uniforms who brought the bags of beans the other day?"

"Of course."

"I found out who they are," he told her grimly.

"Who?" Dread made her skin feel tight. She knew what he was going to say before he even said it.

"Venezuelan Elite Guard," he corroborated.

Lucy's blood flashed from hot to cold. In her mind's ye the lieutenant's fist slammed into her face, making her linch.

"Luce, I think you should leave the mountain," he dded flatly. "We can't risk you running into these guys."

"What? No, I'm not going to leave." The idea was nacceptable, regardless of the fear chasing through her.

"Listen to me. What if we run into these guys and one f them recognizes you? What then?"

"That's not going to happen," she hissed. "The last hing the FARC want is for our UN team to discover vho's aiding them."

"We can't take the chance."

"No!" She shoved at his chest, pushing him onto his ack as she straddled him, asserting her dominance. "I von't let you do that."

"I already made the call," he retorted grimly. "My uys are clearing it with the station chief."

Lucy glared down at him. "You did that without asking me?" she breathed, outraged but at the same time ainfully aware of his naked body trapped between her highs.

In the cubby next to theirs, Carlos hushed them.

They both froze, dismayed to have been overheard. Catching Lucy's face in his hands, Gus pulled her ear to is mouth. "If anything happens to you, Luce, I'll never orgive myself."

It was hard to cling to her anger in the face of such loy-lty. Teamwork was clearly serious business. "Nothing's oing to happen," she reassured him. "How would you xplain my sudden departure? It's not like I can just hop n the next bus out of here," she added hoarsely. "This

isn't about me. It's about Jay and Mike." If she ran away
like a coward, she would never get her courage back
She'd be all washed up. "Don't you see?"

The hands on her face slid through the skeins of her
hair, over the tops of her shoulders and lower to cup her
breasts with reverence. "I *want* to see," he murmured
convincingly.

Beneath her bra and T-shirt, Lucy's nipples pearled
with a sudden stab of desire. She wasn't above persuading
him to get what she wanted. In this position, she had all
the influence she needed. "You would keep me safe," she
avowed, lowering her lips to bestow on him a toe-curling
promising kiss. "Wouldn't you?" she demanded, rubbing
herself enticingly against him.

His breath caught. "Yes," he admitted hoarsely.

Sitting up, she stripped off her T-shirt and bra, leaving
her nearly as naked as he was. "You wouldn't let anything
happen to me," she whispered in his ear, nipping his ear
lobe before offering him her breasts.

As he licked and suckled them, she reveled in the
silken heat rising between her thighs. With an over
whelming desire to seduce him, she scooted back on her
knees, clasped his turgid length, and pleasured him until
a helpless shudder racked his frame.

There would be no gentleness this time, she assured
herself, no danger of disgrace, no recalling another life
time, another place.

She worked him over till his breath grew ragged, his
muscles convulsed. *Not yet, big boy.* Slipping off her pant
ies, she climbed the length of his body to assuage the hun
ger building inside her. Swallowing a moan, she sheathed
him fully, then she rode him hard, taking what his body
offered to find fulfillment.

"Kiss me," he urged, but she refused, wary of the tenderness his kisses evoked.

But she couldn't prevent him from rolling her nipples gently. He slicked his thumb into the sensitive folds spread wide to him, finding with unerring accuracy the center of her pleasure, speeding her heart rate, spurring her toward her release.

Just as she approached the point of crisis, he jerked to a sitting position, pulled her hips to his, and delved his tongue into her mouth, prompting the wave to crash over her. She came violently and helplessly, moaning into his mouth as he convulsed deep within her, mirroring her pleasure.

Keeping their bodies joined, he rolled her under him, put his mouth to her ear, and whispered without rancor, "You can't manipulate me like some stranger, Luce. I'm your partner. I know you too well."

And there it was, laid bare. Her stock in trade was lies and subterfuge, but Gus would accept nothing less than who she *really* was. No agendas, no plots, no secrets.

Relief she didn't understand rose up within her, bringing a flood of tears to her eyes. *Oh, God, not again.* She squeezed her eyes shut, unwilling to acknowledge that his words had such a strange and powerful effect on her.

For a long moment, he simply held her, gazing down at her as she fought to keep her tears from escaping, scarcely daring to breathe as he painted invisible lines upon her face.

"Okay," he admitted gruffly, at last. "You can stay," he added, "if the station chief allows it."

Lucy snatched her eyes open, hoping the dark would conceal the moisture in them. "Promise?" she asked, transported by a sense of gratitude and belonging, feelings she hadn't felt in so long.

He took his time answering as he settled down beside her. "I promise," he finally replied, pulling her into the circle of his arms. Only he didn't sound too happy with his decision.

CHAPTER 11

The cry of a masked mountain tanager snatched David's head off the pile of sandbags. The rain had passed, leaving him shivering under a plastic tarp, sitting on a stool in a puddle of mud.

Bleary-eyed, he watched the iridescent blue bird shoot through rays of sunlight combing through the trees. Wiping drool from the corner of his mouth, he shook off the tarp and cut a surreptitious glance toward the quiet camp, hoping no one had caught him sleeping.

Up into the hours of dawn, David had debated whether or not to share his observations with the deputy. Buitre was ten years his senior, with combat experience that made him dangerous, quick to pull the trigger. Yet they had shared confidences before. Six months ago, Buitre explained to David how the FARC intended to make a comeback. They had offered the Venezuelans their remaining coca processing plants in exchange for military training and supplies. From that point forward, the FARC's focus had shifted from profit to revolt.

David's dream of an honorable revolution seemed to be taking shape before his very eyes.

A flash of movement up the trail caught his notice, and he called the standard warning, relieved to hear Buitre's reply. The deputy strode into view, pulling Carmen. Maife, and Petra behind him, strung together by a rope.

The girls kept their eyes downcast, their shoulders bowed. David took one look at them and wavered. Could he trust the judgment of a man as unfeeling as Buitre? He liked Luna and Gustavo. He didn't want to see them tortured or killed. He certainly didn't want to see them taken hostage, for that was a tactic of the FARC that he abhorred as much as the selling of cocaine.

On the other hand, he had a dream, a vision that Colombia would, in his lifetime, be ruled by a just Marxist government, one that made no distinction between Indian or *blanco*. He could not allow any outsiders to interfere. "Deputy Buitre," he called, summoning his superior.

Freeing the women, Buitre altered course to cast his shadow over him. "What is it, Squad Commander?"

David's mouth turned dry. For a second, he questioned his suspicions. But then, he was certain of what he'd seen and heard. "It's the couple on the UN team, sir. I think you were right to say they are different than the others."

Buitre frowned. "Go on," he urged as David dug for courage.

"I've overheard them speaking English—twice. American English," he qualified.

The deputy's eyes narrowed into dark, suspicious slits. "Are you certain?" he demanded.

"Yes, sir. There were Americans at my university. I used to practice English with them."

"What else?" Buitre snapped, guessing that there was more.

David's heart beat uncomfortably fast. He hated telling tales, and yet... He had his dream to protect. "I caught the woman leaving your quarters at dawn the other day, soon after you left to meet with the Venezuelans. She claimed the older lady was sick and she was looking for the medicine you took from her backpack."

Buitre's scar paled. His fists curled. "How long was she in my quarters?" he asked, flashing a malignant look at the bungalow.

"I don't know, sir," David answered. "When I saw her, she had just stepped out."

"Did she take anything?"

"I saw nothing in her hands."

With an angry growl, and not a single word of thanks, Buitre turned and stalked to the little shelter. David winced as he made to kick a wandering chicken from his path, only the bird scuttled wisely out of harm's way.

A knot of anxiety coiled in David's gut. What now? He had every right to protect his dream, especially now with the revolution to be waged in more honorable ways. Yet he feared Buitre's temper would cloud his judgment and the Americans—if that was what they were—would pay with their lives.

BUITRE FLIPPED THE SWITCH on his generator, shattering the camp's peaceful quiet. Normally, he roused the troops at dawn with a harsh call for muster, but David's confession had fixed his thoughts on the possibility Luna and Gustavo were spies. He pushed into his quarters, peering suspiciously around the cramped, musty space.

If Luna was a spy, what could she have found that would undermine the rebel cause? He had carried his radio with him that morning. The only other source of information was the officer's log.

He snatched it up, flipping through the yellowed pages, seeing nothing amiss. Snapping on the light, he sat down for a closer look, sifting carefully through the pages. He paused, turned back, noting a discrepancy in the dates. There was a page missing. Running a finger along the bend of the spine, he felt the neatly torn edge.

"*¡Puta!*" he whispered. *Whore.* She had stolen a page out of the log! But which page? What information was she privy to?

He backed up a page or two, reading laboriously, trying to picture the pages, the sequence of events. Hadn't there been a map among these pages, telling the location, in code, of the four main camps on the mountain?

His heart seemed to stop beating when he realized it was gone.

Marquez had entrusted him with the camp's security. It was his duty to update and secure the log. But he'd been sloppy. Not only had he left the camp to cavort with the Venezuelans—warriors who inspired him with their expertise—but he'd left the officers' quarters unlocked. There was nothing of value to steal, he'd reasoned. None of the soldiers but David even knew how to read. He'd never conceived that the members of the negotiating team might be a threat.

But why not? Spies had been trying for decades to infiltrate the FARC.

He dared not tell Marquez about the missing map, especially when its absence could be blamed on his negligence. He would have to rouse his commander's suspicions with news that the couple had been caught speaking English.

Perhaps Marquez would let him torture them for information. He would enjoy humiliating the bitch who'd shamed him before his men. That was when she'd called him *chamo*.

The Venezuelan slang word gave him pause. It made him wonder whether she knew about the FARC's alliance with the Venezuelans.

His radio crackled suddenly and he snatched it off his hip, answering Marquez's salutation.

"The Argentine and I are on our way," the commander huffed. "You may expect us by noon."

"Sir," Buitre interrupted, "I have reason to believe two of the UN team members are American spies. I have overheard them speaking English," he added, giving himself credit for vigilance.

Marquez did not reply.

"Did you hear me, *comandante?* The younger woman and her husband may be spies. I would like permission to question them."

"No," Marquez growled, bringing a scowl to Buitre's face. "You are hasty in your suppositions. That couple works at the United Nations in New York City. Of course they speak English."

"But *comandante*," he protested, devastated not to be able to lay his hands on them at once.

"The Europeans are our guests, Buitre. You presume too much to know whether they are spies or not."

"Then let me question them. I will know within hours if they speak the truth!"

"No," Marquez repeated implacably. "We are only steps away from coming to an agreement."

Agreement? Stunned, Buitre held his tongue for a moment. "Then Commander Gitano will be returned to us," he guessed with an abrupt lifting of his spirits, only to have them dashed by Marquez's next words.

"No. Commander Rojas has decided to accept the Frenchman's offer. We will surrender the surviving hostage and the dead one in return for ten of our captured *compañeros*."

Buitre choked on his denial. "No!" he growled in protest. "Why would we settle for such a small ransom? We need more than men. We need leadership!"

"The Elite Guard will lead us. What we need now is for these strangers to leave the mountain before they learn too much. Enough," Marquez bit out. "I have explained the situation. You will follow my orders and treat the UN team with every bit of respect. This is not their war."

Shuddering with outrage, Buitre hurled the radio to the bed. He lurched to his feet to pace the creaking floor.

Weak! Commander Rojas was too weak to breathe life into the floundering rebel ranks. Only Gitano could have grown the FARC's numbers back into the tens of thousands, returning it to the fearsome entity it was before the bombings, the conversions, the slaughter of its leaders.

With a roar, Buitre pounded his fist into his palm. Still, he would obey his commander's dictates. The key to a strong army was discipline among the ranks. So for now, he would heed Marquez's wishes, regardless of how weak and foolish they seemed.

THE FARC HAD ACCEPTED Fournier's proposal with an added stipulation, a sum of fifty million pesos delivered in cold hard cash via helicopter to an airfield near the base of the mountain.

Lucy shared a quick, stunned look with Gus.

"Can we come up with that?" Bellini asked, a bead of sweat gliding from his dark hairline.

In the wake of the rain last night, the weather was muggy and hot. Cloistered in the officers' cramped quarters, the team members eyed Fournier with varying expressions of hope and skepticism.

Fournier scraped spindly fingers over his silver bristles. "It is possible," he conceded, leading to a chorused sigh from the others. "Given the devaluation of the peso, the sum is not so large."

"It's about twenty-five thousand American dollars," Gus supplied. Everyone looked at him in surprise. "I'm good with math," he added.

Lucy digested the latest news with mixed feelings. Not once had she envisioned the UN team and the FARC coming to an agreement. Still, why not? The FARC were getting ten men in exchange for one man and a body. Twenty-five thousand dollars on top of that was icing on the cake.

It was looking like the SEALs at the JIC wouldn't be needed to extract the hostages, after all.

"However, it would be unethical to agree to such a ransom," Fournier added, causing several faces at the table to fall.

"I agree," said Carlos with a contemptuous glimmer in his eye. "To pay them is to encourage more abductions."

Şukruye and Bellini averted their gazes, keeping quiet. It was clear they'd be happy to hand over the money.

"But, as it happens," Fournier continued, sending an enigmatic glance at the Argentine, "Jay Barnes has an insurance policy that pays up to twenty-five thousand dollars in the event of his kidnapping. All that is needed to secure that sum is for Mr. Barnes to write a letter in longhand requesting it be paid and designating a carrier."

Lucy shot a cynical look at Gus. Insurance policy, my ass. More likely Christians in Action, aka the CIA, had informed Fournier at some point that they were willing to contribute a tidy sum to help secure their employees' release. Fournier had kept that card hidden up his sleeve, waiting for just the right moment to whip it out.

Stunned silence descended over the table.

"So..." Bellini inclined his head with cautious optimism. "We are agreeing to the FARC's counteroffer?"

The Argentine held a hand up. "One more thing," he added belatedly. "All this must be done in forty-eight hours."

Surprised, the members of the UN team turned wide eyes on Fournier. At the mention of a time limitation, he seemed to age a decade.

"What's the hurry?" Lucy demanded. "They've held the hostages for over six months. What difference does two days make?"

Álvarez shrugged. "I only repeat what I am told to say."

"They must be desperate for midlevel leadership," Şukruye surmised, "and for money."

"They have been in steady decline," Bellini agreed. "We have seen firsthand how hungry they are, how poor their weapons."

Until recently, Lucy thought, biting her tongue. They would have food and weapons aplenty, thanks to their alliance with the Venezuelans.

"The time constraint is problematic," Fournier confessed. "I would need to communicate with the outside world, of course. I would have to place calls to the proper authorities, to enjoin their cooperation. Freeing ten captives at once, securing the funds, there is always red tape involved." He rubbed his closed eyelids, looking overwhelmed and agitated.

Şukruye and Bellini seemed to wilt in the face of his pessimism.

Lucy herself was caught in a flux of emotions. She glanced at Gus, reading watchful optimism.

Carlos threw his hands into the air. "When does this time constraint begin? And what happens if the money isn't here in two days, eh? Are the FARC going to kill us?"

The Argentine blanched at the suggestion. "It is not Commander Rojas's intent to kill you," he assured them. "I will tell him you are willing to cooperate but that you require a satellite phone, and more time."

"Exactly," replied Fournier. "We must have more time."

Álvarez nodded, seeming to resign himself to the fact that his services would be needed for a while longer. "Is that your final offer?" he asked.

"Yes," said Fournier. "Tell Commander Rojas that we need three days, at least, plus a reliable means of communication. I cannot gather money or men without a phone of some sort."

"Very well." With a murmured farewell, the Argentine scraped back his chair and stood. They watched him exit through the screen door and cross to Marquez, who sat by the fire eating, to explain that yet another trek to Rojas's camp was in order.

Lucy's gaze slid past Marquez to Buitre, who glared at

her as he ate. Even with several yards between them, she could sense the venom he radiated. Her nape prickled in response to it. What had happened to exacerbate Buitre's dislike of her, transforming it into loathing? Had David said something to arouse his suspicions?

"If they give us more time," Fournier murmured, recapturing her focus, "this will work," he said, reawakening their flagging confidence. "We will have done what we came to do."

Lucy glanced at Gus and wondered if, despite his guarded optimism, he felt the tiniest bit torn that it might soon be over and they would go back to leading separate lives.

What was wrong with her? A peaceful resolution was a good thing. So why was her heart heavy, her mind so cautious? What mattered most was reuniting Jay with his wife, laying Mike's body to rest in American soil. For the whole thing to be over in a matter of days, without a shot fired, was fabulous!

Yet the fine hairs at the nape of her neck prickled with the suspicion that something was amiss. Buitre's dark eyes held secrets she wasn't certain she wanted to decipher.

As they filed out of the brick building, Marquez waved them toward the fire pit, where they sat on tree stumps to consume an uninspired meal of rice and beans.

A strained, uneasy silence fell between the UN team and their hosts, broken only by the popping of firewood.

At last, Marquez put his bowl down and stood, signaling to Álvarez that they were leaving. In the same moment, David called Gus from the fire to help support the roof of the soldiers' shelter while a beam was hammered in place. The lean-to had been sagging since the storm last night.

As Gus got up to help, Lucy's stomach cramped. She looked sharply at the tin bowl in her hand and forced herself to eat another bite. Again her stomach cramped.

"Excuse me," she murmured to the others.

Looking for Gus, she realized he had disappeared from view. With her intestines rumbling, she had no choice but to hurry into the forest alone, to the area where the women were assured some privacy.

Pushing as deep into the vegetation as she dared, she found a tangle of vines to hide behind and hunkered down, well concealed.

She must have eaten something that disagreed with her. Or caught a bug. Or been poisoned...

Surely Buitre wouldn't go that far.

Minutes later, following a clammy sweat and sharp intestinal pains, she felt better. Hopefully, the attack was just a onetime deal and she wouldn't be back in the woods in another twenty minutes.

As she retreated from her hiding place, still buttoning her pants, the hair on her forearms rose to stiff attention and she froze.

She could see nothing, hear nothing. She stood in a fishbowl of vegetation, surrounded by every imaginable shade of green. Not a single bird flitted past her. The jungle stood eerily quiet, but she knew she wasn't alone.

Thoroughly spooked, Lucy headed briskly uphill, her thighs flexing with the urge to run.

"What's your hurry, *chama?*" inquired a silky voice, startling her as its owner stepped from behind a tree, blocking her path. Buitre. He'd followed her, which meant that Gus had to be shortly behind him, only he wasn't.

Lucy willed herself to assume an easy, unintimidated stance as Buitre swaggered closer, using the incline to give him a badly needed height advantage. His glittering black eyes sent a chill down her spine.

"What do you want?" she asked, her voice surprisingly cool. She hinged her confidence on the sound of it, telling herself she could lick this bastard if she had to, so long as he didn't use his gun, loosely held in his right hand and, for the moment, pointed at the ground.

"The map," he said, giving her a cold, hard smile. "The one you took from the journal in my quarters."

Fear leapt out of nowhere, clutching her heart. The jig was up. Buitre had realized the map was stolen, and he'd assumed she'd taken it. *Oh, shit. Oh, shit.* Adrenaline flooded her bloodstream, tripling her heartbeat.

David must have told him he'd caught her leaving the building. What else had David told him?

"I don't know what you're talking about." Her disdain was perfect. Again, she took assurance from her superb acting ability. If she could fool Buitre into thinking she was calm, then she could fool herself. PTSD had nothing on her. The realization slowed her breathing, curbed the adrenaline rocketing through her.

Of course, that didn't mean she wasn't in deep shit at the moment. Buitre wasn't just crazy, he was dangerous.

"You're a liar," he breathed, his eyes glinting with malice as he stepped close enough to expel foul breath across her cheek.

And just like that, her confidence wavered.

Lucy's joints seemed to slowly freeze even as a weak laugh sounded in her head. *Well, yeah, I work for the CIA, of course I'm a liar.*

Where the hell was Gus? Just because she was holding her own here didn't mean she wanted to take on Buitre solo. Didn't teamwork include rescuing the ass of your partner from scumbag rebels?

Without warning, he raised his pistol to her face. The safety was off, one in the chamber, and his finger was on the trigger. Lucy flinched, her thoughts flashing back to the warehouse. Fear punched her in the gut, slowing her thoughts, numbing her extremities.

She was both in the jungle with Buitre *and* back in that warehouse in Venezuela. Two separate events that coalesced without warning to strike her powerless.

"Where did you put the map, eh? Is it here?" He delved a hand into her empty hip pocket, groping her through the fabric, his touch intentionally sexual, intentionally cruel. He circled around her back, growling in her ear, "Or here?" He jammed a hand into the other pocket. Fury simmered in Lucy's veins, but it was the fear that won, keeping her frozen in place.

A simple jab, a grab, and a knee to the forehead would suffice to bring him down, groaning in agony. Only she couldn't move. Like *Oz*'s Tin Man, she was paralyzed.

"Or maybe here," Buitre continued, squeezing her left breast, his fingers biting in to her flesh as he pressed his pistol to her skull.

The jungle kaleidoscoped around her as tears formed in her eyes. The tears, her fear, her helplessness galled her. She couldn't let this bastard get the best of her.

"Luna!" Gus's worried shout reverberated under the jungle canopy.

"I'm here!" she cried in a strained and unfamiliar voice.

"*Carajo*," Buitre swore, stepping away from her, putting his gun away.

As Gus crashed down the hill, slipping and sliding in

his haste to get to her, Lucy felt a measure of her confidence return. She rounded on Buitre, sending him a contemptuous glare. "Like I told you before, Deputy, you're paranoid. Stay away from me, or I'll tell the world how the FARC mistreated me."

"Luna." Gus rushed up to her, clasping her elbow and drawing her behind him. "What's the problem here?" he demanded, facing Buitre with menace in his voice.

The deputy stepped back. He shrugged, seeming to measure his odds of taking on the bigger man, whether it was wise to accuse them both of stealing the map. "Ask your wife," he retorted. Hitching his trousers, he turned away and retreated briskly up the hill.

They watched until he disappeared. Gus then turned to face her. "What happened?" he demanded. "What did he do to you?"

"Nothing," she insisted. "I'm fine."

"You're not fine. You're as pale as a sheet. Did he touch you? Threaten you?"

"Come on, now," she retorted, arching an eyebrow at him. "Don't you think I can handle a man like Buitre?" she scoffed.

Doubt and compassion warred in his golden brown eyes.

"He accused me of stealing the map," she admitted, trembling anew as concern flared in Gus's eyes.

"Jesus," he whispered, hauling her into his embrace.

Caught in the circle of Gus's arms, Lucy felt her remaining fear drain away. *Damn it!* She ought to have been able to handle Buitre by herself. But then he'd done what the lieutenant in the warehouse had done, and it had come flooding back.

"It's my fault," said Gus, unaware of her self-ecrimination. "I'm the one who took the map."

"And I'm the one who followed you into Buitre's quar-ers," she argued, wresting free. "Look, what matters is hat David reported suspicious behavior to Buitre, who now suspects us both."

"I should've realized David's calling me to help with he roof was a ploy. I'm sorry," he apologized, his jaw umping.

"It's okay," she reassured him, worried that he might again insist that she leave the mountain early. "All Buitre has are his suspicions," she reasoned. "He can't prove we ook the map, can he? Besides, in seventy-two hours we'll be out of this hellhole."

"You sound pretty sure of that," said Gus, his gaze dubious.

She wasn't, but she wasn't about to give him any excuse to get rid of her. "I'm positive," she lied, giving him a playful shove. "The rebels want us gone before we run into any Venezuelans and guess their little secret."

Ten rebels burst into the bungalow at midnight with their AK-47s locked and loaded.

Lurching from a deep sleep, Gus reached for Lucy, drawing her closer, his heart hammering.

"Find the bitch who took the map." Buitre's voice swam out of the darkness.

Footsteps sounded on the rough-cut planks. Cubby by cubby, the rebels searched the bungalow, startling the other team members.

Beside him, Lucy lurched awake. He covered her mouth to stifle her voice. They couldn't stay here. They needed to flee. "Let's go!" he rasped. Using Buitre's knife, the one he kept hidden between the floor and the leafy wall, he slashed a hole for them to escape through unseen. "Go!" he urged, pushing her through it.

With his every sense cranked to high, he intuited his mistake before he saw it with his own eyes.

Slipping through the ragged edges of the sliced wall, he found Lucy struggling in Buitre's embrace, her eyes wide with terror above the hand that covered her mouth.

"Do you take me for a fool, norteamericano?"

"Let her go," Gus pleaded, taking a step closer. He froze as Buitre raised his pistol to Lucy's head, flicking off the safety. "I told her to take the map," Gus insisted. "I am the spy. She is innocent!"

"Out here, no one is innocent," Buitre contradicted him, causing goose bumps to spike on Gus's forearms. "That's why both of you must die. But you first."

Without warning, he swung the pistol at Gus and fired.

Bam! The explosive impact rocketed Gus to an upright position. He was relieved to feel his heart galloping in his chest.

Next to him, Lucy placed a steadying hand on his back. "Hey."

He swallowed against a parched mouth, blinking rapidly to clear his head. Was he okay? He felt like he'd taken a bullet to the chest. It was just a dream, but... What if it was a warning to grab Lucy and flee into the jungle with her?

He lay back down, stiff with lingering horror and uncertainty.

"Bad dream?" she asked him, stroking a comforting hand along his beard-roughened cheek.

He grunted his acknowledgment, but his uneasiness remained. Last night he'd promised Lucy he'd protect her with his life. What if Buitre killed him first?

He couldn't save her if he was dead.

He wished he hadn't told Lucy she could stick around. He'd rather err on the side of caution than watch his premonitions become manifest.

Ultimately, the decision would be Whiteside's. Lucy couldn't blame him if the station chief made the call to pull her out. Of course, this late in the game, pulling her out could disrupt the negotiation progress. Damn, but the situation was getting sticky, and Gus had a sinking feeling it was about to get even stickier.

CHAPTER 12 ════════════

Fournier leaned into Gus and Lucy's cubby the following morning, startling them. "Wake up, sleepyheads. We're leaving camp in twenty minutes!"

Jarred from a deep sleep, Lucy raised her head to blink at him in confusion.

"Heading where?" Gus rasped, the first to recover.

"Down the mountain," Fournier called back cheerfully. They listened to him push through the rear flap, stepping out into rain that fell in such a steady downpour it was a marvel their leafy roof didn't leak.

With a moan of reluctance, Lucy snuggled more deeply in the cocoon of Gus's arms. It felt too dry and warm under the blankets for her to want to dress in damp clothing and hike down the mountain in the pouring rain. Her aching hip didn't look forward to the trek, either. She'd rather just stay in bed, in Gus's embrace, and never leave.

The feel of his hand sliding between her breasts roused her several degrees. At the same time, he pressed his hips to the curve of her bottom, introducing her to his predicament, the result of sleeping naked. Better yet, she'd rather stay in bed *and* have sex than venture out into a wet monsoon.

Turning her head to glance invitingly back at him, she found his gaze both turbulent and intense. Anxiety bloomed immediately within her.

"Did you sleep okay?" she asked, remembering how he'd lurched from his sleep around midnight.

"Not really," he admitted. "You?"

"I was until Fournier woke us up."

The stiff column against her backside couldn't be ignored. The desire to join with him one more time had Lucy reaching back, stroking his velvet turgidity, then guiding him to her warmth. He entered her with the same serious intensity that was in his eyes. Together they writhed and rocked, milking deep, honest pleasure from their intimacy.

It might be the last time.

The realization pressured Lucy's chest as she melted around him, savoring each deep thrust until he echoed her bliss, gripping her fiercely to him.

As their breathing slowed and their hearts beat more regularly, he held her tightly in his arms, gazing thoughtfully down at her, his gaze still troubled.

This was the most vulnerable she had ever seen him. His worry was so palpable, she could feel it affecting her own thoughts. "It was just a dream," she reassured him. "We're almost done here. Nothing's going to happen to us."

"Just stick close to me these last few days," he countered.

Nothing would please her more, a circumstance that worried her greatly. The time was fast approaching when she'd have to be self-reliant again.

"And if anything happens to me, just get the hell off

the mountain. Find water and follow it downstream. The guys at the JIC will eventually find you."

"Stop," she ordered, shaking off the talons of fear that sank into her neck. "You're worrying for nothing," she reassured him. "Watch, we'll fly out of here together having accomplished everything we set out to do." That was what *had* to happen. Anything less would suspend her healing, leaving her permanently debilitated.

"Right," he agreed, reaching for the knife he kept hidden by their mat. Seeing it curled into the palm of his hand sent a ripple of premonition through her. "Let's go," he said.

She missed him the moment he tossed off their blanket. Even as they rushed to get dressed, she wondered if he felt it, too—regret that they were leaving the nest where they'd rediscovered each other.

She tried to shake it off. Their so-called intimacy had been an act in the first place, a temporary arrangement meant to fool the enemy, not herself. Still, as he made to move past her, she found herself reaching for him. Standing on tiptoe, she pressed a fervent kiss to his lips. "Be careful," she whispered, feeling suddenly anxious, suddenly vulnerable.

"I'll be right behind you," he promised, banding his powerful arms around her in a swift, fierce hug.

"Teamwork," she added, dredging up a smile.

He seemed about to comment on the word, then changed his mind. "That's right," he replied with a forced smile.

"SIR? THEY'RE MOVING."

Chief Harlan's warning tore Lieutenant Lindstrom

from the program he was executing. He shot from his seat to study the topographical map over Harley's shoulders. Sure enough, the two colored dots, red for Gus, blue for Lucy, were creeping down the mountain, making slow but steady progress.

"Track their movements. Let me know when they stop," Luther said, watching a moment longer.

In the past two days, he had run the names of the camps through his encryption program, eliminating all but two sets of data. If Gus and Lucy stopped at coordinates matching any of Luther's results, he'd know which data set was accurate. Then the SEALs would have the exact coordinates of four FARC camps, all but the one unnamed at the top of the mountain.

Added to the shortwave communications and thermal images uploaded to satellite by Predator, their intel on the rebels was growing by the hour, corroborating Gus's latest news that the Venezuelans had allied themselves with the FARC. Pictures of cargo trucks creeping up the side of La Montaña and snatches of conversation involving drugs and weapons shipments all confirmed their insiders' report.

Vinny, loaded down with coffee and donuts from the cafeteria, crossed from the door to Luther's elbow. "What's goin' on?" he asked.

"They're moving," Harley relayed.

"Should we be worried, sir?" Vinny asked, slanting him a look.

The aroma of fresh coffee wrested Luther's attention from the screen. "Not yet," he said, plucking a paper cup off the cardboard tray. "The FARC are famous for relocating."

He carried it back to his desk and sat down, keeping his concerns to himself.

He'd neglected to relay Gus's concern to the station chief. Whiteside was tightly strung as it was. He didn't want to raise the man's blood pressure by suggesting that the Venezuelans might recognize Lucy, should they run into her. In an area the size of La Montaña, the odds of the UN team and the Elite Guard crossing paths were slim to none in the first place.

Luther had faith in statistics. As the ops officer for Team Twelve, he'd made plenty of decisions based entirely on stats, and the odds hadn't beaten him yet. Besides, how could they wrest Lucy off the mountain and not take Gus, also? Whiteside would want them to see the exchange carried through.

So they both stayed. Hopefully this little jaunt down the mountain, which, incidentally, was taking them straight toward the frenzy of activity on the southeast side, would not result in an unwanted encounter.

RAIN GUSHED THROUGH THE JUNGLE CANOPY, turning the path under the boots of the UN team members into a gulley.

Buitre set a grueling pace, threatening to leave behind those who couldn't keep up. As with their earlier trek into the jungle, Bellini, Fournier, and Şukruye floundered. It was up to Gus, Carlos, and Lucy to keep them on their feet as they slipped and slid down the tortuous, often near-vertical path. Distracted by Bellini's clumsiness, Gus fought to keep his eyes on Lucy, his instinct for danger twitching.

This was the path he'd stumbled along the other night. It led straight to the camp of the Elite Guard. Surely Buitre wouldn't flaunt the FARC's secret weapon in front of the

UN team members. Surely the Elite Guard had packed up and moved on, and the team wouldn't just walk up on them.

If they hadn't, and one of them recognized Lucy, the shit was going to hit the fan.

"Luna!" He wanted to warn her that they were getting close, only she was several yards ahead of him, fighting to keep Şukruye upright. Rain drowned out the sound of his voice. In the next instant, he spotted the camp, a little ways off the path, half-concealed by the vegetation. To his dismay, several soldiers were visible, hunkered under tarps strung between the trees.

Keep your head down, he willed Lucy.

Maybe they'd just march right past and his concern would be unwarranted.

"Chamo!" called a voice from higher ground.

The greeting cut through the pounding rain, startling the other team members, who hadn't noticed a platoon of men hiding in the trees.

Buitre hollered back, and two men detached themselves from the group to approach him.

Oh, fuck, thought Gus.

LUCY KICKED HERSELF for being caught off guard. If the Turkish woman hadn't needed so much help hiking, she'd have seen the soldiers hiding just off the trail. A flash of pea green alerted her immediately to who they were. Now all she could do was to turn her back on them, affecting concern for her companion, who was battling a cramp.

"You're okay," she said to Şukruye, who doubled over, pressing a hand against her side.

Lucy's heart galloped. Over the Turkish woman's

gasping complaints, she strained to hear what Buitre was telling the Venezuelans. Something about shelter being available for the officers, up at Cecaot-Jicobo.

That was the camp they'd just vacated.

Buitre was offering their bungalow to the Elite Guard. A vision of them sleeping in the corner cubby she had shared with Gus put a bitter taste in her mouth.

"¡*Vámanos!*" Buitre shouted, and she was forced to turn around. She kept her face averted, kept her eyes on Şukruye's unsteady, mud-stained boots.

The two Elite Guards were still standing to one side of the path, watching them file by. *Damn it!* Didn't they have anything better to do?

As she squeezed past them, shrinking inward to make herself invisible, a cold wave of panic washed over, shortening her breath, causing her to squeeze Şukruye's arm with too much strength.

The Turkish woman glanced at her sharply. "What's wrong?" she demanded.

Lucy gave an infinitesimal shake of her head and compelled her forward. "Keep moving," she urged through lips that felt bloodless. Her scalp tingled as she felt curious eyes slide over her.

Her heart didn't cease to thud until they'd floundered another mile or more without a hue and cry raised. In her soaked jacket and pants, Lucy shivered with belated relief. Her weak knees trembled to support them both as Şukruye leaned on her heavily.

Once the path gave a sharp turn, she cut a look back at Gus, who all but pushed Bellini from behind up a slick incline. Across the distance between them, he sent her a faint, encouraging smile, one that meant, *All is well. I'm right behind you.*

His eyes, however, still reflected turbulence.

With that unexpected encounter behind them, little else could go wrong, she assured herself. The exchange was cut-and-dried. Fournier seemed confident of fulfilling the team's promises within the seventy-two-hour time limit. All the rebels had to do was bring Jay and Mike's body down from Arriba, force Jay to write his insurance company requesting the ransom money, and hand the note over to Fournier, who would take it from there.

In seventy-two hours they'd be back in Bogotá, and Lucy would be soaking her aching hip and her bug-bitten body in a hot tub in a five-star hotel.

Of course, that was if everything went as planned, and when was the last time *that* had happened?

BUITRE'S RADIO CRACKLED. "Deputy Buitre?" Recognizing the voice of the Elite Guard leader, Buitre groped under his soaked poncho and put the radio to his ear.

"*Sí, capitán?*" he inquired smartly. Now, here was a leader worthy of his respect.

Rainwater spattered the hood of his poncho. It was hard to hear Captain Vargas's question while hiking up a steep grade. Something about a woman. "Say again, sir?"

"Who is the younger woman behind you?" This time the words reached him clearly.

Buitre resisted a backward glance. "She's part of the United Nations team. A Spaniard. Why?"

"I've seen her before in my country. And she's not a Spaniard. She's American—a spy."

Triumph exploded in Buitre's bosom, filling him with dark satisfaction. He *knew* it. He'd just known the woman was a spy. She had been too confident from the first, too alert. "Captain, sir," he pleaded, as righteous fury swirled in him, "you must tell me everything you know."

By the time Buitre put his radio away, his mind was filled with visions that made him grind his teeth. The bitch had been caught by the Elite Guard, snooping around a weapons depot in northern Venezuela last year. They had left her beaten and bound, intending to blow up the warehouse with her in it. Only American aircraft had swooped down on them like a mother eagle defending her young. The gunships had destroyed the Elite Guard's convoy, killing all of them but two: Captain Vargas and a man named Santiago.

Buitre seethed. He couldn't resist a quick glance back. Certainty ripped through him as the bitch met his gaze, her eyes cool and watchful.

He'd known she was different from the start.

But what about Gustavo, Luna's soft-spoken husband? Was he also a spy? Buitre glanced back at the bigger man. Oh, yes. He pretended to be myopic, clumsy, unskilled in shooting a weapon, but he was powerfully built, athletic enough to keep both himself and the burly Italian from slipping on the muddy trail. Buitre had glimpsed firsthand his perfect calm in the face of a threat. He had no doubt Luna and Gustavo worked together, had no doubt who they worked for.

The CIA had aided the Colombian army for decades, helping to destroy the rebels' coca crops, helping to pinpoint their cocaine laboratories hidden in the jungle. And now Luna and Gustavo—no doubt fabricated names— had stolen the map that specified the location of the last four rebel camps!

¡Carajo! If they managed to convey that information to the CIA, it would spell disaster for the FARC. Yet

Buitre dared not mention the map's disappearance. It was his fault he hadn't secured his quarters that morning.

He would have to persuade his commanding officers that the couple were frauds, American spies. If the FARC intended to prevail, then those two could not be allowed to leave La Montaña alive.

"NO SATELLITE PHONE, NO RADIOS," the Argentine explained as they stood inside a bare brick shelter dripping rainwater on the dirt-packed floor. This *casita* where the Argentine slept lay just a mile or two short of Commander Rojas's camp, he alleged. Given the pile of hammocks dumped inside the door, this was where the UN team would all sleep tonight.

"I don't understand," Fournier stammered through chattering teeth. They were all soaked and miserable, except for Gus, who seemed impervious to the chill.

"The front commander is a very private man," Álvarez explained without resentment. "The use of modern communication would give away his global positioning to the enemy."

Too late, Lucy thought. He should've stuck with carrier pigeons and ditched the radios.

"Then how am I to reach my contacts and fulfill our end of the agreement?"

"We will be escorted down the mountain to a landline telephone."

"More walking?" Fournier exclaimed in dismay.

"No, no. They have all-terrain vehicles. We will ride."

Fournier looked relieved. "All of us, or—"

"Just you and me," said the Argentine.

Gus spoke up. "Wouldn't a younger man be more

comfortable on the back of an ATV? Perhaps Carlos or I could take your place," he suggested to the lead negotiator.

Álvarez shook his head. "Only Mr. Fournier," he insisted. "He is the one with the contacts."

"When do we go?" asked Fournier. "Our time is limited."

"We go now," said Álvarez. He turned to the rest of them. "Please, make yourselves comfortable. There are hooks on the wall for your hammocks, firewood for the fireplace. You may boil rice twice a day, but the fire must be extinguished by sunset."

"How far away is Rojas's camp from here?" Lucy spoke up, earning a frown.

"I don't know," said Álvarez, heading toward the door. "I don't ask questions."

Asking questions was dangerous, obviously. But inquiring minds wanted to know. Would they get to meet Commander Rojas, or would the Argentine always speak for him? How far away was Rebel Central? Was Rojas hiding something he didn't want the UN team to see?

As they went to hang their hammocks on the pegs, she peered through the smudged pane of a window and realized only Estéban and Manuel had been left to guard the UN team. The rest had departed with Buitre.

Catching Gus's eye, she ascertained that he had noticed the sudden laxness in security. Giving Dumb and Dumber the slip in order to get a peek at Rebel Central was a distinct possibility.

"Only two more days," Gus murmured. Seeing her shiver, he drew her into his arms to warm her with his body heat.

Accepting his embrace, Lucy envisioned the exchange going off without a hitch. She pictured her and Gus on helicopter, sailing up and over the lush jungle canopy, eturning to civilization, to the life she'd led before the nission.

Why, she wondered, did envisioning the best-case sce-ario leave her feeling cheated? Why the emptiness, the ense that her potential hadn't been fully realized?

Perhaps it had to do with the fact that only one of the ostages would be coming home alive. The job would be moderate success at best, denying her a full sense of ccomplishment.

God forbid this nagging emptiness had anything to do vith Gus. There wasn't room for tenderness on the battle-round against terror. She was wasting her time thinking naybe there was. This assignment was a onetime deal, an pportunity to relive a simpler era when loving Gus was ll that mattered. She wasn't the same girl she was back hen. Of course, she had feelings for him. But feelings idn't count when the world was falling apart.

COMMANDER ROJAS USED a forty-foot watchtower as his eadquarters. The structure afforded him an inspiring iew of La Montaña. Up here, where the air was moist nd sweet and highly oxygenated, he enjoyed a sense of oftiness and security. Using shortwave radio only for mergencies, he had managed to elude both the Colom-ian army and the CIA.

Until now. Deputy Buitre's testimony made Rojas's lood run cold. "You are certain you have overheard them peaking English?" he inquired, his voice gruff with isappointment.

"Yes, sir," insisted the scarred soldier.

Deputy Buitre had been a rebel since his teens. His

experience made him an asset to the FARC. He had n
reason to make up lies. Nor did the Venezuelan captai
for that matter.

"Bring Captain Vargas to me," Rojas decided. "I wis
to hear his testimony in person."

"I will, Commander," the deputy promised. "Imme
diately."

Commander Marquez, standing next to the deput
wrung his hands together, waiting for a moment to chim
in. "Commander," he cautioned, "even if there are spie
within the UN team, we cannot harm them. The worl
would consider us barbarians," he insisted.

Rojas sat back, crossed his arms, and thought. Ma
quez was right, of course. If he seized any one of the U
peacekeepers, it would appear to outsiders that the rebe
acted with unwarranted hostility toward a neutral entity.

On the other hand, if the couple were spies for th
CIA, then letting them go could spell ruin for the rebel
depending on how much they had discovered during the
stay on La Montaña.

Did they know of the FARC's plans for resurgence?

Could they lead the enemy to the FARC's hidde
camps?

Twirling a pen between his thumb and forefinger, h
turned his head to survey the canopy, which was toppe
by a thin mist. As he drew a breath of oxygen-rich air,
plan began to form in his head.

"You are right," he said to Marquez. "*We* cannot har
them."

Disappointment seized the planes of Buitre's face, an
Rojas realized here was a man who enjoyed inflicting pai
on others. Nor was he bright enough to realize what h
leader had in mind. Putting his weight on his elbows, h

leaned forward to enlighten the deputy. "Tragically, in the jungle, there are many accidents that may befall an individual. Especially," he added, bringing a glint of comprehension to Buitre's eyes, "when there is a war underway."

SPRAWLED ON A CARPET OF WET MOSS, Lucy peered over a rocky ledge at Front Commander Rojas's compound. "It's bigger than I thought," she admitted to Gus, her heart thumping in the wake of their sprint through the jungle, her blood thrumming with excitement.

They hadn't had to trick Dumb and Dumber, after all. Estéban and Manuel had simply dropped off to sleep by the fire inside the *casita,* and Lucy and Gus had excused themselves, supposedly to heed the call of nature. They'd run the instant they were out of sight, slipping and sliding down the path, as giddy as kids escaping from school, until they heard it—the bustle of Rebel Central.

Veering off the path, they'd pushed through a tangle of vegetation, coming to this rocky ledge where they got their first glimpse of Rojas's hideout.

Buildings with corrugated tin roofs peeked through a thinned canvas below. The camp buzzed with activity, but the thin drizzle and tree branches made it hard to see what the fuss was all about.

Still, they were lucky to view the camp at all. Journalists, the CIA, and the entire Colombian army had been searching for Rojas's new headquarters for over two years now.

"Check out the watchtower," said Gus, pointing.

Following his finger, Lucy spied a structure roughly five stories high, just clearing the canopy. It had been painted green and draped in nets to keep it camouflaged.

She hadn't even seen it till he showed it to her. Bravo
Gus for noticing first.

"I'd like to see the view from there," he added, regard
ing it through narrowed eyes.

"Me, too." Well-being flowed through Lucy's vein
For once, she felt like Gus's equal, his true partner, not
woman he had sworn to protect. "What the hell is makin
that noise?" she added, searching the camp for the sourc
of the sawing sound. "Are they clearing the forest?"

"I think those are the ATVs Álvarez mentioned. Loo
there's one right now." Just then, an ATV shot into
thinned area below them, pulling a trailer behind it.

Men rushed forward to unload the trailer.

As Lucy strained for a better look, Gus twisted th
heel of his boot and pried the phone out. "The camera ha
a telescopic lens," he said, pressing a button to power
up. "Let's see what they've got."

"Crates," she answered, catching a glimpse of a lon
pine box as it was pulled from the trailer. "Long enoug
to carry rifles. Or stinger missiles."

Next to her, Gus swore quietly, and she glanced at hi
askance. "What's wrong?"

"Battery's dead," he said flatly.

As he fetched the spare battery from his right heel, sh
made a mental note—they were now down to eight hou
of battery power. "Five crates unloaded," she murmure
keeping an eye on the activity below. "The ATV just too
off again, back the way it came."

Gus's silence recaptured her focus. She found hi
frowning at the phone with a tense expression that mad
her stomach cramp. "What is it?" she asked.

He pulled out the new battery. "It's not the batter

that's dead. The phone has water in it. There's too much moisture here," he added.

Worry pricked Lucy's bubble of contentment. "So we have no communication," she realized.

"For the time being. The phone isn't completely shot. If it were, there'd be a red dot inside the battery casing. If it dries out it'll probably work again."

If. Probably. To Lucy those words weren't particularly comforting.

"Uncooked rice," Gus murmured thoughtfully.

"What?"

"I can stick the phone in a bag of uncooked rice, and that should draw the moisture out."

Should. "But what if someone goes to cook up breakfast and finds it?" she asked, her agitation rising.

"That's a chance we'll have to take," he answered with a grim look. "I promise I'll keep an eye on it." Putting both batteries back in his boot, he pushed the phone deep into his pocket. "We'd better get back," he said, sending one last glance toward the lookout tower. The dead phone, and the lack of communication, was dampening enough to etch lines of worry on either side of his mouth.

"Right." Lucy, who'd wondered whether to tell him about the worsening pain in her hip, filed it away for when the mission was over. Thank God they were heading out of the jungle soon.

"So what's our story?" he asked, reaching for her hand. "We got turned around and headed the wrong way?"

"Sounds likely enough," Lucy agreed, sending a final glance at Rojas's watchtower. If she were the rebel leader, she'd be up inside that sucker, making big plans.

CHAPTER **13** ═══════

All night long, the satellite phone lay buried in the sack of dry rice in the corner of the *casita*. Gus slept with one eye open, prepared to leap up and intervene should any one of the team members decide to measure out rice in advance of the morning meal. If all went well, the moisture in the phone's casing would be gone by morning.

With the first hint of daybreak brightening the house's single window, Gus rolled out of his hammock and stealthily retrieved it. Casting a glance at Lucy, asleep in her own hammock, he slipped outside.

Yesterday's rain had finally moved on, leaving droplets of moisture winking like diamonds on every leaf. The jungle was drenched in birdsong and monkey chatter, creating a joyous cacophony, through which Manuel and Estéban slept, wrapped in tarps, their hammocks slung between trees.

Gus moved stealthily past them up the path before veering into the woods. Positioning himself beneath an opening in the trees, he removed the battery from his right boot, inserted it into the phone, and held his breath.

As the logo jumped onto the black screen, he closed his eyes briefly. Thank God. He'd worried that his nightmare had been a premonition of awful things to come, like one of the Elite Guardsmen recognizing Lucy on the trail. He hadn't been able to tell if any of them had or not. But at least he was getting a clear signal from the satellite now—a reassuring turn of events. Here was his chance to touch base with the JIC and inquire whether Whiteside had decided to pull Lucy off the mountain.

The phone rang once before it was snatched up. "That you, Ethel?" Vinny asked in a perfect imitation of Fred.

"I need to keep this short," Gus murmured, peering cautiously around him. "Listen, I'm about one click away from Rebel Central, which means my coordinates should be close to one of those camps."

"Roger that, Gus." It was the OIC. "We suspected that yesterday when you approached the coordinates for Ki-kirr-zikiz. We thought maybe you'd try to call in. What's going on over there? Over."

"Sorry, sir. The sat phone's been out of commission. To bring you up-to-date, the lead negotiator has cut a deal with the FARC and is currently off the mountain trying to work out the details. There may be an exchange taking place here, in the next couple of days."

"We've heard rumblings to that effect, Gus. Do you think Fournier can pull it off?"

"He's got the experience," Gus reasoned. "Plus the FARC are eager to ship us out of here. Commander Rojas has the Venezuelans funneling him weapons faster than they can unload them."

"The Predator has images of that," the OIC corroborated.

"Any word from Whiteside on pulling Lucy out early?"

Gus asked. "We crossed paths with the Elite Guard yesterday. I don't know if any of them recognized her, sir, but I'm not sure we should take any chances."

"Well," Luther countered, sounding suddenly uncomfortable. "The negotiation is this close to resolution, Gus. It might throw a wrench into the process if Lucy were to disappear all of a sudden," he reasoned.

Gus had to admit that was true. Still, recalling the conjecturing look on the Venezuelans' faces, he couldn't shake the nagging fear that Lucy's encounter with them in the warehouse last year would bite them in the ass. "Yes, sir," he murmured.

"So proceed as you are, Gus, and good luck. We'll be monitoring things on this end. Anything else?"

"No, sir, that's it."

"Hope to see you soon, over."

"Thank you, sir. Out."

With another peek around the tree, Gus stowed the phone in his boot before turning to water the tree.

Still weighted with foreboding, he hurried back to camp, relieved to find Manuel and Estéban just stirring. Carlos and Bellini met him at the door as they headed for the trees. Inside the *casita,* Şukruye knelt by the fireplace, pouring rice into a tin bowl. But Lucy was still in her hammock, apparently lethargic after a restless night's sleep. He crossed the room to gaze down at her. "Morning," he said, noting with a touch of alarm that she seemed more pale than usual.

"Hi," she said shortly, rubbing crust from the corners of her eyes.

"Tough night?"

She refused to answer, rolling stiffly to a sitting position. She'd pleased him by asking to share a hammock with him last night. They'd tried, only to end up hitting the dirt-packed floor when they both tumbled out. Lucy had then moved to her own hammock, where she obviously hadn't fared much better. The thought that she might have missed him broke over him like a warm morning sunrise.

Just then Şukruye left the *casita* to fetch water for the rice. They had the place to themselves. He sought the courage to voice the question that had been building in him lately.

"Did you check the phone?" she asked before he had the chance to speak.

"Um, yeah. It works again. I just called in and brought the guys up-to-date."

"Good," she said, a hint of color returning to her face.

Gus swallowed hard. It was now or never. "You know, when all this is behind us..."

She looked up at him sharply, suspending his suggestion. "What?" she prompted impatiently.

Maybe she wasn't in the right mood for him to suggest a date. She seemed a little irritable. "Nothing. It'll wait," he decided.

With her hip throbbing painfully, her eyes burning from lack of sleep, and her stomach rumbling for the meal of rice that wouldn't be ready for another half hour, Lucy's patience was too thin for her to tolerate guessing games.

"Just tell me," she insisted, feeling crabby and angry at herself. Damn it, she couldn't even sleep without the comfort of Gus's arms around her. What happened to being completely self-reliant?

He sent a nervous glance at the door. "Well, I was thinking, when this was over, we could maybe see each other, socially," he suggested with watchful wariness.

He sounded like the shy college sophomore who'd asked her out when she was just a freshman. Even as her heart took wing, Lucy's stomach sank like it was weighted with concrete. She stared at him, speechless. They were in a war zone, living on borrowed time if the Elite Guard outed her, and he was trying to ask her out on a date? If they both lived through this op, the chances of them staying on the same continent for the next assignment were slim to none. How the hell was romance supposed to fit into that picture?

At her continued silence, Gus shifted uncomfortably. "You still like pizza, right?" he continued bravely. "I know this new pizza place near Tyson's Corner—"

She put a hand up, suspending his persuasions. "Stop," she begged. "That's enough. Just... don't say any more."

Jamming his hands into his pockets, he frowned down at her. "You're the one who insisted I spit it out," he added, his eyes dark with disappointment.

"My fault," she accepted. "And don't look at me like that. It's nothing personal, okay? People like us don't do relationships, Gus. I can't even keep a houseplant alive."

Rolling out of the hammock, she pushed abruptly past him, afraid he'd see the confusion in her eyes and pounce on it. Her knees felt strangely weak as she headed toward the door to jam her feet into her boots. A part of her longed to turn back, to hurl herself into his arms and say, "Yes, I want to date you!" But the smarter half prevailed. Squaring her shoulders, she marched out of the *casita* without a backward glance, nearly knocking down Şukruye, who was on her way in.

"Careful!" the woman cautioned as Lucy bumped her bucket of water.

"Sorry," she muttered, fleeing the building. Hurrying past the others, she pushed blindly into the blur of vegetation, remembering at the last second to mark her trail by bending branches.

Gus's suggestion, coming on the heels of a poor night's sleep, had thrown her thoughts into turmoil.

Hell, she had nothing against casual dating. She'd been known to dazzle the opposite sex from time to time. But there would be nothing casual about seeing Gus socially, as he'd put it. This adventure in the thicket made it glaringly obvious that they felt comfortable together as boyfriend and girlfriend. If she dated him again, she'd become as wrapped up in him as when she was younger. She'd be picking and choosing her assignments so she could see him, distracted from her primary objective.

Worse than that, she wouldn't be self-reliant ever again. She would *need* him to feel complete, just as she had in college. It had taken years to stop missing him.

Oh, no. She'd taken this assignment to find her courage so she could be strong again. She wasn't going to cash all that in just to grow weak in other ways.

It was best if she didn't see Gus at all.

The thought stripped her of all happiness, making her realize how far gone she already was. *Hey, at least we work for the same people,* she comforted herself. *We're bound to run into each other.*

Upset with herself for even needing consolation, she snatched a vine out of the way, upsetting the monkey that was clinging to it. Then she whirled around, hunting for a soft-looking leaf to wipe with on the carpet of spongy decay.

God, what she wouldn't give for a real roll of toilet paper!

Ten minutes later, Gus seemed to have forgotten both his proposition and her flat-out rejection. He sent her a long, thoughtful look as she reentered the *casita,* but then he was right back to playing her courteous and attentive husband. The fact that he'd accepted the situation so easily did nothing to improve her mood.

For once it wasn't raining, but blood-seeking mosquitoes kept the UN team members indoors, where they lolled in their hammocks sharing reflections and personal memories.

"What's the first thing you intend to do when you return to civilization?" Carlos asked, prompting fantasies in Lucy's mind of a warm bath and a full-body massage.

"Open a bottle of my best pinot grigio," said Bellini, who owned a vineyard.

"Get a pedicure," said Şukruye, glancing wryly at her battered feet.

"Take my wife on a honeymoon," said Gus.

Everyone looked at him in surprise, including Lucy, who quickly swallowed down her startled, "What?" He'd gone from suggesting a date this morning to planning a full-fledged honeymoon? Talk about a fast courtship.

"You haven't had a honeymoon?" Bellini exclaimed in dismay.

"No, no, Luna was too busy working to take time off," said Gus with a doleful shrug.

"That's right," Carlos agreed, backing Gus's allegations. "I told her to take a vacation after the wedding, but she refused."

Bellini beetled his eyebrows at Lucy. "For shame!" he cried, causing Lucy's face to heat. "Love is a rare gift. You must make the most of those magical first months. Where will you take her, Gustavo?" he demanded.

Lucy arched an eyebrow at Gus. *Hurry up. Think fast.*

Gus shrugged. "Oh, I don't know. Somewhere warm. A five-star hotel on a sandy white beach?"

A vision of them sprawled on deck chairs sipping mai tais sent a wave of yearning through Lucy.

"What do you say to that, Luna?" Carlos prompted, his dark eyes dancing with secret mirth. "Will you take your honeymoon or not?"

"Of course," she said, sending Gus a deceptively warm and loving smile. She then lay back in her hammock, her smile fading as she seethed inwardly.

That was a low blow, she thought, instilling in her yearnings for things that couldn't be. Marriage to Gus. A honeymoon. Did he seriously think she could luxuriate at a seaside resort while bad guys plotted ways to strike the innocent?

And yet...once envisioned, the image refused to go away.

Damn him for putting it in her head in the first place. Just because he was her partner on this assignment didn't mean he was her partner for life.

She wouldn't need him to watch her back much longer. Hell, when this assignment was over, she could use mirrors for that.

THE SUNLIGHT WAS JUST BEGINNING to wane when the door of the *casita* crashed open, startling its dozing occupants. "Someone is coming!" Estéban announced, ducking out again.

Gus leapt up to watch through the window. The others shared hopeful glances. "It's Buitre and Fournier," he finally confirmed.

The negotiator had been gone for over twenty-four hours.

They greeted him at the door, enthusiastic in their

welcome. "I have much to tell you," the Frenchman cheerfully announced as he stepped across the threshold.

They drew him toward the fireplace, where embers
still glowed in the wake of their evening meal. Buitre shut
the door, keeping the younger rebels out, himself inside.

"Is it done?" the Italian asked, his face alight with
hope.

"Tell us everything," Şukruye pleaded. "You've been
gone so long, Pierre. We were growing worried for you!"

"It is done," said Fournier, darting an uncomfortable
glance at the deputy. Buitre had placed his back to the
door to watch them with a coy expression. "Well, at least,
the process is underway," he amended.

"Where is Señor Álvarez?" Carlos asked, drawing
attention to the Argentine's absence.

"He was released earlier this afternoon," Fournier
relayed. "I imagine he will soon be with his family."

Şukruye clasped her hands to her heart. "Then we
must be leaving soon, as well," she breathed.

"Yes, yes," said Fournier with another uncomfortable
glance at the door.

Lucy slanted Buitre a look of her own. There was
something creepy about him just standing there, holding
a jug in one hand. Why did she get the sense that he was
gloating, his dark eyes focused for the most part on her?

As the Frenchman gestured for them to gather nearer,
Gus looped an arm around Lucy's waist, drawing her stiff
body closer. Weakness undermined her determination to
remain aloof. She caved in to it, forgetting his presump-
tion, as she let the memory of his touch burn a lasting
impression in her mind, to cherish later.

"We went all the way to Puerto la Concordia," the
Frenchman divulged at just above a whisper. "There we

met a lawyer, a FARC supporter, who had a telephone, a fax, and dial-up Internet. I was able to fax Jay Barnes's request for payment to his insurance company."

The kiss Gus placed on Lucy's temple briefly distracted her. Another memory, filed away for later.

"The money will be wired to a bank in Bogotá," Fournier added, his gray eyes alight with optimism, "where one of my associates will pick it up. In addition, the ten FARC prisoners will be released and delivered, under guard, to my associate. Both the officers and the money will be boarded on a Red Cross helicopter and delivered tomorrow afternoon to the airfield at the foot of the mountain, where Commander Marquez will be waiting to relinquish Jay Barnes and the body of Mike Howitz."

"Tomorrow!" Şukruye exclaimed, her eyes glimmering with tears of relief. "Oh, you have done well, Pierre!" she praised him.

It seemed a little premature to dole out accolades, thought Lucy, resisting a glance up at Gus. What about the red tape Fournier had mentioned the other day? A whole host of things could go wrong, delaying the helicopter's arrival.

"Not I. All of us," Fournier insisted.

"Then you must celebrate," Buitre spoke up abruptly, interrupting. Pushing off the door, he swaggered closer, extending the jug in his hand. He thrust it at Fournier. "A gift from Front Commander Rojas," he announced.

"Thank you," said Fournier uncertainly. "What is it?"

"*Chicha*," said Buitre with an enigmatic smile.

"Fermented cassava," translated Carlos with a guarded expression.

What was the deputy up to? Lucy wondered.

"Try it," he insisted. "It is better than *panela*."

Never one to offend a host, Fournier removed the cork and took an obliging sip. He swallowed, wheezed, and cleared his throat. "Not bad," he decreed. "A bit like English cider. Thank you, Deputy Buitre."

Buitre inclined his head. "Everyone must try it," he insisted with a steely smile.

Lucy considered the offer. Was this a friendly gesture on the rebel's part, or a hostile one? The FARC had nothing to gain from harming them, not when they'd yet to receive their ransom payment. On the other hand, she could not forget Buitre's suspicions, nor his hostility when he confronted her about the map.

To her incredulity, she watched Gus take a hearty swig. Was he that certain the drink hadn't been laced with poison?

He thrust the jug at her, wafting potent-smelling fumes in her direction. She took a wary sip. Liquor seared her throat and left a sour-sweet taste on her tongue. *Chicha* wasn't bad at all. She hoped it would ease the ache in her hip.

The others followed suit, all but Şukruye, who declined. "I don't touch liquor," she explained.

"Drink," Buitre cajoled, but the woman refused, withdrawing quietly to her hammock.

"You must toast Señor Álvarez," Buitre suggested, his voice, his mannerisms friendly. Then again, even serial killers had their charming moments.

As the floor seemed to shift beneath her feet, Lucy reached for Gus, who looked down at her sharply.

"To Señor Álvarez," said Fournier. His eyes seemed brighter than usual as he passed the jug to Gus.

The jug made another round. Lucy was pleased to feel the ache in her hip subsiding.

Bellini spilled some and giggled.

Gus suddenly staggered, lost his footing, and made a grab for Lucy. Together they crashed onto the dirt-packed floor.

Buitre roared with laughter. "You like that, eh?" he asked, bending over them with a grin. The room's shadows turned his face into a grotesque mask.

"Sorry," Gus muttered, his speech slightly slurred. Amazingly, he'd managed to keep his weight from crushing her.

"I'm okay," said Lucy, rolling away and helping him to his feet. "That's enough for us," she announced, guiding Gus to his hammock. He fell into it, lifted his feet, and rolled right off the other side, landing on the floor again.

Buitre roared with appreciation. Lucy set her teeth.

"Gustavo has no tolerance," she explained, even as it occurred to her that Gus was intentionally putting on an act. He didn't trust Buitre's intentions any more than she did. And one way to satisfy the deputy was to feign inebriation.

"We should all retire," Carlos suggested, taking the jug from Bellini, who tried to sneak another swig. "The sun is almost down," he added, tossing water onto the embers to quench the fire.

"We hung a hammock for you, Pierre," chimed in Çukruye, beckoning him to the other corner.

As the team members backed away, Buitre threw a final smirk over his shoulder and left, bearing the jug with him. With a curt word to the rebels outside, the deputy departed. Minutes later, darkness descended with breathtaking speed. The vibration of insects filled the air.

"Buitre meant no harm, I'm sure," Fournier commented, breaking the thoughtful silence.

"Are you okay, Gustavo?" Carlos inquired.

Gus's only reply was a subtle snore.

"He's sleeping," Lucy told the others, knowing h
wasn't. Buitre had hoped to see them make fools of them
selves. Gus had given him what he'd wanted, sparing th
others and managing, at the same time, to speed him o
his way.

She had to admire his quick thinking, his self-sacrifice
She reached over, intending to give him a quick pat. Fas
as a trap, he caught her hand, proving himself still awake
To her bemusement, he lifted it to his mouth and placed
warm, tender kiss on her palm.

Lucy's breath caught. James used to do the same thing
murmuring, "Love you, Luce."

She loved him, too. But she was never going to say
out loud to him and mislead him into thinking they ha
a future together. If she made promises now, what woul
happen when she couldn't keep them? And worse, if sh
did try to keep her promises, how much would they bot
have to give up to make their relationship work?

One of them had to be realistic, and at the moment
looked like it was going to be her.

So if the exchange went off as planned tomorrow, thi
was their last night together.

The realization smothered her like the impossibl
darkness.

In a moment of sentimentalism, she savored the crea
of the ropes beneath her, the feel of Gus's chest rising an
falling under her hand, her fingers loosely twined with his

Anyone could fall in love, she reasoned. But lov
should not require the surrender of everything she'
worked for and believed in. A strong woman didn't need
man to feel whole.

*   *   *

HE DESCENT TO THE airfield at the base of La Montaña
egan with a harrowing ride on ATVs that bumped and
shtailed down winding, rutted paths. The muddy tracks
an up and down the mountain like veins linking Rebel
entral to the Guayabero River.

It was a glorious day for a hostage exchange.

Patches of blue sky flashed here and there where the
anopy thinned. The air felt crisp and cool in Gus's face.
was tempting to just hold on to Lucy, seated between
im and David, and enjoy the ride. But seeing a pile of
rates hastily concealed under cut branches, he tried to
x their coordinates in his mind, thinking they should be
eized before the rebels got the chance to use them.

He pointed it out to Lucy, who sent him a subtle nod.
he'd already seen it. He admired that about her—her
wareness, her instincts. What drove him crazy, though,
as her stubborn insistence on isolating herself. She was
till a victim of survivor's guilt. It was perfectly plain to
im. Her refusal to plan a date with him, let alone a hon-
ymoon, had nothing to do with the rigors of her job. She
idn't think she had a right to be happy again. It was really
aat simple, that sad.

The path forked, and David broke right, followed by
stéban, Manuel, Julian, and Buitre, who carried the
ther four team members on the backs of their vehicles.
Iinutes later, they passed the hidden stockpile a second
me, and Gus realized the rebels were driving them in
ircles to disorient them. The airfield probably wasn't as
ar away as they wanted them to think.

David forked left this time. Several hundred meters
ater, he pulled off the trail and cut the engine. The drivers

behind them did likewise. And that was when Gus hea
it, the roaring of a river. Helping Lucy off the ATV, he fe
tension in her fingers. He couldn't blame her, either.

Given the looks of the other team members, the
dreaded a river crossing. Reluctantly, they trailed Buit
toward the break in the canopy.

A gushing expanse of café-au-lait-colored water ha
carved a canyon of mud out the side of the mountain,
least thirty feet wide. Sticks and branches swirled dow
river, caught up in its torrential current.

Seeing the bridge that crossed the canyon, the tea
members moaned in dismay. At least they wouldn't t
crossing via a steel box on cables. But the bridge itself wa
narrow and fraying. A fine mist, rising from the seethir
water, dampened both the rope and the boards, makir
them slippery, subject to decay.

No way had boxes of weapons been carried across th
bridge. There had to be another way down the mountai
Gus realized.

But either Buitre didn't want them running acro
Venezuelans on the main path, or he got his jollies out
scaring them.

"Not to worry," Fournier reassured them while keep
ing hold of Şukruye's arm. "Just picture the helicopt
coming to take us home."

Pale with fear, she nodded and clung to him.

The team members lined up. "Only two at a time
Buitre cautioned. "You're last," he added as Gus took h
place in line.

Uneasiness feathered Gus's spine. *Why last?* he wo
dered, sending Lucy a reassuring nod as she glanced
him sharply.

The worry that creased her forehead was a comfor

ng sight. She could pretend all night and day she didn't
ave feelings for him, but he knew otherwise. Whether
e could convince her that she deserved happiness was
nother question altogether. How could he compete with
er survivor's guilt?

At least her self-destructive tendencies had been tem-
ered by wariness, thanks to PTSD. The longer she lived,
he more he stood a chance of winning her back.

"Hold the rails and walk across quickly," he advised the
thers. "Try not to leave the bridge shaking." The oscilla-
ions would get worse with every crossing. "Fournier and
;ukruye should go first," he added.

"I will give the orders," Buitre sneered, sending
cross David and Manuel, who made the crossing look
asy. Julian and Carlos were told to cross next, followed
y Estéban and Bellini, who sent the bridge rippling but
afely reached the other side.

It was up to Fournier to coax the Turkish woman across
he writhing suspension. She wailed with every step, rac-
ng the last few feet to arrive on solid ground. Only Lucy,
;us, and Buitre remained.

"Let Luna go," Gus insisted, sensing a trap.

Buitre sent him a careless shrug. "Of course," he said.

Maybe the trap was just in Gus's head. "See you on the
ther side," he whispered, dropping a kiss on her soft lips.
The worry in her wide eyes was unmistakable.

"I'll be right behind you," he promised, repeating the
vords he'd said a few days back. He meant them with
verything that was in him.

As Buitre barked at her to get going, she backed away
rom Gus, drew a deep breath, and stepped bravely onto
he undulating bridge. With his heart thudding heavily,

he watched her power her way across. If something hap
pened now, he'd be hard pressed to help.

When she was two thirds of the way across, Buitre fol
lowed her. Gus watched his every move with suspicion
but he trailed Lucy without incident, and soon she stood
on the opposite shore, waving back at him.

If this wasn't a trap, then why was his intuition scream
ing at him to beware? Buitre hadn't messed with Lucy.
Maybe he intended to mess only with Gus.

Remembering his nightmare, Gus stepped onto the
lurching bridge with tension in every muscle. He'd com
pleted dozens of obstacle courses throughout his train
ing. If Buitre thought he was going to shake him off the
sucker, he had another thing coming.

Through narrowed eyes, he studied Buitre's every step.
As the deputy neared the opposite shore, he paused and
glanced back, putting both his hands on the railing that
faced downriver. Buitre's fingers seemed to dance over a
knot in the rope. But then he turned away, moving casu
ally toward shore.

A subtle shudder whipped along the length of the
bridge. Suddenly, the rope under Gus's right hand went
slack. He dropped it, groping for the left side, as the slat
under his feet tipped forty-five degrees.

If not for his quick reflexes, he would have slipped into
the river racing ten yards below him.

He could hear his teammates shouting in consterna
tion and alarm, their cries scarcely audible over the sound
of rushing water.

Stunned, stuck halfway across the bridge, Gus met
Buitre's gloating gaze and knew. The man had tried to
dump him in the river. *The son-of-a-bitch.* Suddenly, the

nightmare Gus had suffered the other night seemed all too much like a warning he had ignored.

Too bad for Buitre, he could still make his way across with what was left of the bridge. But would Buitre try to shoot him then, as he had in his dream?

A blur behind the deputy caught his eye. He realized Lucy was fighting Carlos's hold in an attempt to climb onto the distressed bridge and rescue him. He'd never seen a look of pure terror on her face before.

He tried to send her a reassuring wave, but the bridge was rocking violently. The rope that had served as a railing now trailed into the water. "Stay back!" he shouted, projecting confidence so she would know not to worry.

Carlos kept a firm grip on her, which, Gus knew, was no small feat. He hoped he could count on the Spaniard to keep the upper hand.

Right now he needed to focus on a plan.

The bridge now resembled one of those trick ladders strung up for kids in amusement parks. Gus was confident he could apply the laws of physics to keep the bridge from tipping over too far. On the other hand, did he trust Buitre not to shoot him if he made it to the other side?

A violent shudder had him glancing up, distracted.

Buitre again. The man was climbing out, presumably to rescue him.

Bullshit. More likely he was going to try to hurl him into the giant wash machine below.

"Get back!" he yelled, but the deputy's eyes glittered with malice as he inched closer. With rising dismay, Gus realized Buitre was headed to a knot similar to the one he'd manipulated on the other side.

He was going to release the other railing. And suddenly Gus knew: this bridge had been designed to be dismantled, so the FARC could dump the enemy into th river.

He watched with rising consternation as Buitre ease a loop over the head of the knot while at the same tim extending his free hand, so that, to the others, it looke like he was helping.

The bridge gave a familiar lurch. Before the rope coul slacken under Gus's hand, he dropped onto his stomacl wrapping his arms and legs around the wooden slats. wet mist coated him as the bridge swayed, jerked dowi ward by the falling rope. Tipping ninety degrees, he clun like a cat in a tree, wondering what his odds were if he fe into the seething water.

Glancing up, he met Buitre's mocking gaze, rea the cruel smile on his face, and realized the man full intended to kill him. Somewhere along the line, he'd cor vinced himself that Gus and Lucy were spies. Had he cor vinced the FARC leadership, as well? Was he acting o orders to destroy them?

If so, then Lucy was his next target.

Oh, hell no.

Adjusting his grip, he began to drag himself towar Buitre, toward shore. He would have to pretend to tak Buitre's hand, then rip him off the ropes and throw hir into the water before the man could pull a gun on him.

Then he and Lucy would have to detach themselve from the rest of the team, call the JIC, and get the hell ou

Grimly determined, one part of him aware of Lucy hysteria and Carlos's battle to keep her contained, Gu pulled himself inch by inch over the slick, swayin boards.

Suddenly, with a loud squeak, the board under his le arm tore from the track beneath it. Gus groped for a di ferent board to clutch, but it was too late. His upper body had twisted too far. Gravity had hold of him now.

The rubber of his boots squeaked as he slipped. He knew he was going to fall. There was nothing left to do but ensure he hit the water at an angle that wouldn't kill him.

With Lucy's scream sounding in his ears, he plummeted toward the river, somersaulting.

CHAPTER 14

Splash! With catlike agility, Gus managed to enter the river feet-first. Water slammed up his nostrils and closed over his head with the force of a collision. Immediately, the current seized him up, projecting him downstream at a frightening clip.

To protect his limbs, he curled into a ball. He could see nothing under the water but shades of dark brown. A log clipped the side of his head, leaving his ear ringing. He slammed into a boulder and glanced off of it. The current dragged him through the branches of a fallen tree.

Desperate for air, he clawed for the surface and realized his boots were weighing him down.

The boots with the sat phone that had finally worked.

The electronics in his heels were probably ruined by now. He wasn't going to be calling the JIC anytime soon.

Plus, if he shucked the boots, he'd get to breathe.

Breathing was good.

Sluicing along underwater, he struggled with the laces and tugged the boots off, his lungs and his nasal passages burning.

He used his jacket to slow him down. Tearing it open, he dragged it behind him like a parachute, then shook it off and strained again for the surface.

At last his head broke free. He gasped for air, only to be yanked under again. But he'd glimpsed enough of his surroundings to determine where the shoreline was, in which direction to swim.

Minute by minute, he made his way toward the dark mud and bowed branches at the river's edge.

After what seemed like hours but may have been as little as fifteen minutes, Gus crawled onto shore, gasping and weary. He pulled himself onto the embankment and staggered to his feet to survey his surroundings. Swiping a hand over his eyes, he couldn't believe what he saw.

On the other side of the river, La Montaña rose skyward in a precipitous tangle of vegetation. But on this side, the terrain was as flat as a prairie, dotted with banana and papaya trees, as far as the eye could see.

Knocking water from his ears, Gus turned full circle to get his bearings. Pebbles and sticks gouged his feet. Looking down, he saw that one of his feet was encased in a muddy sock; the other was bare.

Great. Perfect. He was miles from Lucy and shoeless.

If Buitre had acted under orders, then the FARC had come to suspect him and Lucy, enough to try to dispatch them. And that meant Lucy was next. Oh, fuck no. He had to get back to her and save her before it was too late.

A shudder of disbelief racked his body. He hugged himself to ease his shock. *Why am I even surprised?* he asked himself. His nightmare had been a warning that he'd foolishly overlooked. He'd sworn to Lucy that he would protect her. Goddamn him for being an idiot! How was he supposed to do that when they were miles apart?

*   *   *

"WHAT THE HELL?" SAID VINNY, who was looking forward to his watch ending in eight minutes. Pulling his
limbs in from a full-bodied stretch, he sat forward, eye-
balling the red dot that was Lieutenant Atwater as it
moved with amazing speed away from Lucy. "Sir, you
need to see this!" he exclaimed.

Within a second, Lieutenant Lindstrom loomed over
him. Harley and Haiku abandoned what they were doing
to gawk over his other shoulder.

"What's he doing?" Harley demanded.

"He's on a river," Vinny realized. "Maybe he's in a
boat."

"Not unless he's whitewater rafting," countered the
lieutenant. "How fast is he moving?"

Vinny drew a line on the monitor and hit two buttons.
"Like twenty miles an hour."

With silent concern, the SEALs watched the red dot
travel farther and farther from the blue dot. Not one of
them voiced the possibility that Lieutenant Atwater might
be dead. Moving through water at that speed without a
helmet or life vest was asking for trouble.

"Haiku, call the station chief," commanded the OIC,
suddenly decisive.

"Sir, he's slowing down," Vinny alerted him.

Lieutenant Lindstrom leaned in. Chief Harlan did the
same. Haiku crossed the room to make a phone call.

"Can you zoom in any closer?" asked the LT.

"A little," said Vinny, tapping the appropriate key.

"Come on, sir," muttered Harley as they waited on
pins and needles for any indication that Lieutenant Atwater was still alive.

The red dot moved, no more than a millimeter, but it definitely moved. "He's good," Vinny declared.

"Sir, I've got the station chief on the line," Haiku announced.

"Just a second," the lieutenant murmured, keeping his eyes glued to the red dot.

It moved again.

"He's got to be walking. He just covered five yards," said Vinny, having drawn a line to determine the distance.

With a nod, the OIC moved to the phone to update Whiteside. He hung up a minute later, looking thoughtful.

"What'd he say, sir?" Vinny asked, too impatient to wait.

The lieutenant's jaw flexed. His dark blue eyes looked troubled. "He says we wait an hour for Gus to contact us. If we don't hear anything by then, we go in for an extract."

"Uh..." Harley was the first to point out Whiteside's idiocy. "Sir, if the sat phone went down the river with the lieutenant, he won't be using it to call anybody."

"Right," said the OIC, sliding his hands into his pockets. He deliberated for a split second longer. "Haiku, get the rest of our guys in here, ASAP. We need to move on this."

THE SHRIEK THAT HAD ERUPTED from Lucy's throat when Gus plummeted toward the water had been the last utterance she'd made. Even when they'd spent hours searching for him, putting off the exchange at the airfield to scour the shoreline, she had retreated deeper and deeper into her thoughts, keeping silent.

The team members—all but Fournier—had rallied

around her, embracing her, offering words of reassurance to which she was incapable of replying. She knew she was in shock. For the first time in her career, she didn't know who was standing where; where to find the closest option for cover in the event of sudden violence; how far they had traveled looking for Gus.

Her thoughts scurried through her mind like a rat in a maze, seeking answers and not finding them. How had the bridge suddenly and mysteriously collapsed when it had felt stable just minutes before?

Instinct told her Buitre was to blame. Only how? He'd still been crossing when the first side collapsed. And then he'd risked his life by venturing back out to reach for Gus's hand. Helping, or hindering? For then the second side had collapsed, and Gus had lost his grip, slipping into the water.

He'd been missing for hours now. The team members had called his name till they were hoarse. They'd squandered precious time searching for him until, at last, Fournier announced they would continue to the airfield or risk forfeiting their agreement with the FARC.

To Lucy, he'd muttered an apology and the promise to send a search party back for Gus. But the odd look in his eyes told her the incident had solidified certain suspicions in his mind regarding her and Gus. He made no overt accusations; still, a coolness in his demeanor left his promise sounding hollow.

Fournier's suspicions resurrected her own. Had Buitre tried to kill Gus in such a way as to make himself look blameless?

If so, he was in for an unpleasant surprise. Navy SEALs didn't drown, not if they were conscious. And she'd seen Gus hit the water in a controlled manner, feet first. Of course, that was that last she'd seen of him.

But she had faith that he had escaped the torrent farther downriver. She envisioned him climbing ashore miles from where they'd searched. She knew he'd return for her, if he was able. That's what partners did.

"Come," said Carlos. Linking his arm with hers, he appointed himself her protector in Gus's stead. Given the watchfulness in his dark eyes, he, too, was worried that the FARC had guessed Gus and Lucy's true identities.

She needed to stay vigilant. She needed to expect the worst. But shock held her in its icy grasp. She followed his lead, blindly, down a worn path that wound toward the base of the mountain. Despite Carlos's reassuring grip, isolation and fear took up residence in her heart. She felt Gus's absence as she would a missing limb.

Thank God for the microchip that jarred her hip with every step. The JIC still had her on radar. Gus, too, for that matter. They could see that they were separated. They were bound to respond.

Hurry! She thought, sending them an anxious, kinetic message. *Get here quick!*

The trees thinned abruptly and the sun grew brighter. With a start, Lucy realized they had descended to the valley. Branches gave way to a clearing of wild grass, about the size of a football field, illumined by a hot sun.

"We're here," Fournier announced, looking straight through Lucy as he glanced back at the others.

He led them into the field and stopped, peering around. A cinderblock building with a red-tiled roof stood baking under the naked sun, a clear landmark to pilots. Grooves worn into the tall grass indicated that the field was used as a runway.

"There's no helicopter," Şukruye remarked with worry.

"Perhaps they came and left already," added Bellini anxiously.

"No, no," Fournier reassured them. Shading his eyes, he peered upward at the cloudless sky. "They haven't come yet."

Jumpy with suspicion, Lucy peered behind her and watched Buitre give orders to David, Manuel, Julian, and Estéban. She strained her ears to overhear what he was telling them. David's stunned expression corroborated her fear that Buitre was sending them back to hunt for Gus, to kill him if they found him. In the next instant, the four youths turned and melted into the forest.

Buitre sauntered over to the Europeans. "You will wait here," he commanded, pointing down at the sunny grass. "Comandante Marquez awaits in there," he added, gesturing toward the cinderblock structure. "When the helicopter arrives, our *compañeros* must be presented to us first. Then you will bring us the money. If we are satisfied you have not cheated us, we will release the living hostage and the dead one."

He glanced briefly at Lucy, his dark eyes cruelly mocking.

Fournier eyed the cracked and filthy windows of the cinderblock building. "Perhaps," he suggested diplomatically, "you could assure us that the hostages are here?" The building appeared deserted.

Turning a deaf ear on his request, Buitre shouldered his rifle and marched through the knee-high grass to join Marquez inside the building.

Relieved that she hadn't been overtly threatened yet, Lucy gave in to her shaky knees and sank gingerly down on the soft grass, bearing her weight on her good hip. The others followed suit, their gazes fixed on the sky for the arriving helicopter.

Where are you, Gus?

He'd warned her that if anything should happen to him, she should find water and follow it down the mountain to await rescue by the Navy SEALs. But she was already down the mountain, so now what? All she could do was to continue as a participant in the hostage exchange and hope she would be allowed to leave without incident.

But how was she supposed to leave without Gus? Partners weren't supposed to abandon each other.

Just keep your head in the game, Luce. Keep vigilant.

She knew to expect the worst. At the same time, she had a job to finish. She had sworn to herself she would get the hostages home, one dead, one alive. Whatever happened, she was obligated to fulfill that promise.

IN THE TIME THAT IT TOOK to retrieve his jacket from the river, where it had snagged on the branch of a fallen tree, the voices calling for Gus had faded.

Throwing himself down on the muddy riverbank, he used the knife still in his pocket to shred the jacket into strips, his movements precise and calm, a result of his training.

Inwardly, his heart was screaming at him to hurry.

In seconds, he had fashioned booties to protect his feet, already bruised and bleeding from the short distance he'd walked. The sturdy canvas would offer moderate protection, at least. To keep himself camouflaged, he draped his head with the remaining material and resumed his chase, moving stealthily upriver.

They couldn't have gotten too far ahead of him, he assured himself.

Nor did he blame Fournier for abandoning their search. The UN team's priority today was to make certain the exchange took place the way it was supposed to. Come what may, they had to meet the helicopter at the airfield. That was the agenda.

It was Buitre's agenda that worried Gus now. No doubt he hoped to prevent the map, or knowledge of the map, from escaping. In order to do that, he would try to kill Lucy next. Too bad the information had already been disseminated and decoded. The FARC didn't stand a chance.

But that didn't increase Lucy's odds any.

With a fierce grip on the knife, Gus cut diagonally through the jungle, hacking at branches and vines to save time. Sweat trickled between his shoulder blades. Thorns and spines scratched his bare arms, drawing blood. Mosquitoes swarmed him.

When he stumbled across a path lined with fresh prints, he nearly wept with relief. Now he could cover ground faster.

The booties lent him both stealth and speed. He raced down the path, confident of his ability to catch up. Already the sun was edging toward the mountain's peak. Shadows crept like mercury up the trunks of trees. Gus ran faster, nearly plowing into the squad of rebels meandering up the trail ahead of him.

With a jolt of adrenaline, he darted off the path, hiding behind a bush, slowing his heavy breathing. Goddamn it! What were David and his squad doing coming back this way?

"But why would we kill him?" Estéban was asking. "I like Gustavo. He helped to repair our shelter."

"He is a spy," insisted David in a torn and emotional voice. "And so is Luna. They are both spies."

Oh, shit, thought Gus. If the four kids caught sight of him, they apparently had orders to mow him down.

At that very instant he heard in the distance the *whop, whop, whop* of an approaching helicopter. The exchange was about to go down in a location not too far from his hiding place.

But until these kids moved past him, he was pinned down, forced to hold perfectly still, ignoring the mosquitoes swarming him. *Goddamn it!*

"THERE!" FOURNIER CRIED, pointing as a Red Cross helicopter burst into view from behind the mountain with a reverberating crescendo. The UN team members, who'd come to their feet at the first hint of its approach, waved a frantic greeting.

Lucy's eyes stung at the heartening vision of a red cross emblazoned onto the sides of the reconditioned Huey UH-1 Iroquois. If Gus were safely with her, she would get satisfaction out of watching its tail flare, watching the grass ripple like rings on the surface of a disturbed pond as powerful winds whipped her hair in her eyes.

For ten days she'd craved her return to civilization, only Gus's disappearance had stripped her of her anticipation. She didn't know if she could leave him here.

As the bird nestled onto the airfield and the thunder of the rotors diminished, Fournier held them back. "Wait," he advised.

With a clank and a rumble, the helicopter door slid open. A man wearing a dark uniform leapt to the ground,

assault rifle cradled in the crook of one arm. Scoping th
area uneasily, he waved them over.

"Who is he?" Lucy asked Fournier as they struck ou
across the field. Glimpsing movement behind the windo
in the little building, she ducked behind Carlos, who kep
a firm grip on her arm.

Here they were, out in the open, while the FARC wer
barricaded in a concrete building, possibly heavily arme
The Huey's mounted gun and torpedo launchers had bee
removed, leaving it utterly defenseless.

The situation didn't feel right. Then again, nothing ha
felt right since Gus had plummeted into the river.

"Prison guard..." Fournier informed her. The win
snatched away the remainder of his words.

They approached the helicopter in an uneasy kno
and Fournier shook hands with the guard, instructing hir
to release the officers and send them into the red-roofe
building. Peering into the chopper, Lucy eyed the ten fo
mer rebels, sitting back to back under the armed watch o
a second guard.

One by one, they struggled up. Wearing orange priso
suits with their wrists still cuffed, they jumped from th
helicopter and trotted toward the cinderblock buildin;
The door swung open and they swarmed inside, but Luc
could see nothing in the shadowy interior to indicate tha
Jay was inside, chafing for freedom.

With her mind still numb with shock, it was hard
get a clear read on the situation. Aside from what had hap
pened to Gus, everything was happening according
plan, yet she had a terrible suspicion they were all bein
duped.

"Now what?" the prison guard shouted down
Fournier, looking worried.

The enemy now outnumbered them ten to one.

"Where is the money?" Fournier asked.

The second guard swung a briefcase down to him. Hefting it, Fournier eyed his teammates. "Ready?" he inquired, indicating they should follow him.

Uneasiness congealed in Lucy's gut. In addition to outnumbering them, the FARC now occupied a strongly defensive position. Their precaution seemed a bit overdone, considering the Red Cross helicopter was stripped of all fighting capabilities.

Unless the FARC knew something Lucy didn't . . .

CROUCHED BEHIND THE BROAD-LEAVED BUSH, Gus kept his eyes trained on the rebels as they ambled past him, close enough that he could have whispered, "Boo!" and they'd have spun around with muzzles blazing.

He weighed his chances of taking them all at once. What he wouldn't give for an assault rifle of his own. There was just one problem. Despite their orders to kill *him,* he didn't want to kill *them.*

His best bet was to let them go.

Only by the time they ambled past, Buitre might have found the opportunity to kill or capture Lucy.

The possibility of the latter had him suffering through hot and cold sweats. God knew what the FARC did to their captives.

A mosquito flew into his ear, another up his right nostril, forcing him to squeeze his nose before it made him sneeze.

The longest minutes of his life ensued as he waited for the quartet to disappear, arguing his fate as they continued back to the river to search for him, never realizing they had gone right by him.

DUCKING THROUGH THE LOW DOOR, Lucy's eyes adjusted swiftly to the darkness. The little building was crowded with men, none of whom had bathed recently, gauging by the odor of unwashed bodies. They lounged around Marquez, who sat behind a little table. At their entrance, a lone man crouching on the cement floor scrambled up, a steel chain swinging from his neck.

Jay! Lucy swallowed her cry of dismayed recognition. As their gazes met, she touched her ear in the standard signal for *You don't know me.* Immediately, he dragged his attention to the others.

"Thank God!" he croaked, staggering toward them, a mere shadow of his former self.

"Jay Barnes?" said Fournier, extending him a formal handshake. "Pierre Fournier, United Nations. I presume you're ready to go home."

"Yes," Jay agreed, casting a fearful glance behind him. Lucy took the opportunity to study him. Ten months in captivity had come close to killing him. Once tall and robust, he was bent and thin, his skin a sickly shade of yellow.

"Bring us the money," Buitre prompted, impatiently waving Fournier forward.

Drawing Jay into their midst, Fournier extended the briefcase to Buitre, who laid it on the table in front of Marquez. "Go ahead and count it if you must," Fournier said. "Only where is the body of Mike Howitz?" he inquired.

Buitre shoved a wooden box across the cement floor. "Don't open it in here," he warned.

Eyeing the crude coffin, Lucy's stomach roiled as she envisioned Howitz's rotting corpse inside. Her hands curled into fists as blind fury exploded through her. The sons of bitches had killed him. And they were getting paid for that?

"Thank you," Jay was saying, shaking each team member's hand, one at a time. He reached for Lucy, gripping her extra hard to convey both his grief and gratitude. She dared not meet his gaze. Buitre was watching them closely.

Marquez snapped open the briefcase, lifted the lid, and sifted through the contents. Rebels leaned in on every side, eyeing the money greedily.

Outside the building, the helicopter's rotors began to spool. With a thud, Marquez closed the case abruptly. He met Fournier's gaze and stood up. "Take the Americans and go," he shouted over the noise. His dark, flat gaze betrayed no emotion whatsoever.

Glancing at the other rebels, Lucy read the same secretive look in their eyes. Splinters of suspicion sank deep beneath her skin. Something was happening. If only she could predict what.

But why would the rebels jeopardize the exchange when they'd gotten what they wanted? Was it just to punish her? Wasn't trying to kill Gus enough of a punishment?

"Remove Mr. Barnes's chain," Fournier replied, frustrating Lucy's instinct to retreat as fast as possible.

A soldier stepped forward with a key, and the deadbolt that kept Jay chained like a dog fell open. It dropped to the dirt floor with a heavy *chink*.

Fournier nodded. "Bellini, Carlos," he said, waving them toward the box. "Help me with this."

As the three men struggled to lift Mike's coffin, Şukruye

held the door. Lucy grabbed Jay's sleeve to escort him as quickly as possible into the gale force of the helicopter's rotors.

WITH THE YOUTHS FINALLY OUT OF SIGHT, Gus bolted from his hiding place, crashing downhill toward the rising thunder of the nearby helicopter.

Leaves brushed at his face. The ground felt as slick as mud beneath his flying feet. God forbid he was too late!

If Buitre had already harmed Lucy, what then? Gus would rather snatch his own heart out of his chest than discover that he'd failed her.

He nearly burst through the tree line, exposing himself to view. At the last second, he skidded to a stop, then scrambled up and out of sight. From behind a kapok tree, he peered out at the field, searching for Lucy, unable to see her.

The large grassy field seemed to dance beneath a hot sun. A Red Cross helicopter idling yards away from a building was clearly preparing for liftoff, only Gus could see no one inside it but the pilots. Where was Lucy?

Suddenly, the door to the building popped open. To Gus's relief, Fournier stepped into view, bearing one end of a box. Carlos squeezed through the door while supporting the box in the middle, then Bellini appeared carrying the other end. *Howitz's body,* Gus supposed.

When Lucy and Şukruye appeared, bearing a skeletal figure between them, he released a shuddering breath of relief. The exchange had gone off without a hitch. Poor Jay, he thought with a pang of pity. The man was scarcely recognizable from his picture.

With cautious optimism, Gus watched the UN team

move in a slow parade toward the helo. Again the grass in the field seemed to dance. He rubbed his eyes, certain his vision was playing tricks on him.

But then the field came alive, and he realized with dawning horror that an army, hitherto disguised by blankets of straw, had been hiding there all along. Throwing off their camouflage, soldiers leapt to their knees, raised rifles to their shoulders, and opened fire on the building.

Rat-tat-tat-tat-tat! A barrage of semi-automatic gunfire cut through the helicopter's thunder. Astonished and terrified, the team whirled, stared, then raced toward the helicopter, seeking cover.

Who the hell? Gus wondered, his chest swelling with fear as the red-roofed shelter fell under attack.

From within the building came an answering volley.

The bizarre vision made no sense. Horrified, certain to be shot if he interfered, Gus kept his eyes on Lucy as she and the other team members struggled to lift the box into the helicopter. The engines whined as the pilot pushed for speed in an effort to escape the unexpected melee.

Colombian army, Gus realized, recognizing the distinct uniforms of the soldiers who had hidden in the grass. His astonishment mingled with rage. "No!" he ground out, his guttural cry drowned out by the firefight.

The army had nearly jeopardized the start of this mission. Now they were wreaking havoc on its successful resolution. Why? Of course they resented the release of the ten FARC officers, but would they risk the lives of UN peacekeepers just to keep those officers from reintegrating?

Get in, Lucy! With his heart in his throat, Gus watched as Lucy helped Jay into the helo.

Thank God the army's ammunition was being aimed

at the building. For the moment, the FARC inside were pinned down, unable to return fire. The helo stood a fair chance of taking off, if Lucy would just get in!

Carlos, kneeling in the doorway, reached out a hand to pull her up. She'd helped everyone else, making herself last to board. But Lucy hesitated, throwing one last look over her shoulder.

With a pang of insight, Gus realized she was looking for him. *Go, Luce!* he wanted to shout. *Go!* But between the roar of the rotors and percussion of artillery, she would never hear him.

Movement within the building caught his eye. Suddenly, the muzzle of an AK-47 poked through a shattered windowpane, and Gus's blood turned to ice water. Even before a crack shattered the staccato of continuous gunfire, he knew that Lucy was the target.

She crumpled where she fell.

Gus stifled a hoarse shout. *No!* He watched helplessly as Carlos leapt from the doorway to snatch her up, but the weapon that had fired upon her discharged again, spewing rounds that clanked into the side of the helicopter. Struck by a bullet, Carlos reeled and dropped. The helo began to rise.

Carlos groped for a running board. He reached for Lucy, but with only one good arm he couldn't pull her with him. As the Huey made its ascent, Carlos was clinging for dear life.

Slowly, slowly it gained altitude. Bellini and Fournier reached out hands to grab him, and Carlos eventually climbed back in.

They'd left Lucy on the fucking ground.

Every instinct shouted at Gus to run to her.

But common sense kept him pegged to his hiding place. He gasped for breath, battling the impulse to vomit.

Jesus, God, don't let her be dead, he prayed, his gaze fixed on her unmoving figure. This wasn't supposed to happen. He was her partner. He was supposed to keep her safe. But she had looked to her own safety last, using her training to save the others—the very people who'd left her to fend for herself.

Through eyes filmed with tears, he watched the helicopter rise higher and higher, out of range of rifle fire. Its shadow streaked across the golden grass, then it listed sharply to one side, shaking the earth beneath him as it thundered toward the mountain and disappeared behind the sharply rising canopy.

WITHIN THE HUEY, CARLOS SCOOTED to the middle of the grooved floor and gasped his thanks. "We have to go back for her!" he shouted to Fournier.

The Frenchman's lips thinned. "No," he refuted, his expression flat and guarded. As Bellini crawled to the rear, Fournier leaned forward to add, "You played me for a fool, Carlos. Luna and Gustavo de Aquiler were never one of us. But you already know that," he accused, sitting back.

Stunned, Carlos gazed up at him, still trembling in the wake of his close call. He sent an uncomfortable glance at the other team members. Together with a prison guard, they hovered over the freed hostage.

"For your sake, I will say nothing," Fournier added, "for I have long considered you my friend. But I will not put my people in jeopardy to return for two imposters. They are CIA, aren't they?"

Carlos refused to answer.

"Let the CIA get them out," Fournier decreed, veins appearing beneath the transparent skin on his forehead.

Swallowing convulsively, Carlos turned his head to look through the helicopter's open door. From this altitude, La Montaña had never looked more darkly menacing. With the sun sinking behind its mass, this side was a wall of dark vegetation, hostile and obscure.

And Gus and Lucy were both alone down there.

God help them both, Carlos thought.

CHAPTER 15

The field fell suddenly and inexplicably quiet.

Staring at Lucy's prone body through the lingering smoke and tear-filled eyes, Gus realized the Colombian army had ceased firing on the little building. Standing vulnerable to counterattack, they lowered their guns and waited, as if expecting—what, the FARC to surrender?

It felt all wrong.

Suddenly, the door of the beleaguered building flew open, and FARC rebels poured out of it, cheering. *Cheering?*

To Gus's astonishment, the army didn't shoot them; they countered with a cheer of their own, jumping up and down, firing weapons at the sky.

What the fuck?

Gripping the tree in amazement, Gus gawked at the bizarre vision. Amid rebels and government soldiers, Lucy lay sprawled in the grass unmoving. Bile crept up his throat as he pictured her life's blood pouring out of her.

Buitre sauntered onto the airfield to gaze down at her,

a smirk of triumph on his scarred face. He nudged her with a toe, and she stirred.

She stirred!

Swallowing down a cry of wonder, Gus watched as Buitre nudged her again, commanding her to get up.

How could she? She'd taken a hit square in the chest.

But she did. Somehow, miraculously, she did. As soldiers and rebels mingled, exchanging handshakes and clapping each other's backs, Lucy rolled to her knees and lifted her head, looking around her in confusion.

Some of the government soldiers were taking off their uniforms, shaking out of them as if covered in ants.

And that was when Gus realized this was all a setup.

Beneath the colors belonging to the Colombian army, the soldiers wore the pea green color of the Venezuelan Elite Guard. *Son of a bitch!*

The pieces of the puzzle fell abruptly into place. Those weren't Colombian soldiers. They were Venezuelans, the FARC's new allies. *Holy Christ!*

In a sneaky guerrilla tactic that involved dressing like the enemy, the allies had just convinced the fleeing UN team that Colombian soldiers had shot and killed one of their team members while attacking the FARC.

The fallout would be tremendous. Within hours, both the United Nations and the International Red Cross would condemn the Colombian army. The Colombians would fly into a frenzy to prove their innocence—something that could take months to prove. Only by then, the damage would be done. No one would believe the army's claim of innocence. The government would lose big points in popularity.

Gus didn't give a shit about any of that. The only thing that mattered now was Lucy, who'd fallen into the FARC's hands, just as she had in his dream.

Watching Buitre haul her to her feet, he thought again
of how the dream had been a premonition, one he should
have heeded. Buitre had never intended to let him or Lucy
leave the jungle. He should've grabbed Lucy that very
night and spirited her out of there while the getting was
good.

Now she was hurt. Or was she? He searched the front
of Lucy's jacket for signs of a bullet wound. He couldn't
see any stains from here. Nor was she clutching herself,
trying to staunch the flow of blood. It dawned on him that
maybe she hadn't been shot with a real bullet.

Maybe the FARC didn't want her dead. They wanted
another hostage. They'd gotten rid of a dead spy and a
sickly one, and now they had a healthy hostage and fifty
million pesos to boot. Plus they'd tainted the reputation of
the Colombian army, all in one fell swoop. Conniving bastards. He'd see them in hell before he let them take Lucy.

Scanning the area, he calculated his odds. He was outnumbered fifty to one. His only weapon was a three-inch
knife, dulled from hacking through vines. He didn't even
have shoes to protect his goddamn feet.

He watched as Buitre coiled a length of chain around
Lucy's neck and bolted it. Snatching up the dangling end,
he jerked her off her feet, laughing coarsely as she spilled
to her knees. Gus couldn't see Lucy's face, but he didn't
need to. He knew she'd spit in Buitre's eyes if given half a
chance, consequences be damned.

Gus's blood boiled. His temple throbbed with murderous rage. He was going to kill Buitre. There wasn't any
question in his mind. And he was going to enjoy every
goddamn minute of it!

An Elite Guard sauntered over to stand next to the deputy. He was the same officer Gus had recognized the other

night. As Lucy pushed defiantly to her feet, the man caught her face in his hand, turned it left, then right, and nodded. The gesture was clear: He'd positively identified her.

Shit. Things were happening much too quickly. The rebels had clearly had this planned for a while now.

The whine of motors cut into his dark thoughts. In the next instant, six ATVs shot into view around the base of the mountain, bouncing across the field to approach the rebels.

Oh, no, thought Gus, his heart racing as the vehicles came nearer.

But yes. The released officers, Marquez, Buitre, and some select Elite Guards were going to ride up the mountain, leaving the rest of the men to walk. Lucy was about to be whisked away.

Gus leapt to his feet, loath to let her out of sight. He began running, crashing pell-mell into branches and fronds as the ATVs revved and whined and raced back the way they'd come. Approaching the river's edge, Gus paused to catch his breath. *Think,* he ordered himself. *Think, Gus. You can't possibly keep up.*

As motivated as he was to kill the enemy with his bare hands, he couldn't save Lucy on his own.

He needed to wait for his teammates. Goddamn it, they had better be on their way!

A flash of movement had him ducking behind a fallen tree. David's squad, who'd been following the river-bank upstream, looking for Gustavo's washed-up corpse, had stopped like startled deer, scanning the area, guns poised.

They hadn't seen him, had they? Over the rushing of the river and the humming of his eardrums, he strained to hear their conversation.

Risking a peek over the log, he saw to his relief that they were now moving away from him.

If they had searched downriver rather than up, they would have come upon his tracks already. David, raised as an Arhuaco, was a reputed tracker. Gus would have to take great pains to hide from him.

Darting from his hiding place, he slipped back into the jungle, covering his tracks as he did so. Until his teammates flew in to recover him, Lucy was doomed to endure what the FARC dished out.

He hoped to God they wouldn't break her before they managed to rescue her.

PINNED ON AN ATV between Buitre and the Elite Guard captain, Lucy felt her terror rise as they bumped and swerved back up the mountain. Deeper and deeper they pressed, past the shipment of hidden weapons, past Ki-kirr-zikiz, past the ridge where she and Gus had spied on Rebel Central, to the brick *casita,* where Buitre cut the motor at last.

Eyeing the cozy structure where she had slept with her hand on Gus's heart, Lucy now felt his absence keenly.

She could not believe she had been brought *here* to be interrogated, of all places.

She wasn't ready for this.

The last time an Elite Guardsman had questioned her, he'd brought her face-to-face with her mortality. Since then, she had fought to contain her fear, to give courage back its rightful seat. And she had just been winning that battle. Now she was back in the clutches of those who'd traumatized her in the first place. Wasn't life ironic?

When's it going to end for you, Luce? Gus's worried visage swam up from the well of her memories.

Not here. Not now. She couldn't do that to him. She couldn't do it to herself.

She had no choice but to find the grain of courage still within her and hold fast to it.

"Off!" Buitre ordered, and the captain who sat behind her leapt off, tugging the length of her chain to pull her after him. She staggered off, stumbling to find her legs weak with fear.

"Why so pale, *señorita?*" he taunted, tugging her closer. "Or is it *señora?* You had a husband until recently. Was he a spy like you?"

She flicked a glance at Buitre. Then her suspicions were founded. Gus had been dumped in the river intentionally. Only she couldn't begin to picture him dead. She knew he wasn't. She could still feel him inside of her, quietly supportive.

"Spy?" she scoffed, pleased with the fearless tone of her voice. "I'm a human relations officer with the United Nations. And you are making a very costly mistake."

"There is no mistake," Buitre raged, spittle flying from his mouth. "David overheard you speaking English. He saw you stealing from my quarters."

Lucy sighed and shook her head. "I always practice English with my husband. And I was looking for my medicine in your quarters."

Buitre lunged at her, but with a cool smile, the captain stepped between them. "You may leave this to me, Deputy," he promised with frightening calm. "I know just how to make her talk."

Lucy's blood seemed to crystallize. She fought to keep from blanching.

"Step inside," the captain invited her, gesturing genteelly for her to precede him.

As Lucy edged into the shadows of the building, her gaze slid helplessly to the corner where Gus had painted that vision of them on a tropical beach enjoying their honeymoon. Her heart clutched with longing at the vision of them, and with remorse. She'd give anything to be there now!

As Buitre looped the end of her chain over a peg on the wall, Lucy sucked in shallow breaths. This was it. Her recurring nightmare was about to become a reality. It would likely take hours for Gus and his SEALs to rescue her. The only thing that would see her through till then was her will to resist.

Pausing before her, arms folded across his chest, the captain stroked his chin. Light from the single window fell across his face, illumining his thin moustache, his hooded eyes with their sparse lashes. "I will prove to you that she is lying," he promised Buitre.

AT THE EDGE OF THE LANDING FIELD, seated with his back to the kapok tree, Gus watched as the mountain's shadow expanded, swallowing up first the cinderblock building, then the airstrip. Thinking of Lucy and what she had to be enduring, he groaned and rocked himself.

He'd feared it would come to this. From the day they'd been given this common assignment, he'd dreaded the thought of Lucy coming to harm on his watch. It wasn't supposed to happen. He'd sworn himself to protect her, to bear the brunt of the danger so she wouldn't have to.

But somehow his best efforts had backfired, and there was nothing he could do about it, not until his teammates got here.

At any moment they would arrive, he told himself. But the seconds dragged into minutes and minutes into hours, and still his only companion was his unforgiving conscience.

He'd told her he would be right behind her.

"IF SHE IS A SPY," the Venezuelan captain continued, sliding a demoralizing look down Lucy's body, "she will be carrying a tracking device, in which case her government will find her if we do not act swiftly."

Lucy's heart thudded at the accuracy of his statement. A clammy sweat enveloped her.

"Undress her," he commanded of Buitre, and panic streaked through her, causing black spots to swim before her eyes.

Buitre reached for her and she knocked his hands away, her thoughts racing to find a solution to her predicament. If she could just slow the hands of time until Gus and the SEALs came for her.

"Tie her hands if she won't cooperate," the captain suggested, his gaze intent upon her face. She was certain he could see her fear, smell it.

"I'll undress myself," she offered. "I have nothing to hide."

He gestured elegantly. "Go ahead."

Heart pounding, Lucy stalled, removing each button of the jacket with painstaking care.

"Faster!" ordered Buitre, who watched with rabid hunger as she reluctantly dropped her jacket on the floor.

"Now the shirt," purred the captain, enjoying the show.

She'd stripped to her underwear at the start of the journey. This was no different. At least, that was what she told herself as she raised the T-shirt over her head, stringing it on the length of chain that ran from her neck to the peg above her head.

If the right moment presented itself, she could snatch her chain off the peg and run for the door. Only how would she flee quickly carrying twenty extra pounds around her neck?

The captain slanted a knowing look at Buitre. "Did you not consider that the wires in her bra might transmit her location?" he mocked.

Shocked, Buitre eyed Lucy's black satin bra with a frown.

"Remove it," insisted the captain. Lucy balked, drawing deep breaths to keep down the tide of fear constricting her airways.

In a quick move that revealed little more than a flash of pale skin, she shimmied out of the bra and jerked the T-shirt back on. "Here," she said, tossing it at the captain. "You will see there is nothing in the material but wire. I told you, I work for the United Nations. You have me confused with someone else." Having outsmarted him, triumph fizzed in her briefly.

"There is no mistake," the captain assured her calmly. "Cut this open," he said, handing her bra to Buitre. "Tell me what you see."

Approaching Lucy, he stabbed her with a ruthless gaze. "I remember you from the warehouse in Maiquetía," he murmured, causing every fine hair on her body to prickle with alarm. "You were spying then. You are still spying."

Lucy held his gaze defiantly. "I am not who you think I am," she retorted convincingly.

His slap came out of nowhere. One minute he was

standing there looking at her. The next he was rubbing hi
reddened palm with his left thumb.

Stunned by the force of the open-handed blow, Luc
stared for a moment at the floor. Then she jerked he
chin up, her cheek stinging. "Is that all you've got?" sh
taunted, welcoming the heat of rebelliousness. She coul
do this. As long as he just beat her up, she would win. An
Gus would be so proud, so relieved.

The captain drew himself to his full, indignant height
"No, *señorita*," he answered through his teeth, his narrov
moustache twitching, "that is only a taste of the punish
ment you will endure if you are not candid with me."

"Sir, there is nothing in this *sostén* but wire," Buitre
interrupted, sounding disgruntled.

The captain looked briefly surprised. He reconsid
ered Lucy, stroked his chin again, then nodded. "Tie he
hands," he said to Buitre.

Lucy sucked in a breath. "Why?" she demanded. "I'n
cooperating, aren't I?"

"Use your belt," suggested the captain, ignoring he
question as Buitre hunted for something to tie her with.

With blood roaring in her ears, Lucy fought to keep
panic from overtaking her. As Buitre approached he
with his belt in hand, she kicked out, repelling him wit
a heel-strike that sent him barreling backward into th
captain.

"*¡Puta!*" he swore, lunging at her even as the captai
stepped into his path. "Let me question her!" Buitre raged
"I swear I will make her talk."

Lucy welcomed the adrenaline that drove back he
fear. She'd realized that once they stripped her of he
clothing, anything was bound to happen, none of whicl
she was prepared to handle. Her body belonged to Gu

alone. She would fight to within an inch of her life to keep it that way.

"Patience," insisted the captain, pulling a dagger from his webbed belt. "She's a trained fighter. Beating her will accomplish nothing. Now tie her while I hold her still," he instructed.

No! She sought to take the dagger from him, to secure her freedom by arming herself. Only he, too, was trained in hand-to-hand combat. Within seconds his blade pricked her jugular. She stilled, gasping for air, as she submitted to having her wrists bound.

Buitre cinched the belt tight, pricking a hole in the leather to keep it taut.

The captain stepped back to reconsider her. He looked at Buitre. "She was allowed to keep her own boots, yes? Remove them. The device may be hidden in the sole."

Good thinking, Lucy thought, welcoming the reprieve. *Wrong boots.*

With rough, impatient hands, Buitre removed her boots. She stood in her socks, docile now, praying the search would end when her boots came up clean. Buitre turned them over. "I don't see anything," he muttered.

"Give them to me." Starting with the right boot, he poked at the rubber sole with his knife, pried and sliced, but found nothing.

Tossing the boots to the floor, he hooked his thumbs in his belt and frowned, while Buitre circled behind her, salivating like a hungry dog.

"Remove the rest of her clothing," the captain decreed at last.

Lucy's skin seemed to shrink. *No!*

"Sometimes devices are planted under the skin," he

explained, causing fear to ripple up her spine in fluttering electrical currents.

"Like this?" Buitre asked, pointing out the cut on her hip, just above her baggy trousers.

"Where?" The captain edged around her to regard the angry slit, crusty with pus and blood.

Fear ambushed Lucy, strangling the casual explanation that she'd cut herself.

"Exactly," purred the captain, shooting her a gloating look. "You will have to hold her down," he said to Buitre, "while I will cut out the device."

IMMERSED IN TOTAL DARKNESS, Gus still waited, straining to hear the distinctive flutter of the Little Bird, the OH-6A light assault helicopter, over the sonata of nocturnal insects.

He'd willed his teammates' arrival with every beat of his heart, teeth chattering at the encroaching cold, for hours now.

What the *hell* was taking them so long?

Worry kept his muscles locked and aching. His eyeballs felt like they'd been hardboiled, he had stared at the sky so long and so hard.

Then, at last, with his patience about to snap, a flurry erupted overhead. He leapt to his feet in relief, searching the starry sky until he spied the silhouette of a miniature helicopter hanging a hundred feet above the field, no lights.

One, two, three, four dark figures fast-roped to the ground and scattered.

Gus hobbled into the field. With night-vision capabilities, his buddies would have spotted him already.

A shadow materialized from the darkness. Between the black knit cap and the greasepaint, Gus had trouble recognizing Harley. "Sir, you hurt?" The blue eyes and the rumbling baritone gave him away.

"I can walk," Gus answered. *Barely.*

"This way," said Harley, forcing him into a trot that sent shards of pain up his legs. On the far side of the field, well away from the cinderblock building, the SEALs rallied up—Luther, Harley, Vinny, and Haiku. The other four SEALs had evidently remained at the JIC, on call for backup.

"What happened?" asked the OIC as they crouched in a tight circle.

"The FARC have Lucy," Gus grated, a fresh wave of fear rolling over him. "I think one of the Elite Guard recognized her from the warehouse last year. The FARC were already suspicious. They tried dumping me in a river. I lost my boots and the sat phone, but I'm pretty sure they consider me neutralized. We need to get to Lucy," he finished.

Luther glanced down at the tattered remains of Gus's booties. "Vinny, take a look at his feet."

The soft blue beam of Vinny's penlight cut through the inky darkness. Gus pulled off the booties and spared a cursory glance at his ravaged soles. "I'm fine," he insisted.

Opening his medic's kit, Vinny set about cleaning the open lesions.

"We should've pulled you out," Luther reflected.

"No. Sir, I am *not* leaving Lucy on this mountain," Gus growled with heat. "Get me boots, gear, and firepower and I'll be good to go," he insisted. At the same time, his heart sank. The request would take up to three hours to fulfill.

Lieutenant Lindstrom seemed to weigh his options. "Haiku, relay that request to the JIC," he ordered softly.

"Size-thirteen boots," said Gus. He ground the heels of his palms into his eye sockets.

"Rumor has it she was shot," said Harley.

Gus snatched his hands out of his eyes. "You heard that already?"

"The UN team touched down in Bogotá just as we were leaving, delaying our departure," the OIC explained. "We heard all kinds of strange reports."

Gus shook his head. "Whatever you heard was wrong." In a tight, flat voice, he explained the Elite Guard's duplicity, how they'd dressed themselves in lamb's clothing.

"That is fucking brilliant," marveled Harley.

"We trained them," Gus reminded him with a hard look. "That's why they're so good. And if the truth isn't made known, the Colombian army is going to take the rap for something they didn't do."

Why was he even wasting words talking about this? They needed to plan a recon mission and rescue Lucy.

"Haiku, get back with the JIC and pass on that information," ordered the lieutenant.

"Yes, sir."

As Haiku scurried to one side to relay the message, Lieutenant Lindstrom pulled a rugged laptop from his pack. Powering it up, he positioned it so Gus and the others could see. "Here's our position. Gus, this is you," he said, pointing to a bright red dot.

He toggled a key, and the image on the screen jumped, showing a blue dot in a field of neon green. "This is Lucy. The map shows her seven klicks from here, due northwest, at an altitude of three thousand feet. As soon as your gear gets here, we'll go after her," he promised. "Moving at a fast walk, we should be able to assess her situation before sunrise," he predicted. "If the odds look good, we'll plan an ambush and extract on a SPIE rig."

The special-patrol insertion/extraction rig could be lowered by helicopter straight through the jungle canopy, lifting them as a group, clipped to a length of rope via D-shaped rings.

Luther made rescuing Lucy sound like a walk in the park. If that were true, then the SEALs had the easy job.

Lucy's job, withstanding interrogation at the hands of the guerrillas, was undoubtedly tougher. She'd be the first person to insist she could take a licking and keep on ticking. He'd seen her do it. He just didn't know if she could do it again.

Goddamn it! He would never forgive himself for letting this happen.

CHAPTER 16 ═══════

Viewed through state-of-the-art night-vision goggles, the near-vertical jungle seethed with nocturnal creatures, crawling, darting, peering through enormous red eyes at the five Navy SEALs moving as quietly as possible up the twisting path.

They had been traveling for several hours now, moving fast and closing in on whoever held Lucy captive. Stopping every half-hour or so, the squad consulted the laptop, reassured that they were closing in on Lucy's coordinates.

Here and there, an outcrop of stone or roots crisscrossing under Gus's feet struck him as familiar. By his reckoning, they were not too far from Rebel Central or the brick *casita,* where he and Lucy had spent their last nights together.

Along with night-vision goggles, each man carried an MP-5-SD, silenced versions of the classic semi-automatic machine guns. Harley and Haiku, sniper and scout respectively, had rifles mounted with night-vision scopes.

In new boots that cushioned his soles and left barely discernable tracks, Gus tackled the steep terrain with singleminded determination. The protein bars he'd consumed while waiting for his gear countered his flagging energy levels. He had to get to Lucy before they broke or killed her. Anything else was unacceptable.

But what if they showed up too late? His mind refused to accept that as a possibility.

"Alpha squad, rally up." The OIC's whispered command cut through Gus's ragged-edged thoughts.

The SEALs came together in a circular, protective position, dropping to their knees and raising their visors, two by two, to consult the laptop.

Lieutenant Lindstrom's sudden frown, illumined by the soft-glowing screen, made Gus's stomach knot. "She's moving," the OIC announced, swiveling the laptop so they could all take a look.

Sure enough, Lucy's microchip was traveling in a northwesterly direction, away from Ki-kirr-zikiz, headed dead north.

No! Gus inwardly raged. "How fast are they moving?" he wanted to know.

"Almost seven klicks an hour."

That fast? They would never catch up before dawn. The longer Lucy remained a hostage, the more traumatized she would be. "Fuck!" he raged, his temple throbbing.

Four sets of eyes jumped up to regard him with compassion and apparent willingness to fight, not just for Lucy, but in retaliation for the thousands of hostages the FARC had seized throughout the decades.

"Where could they be taking her?" the OIC wondered out loud. "None of the camps lie in that direction, at least not according to the map you uploaded."

Gus had to swallow to find his voice. "Arriba," he said

hoarsely. "Maybe they're taking her to Arriba. That's where the other hostages were kept."

With a thoughtful look, the OIC closed his laptop. "Let's move," he said, simply.

COLD WATER SPATTERED LUCY'S FACE, rousing her from a blissful well of unconsciousness. She sputtered and jerked awake, only to be skewered by sharp, insistent pain radiating from her lower back.

Buitre's scarred face swam into focus as he bent over her. Her gaze flew to the only window, where golden light flooded in, letting her know that it was morning. She'd been lying on the dirt-packed floor unconscious for half the night.

And Gus hadn't come for her.

The realization ripped through, testing her faith that he was still alive. What if he was dead or injured and alone in the jungle? Surely she would sense it if something awful had happened to him.

In the same instant, memories of the prior evening raked her tender consciousness. Inflicting agony, Captain Vargas had dug in her hip for the microchip until she'd passed out cold. She assumed he'd found it and cut it out. She couldn't remember.

She felt desecrated, violated, numb. A glance back at the ravaged flesh on her hip made her head spin. Dried blood encrusted the material on her trousers, but at least she still wore them. That wouldn't be the case, would it, if they had raped her?

"Get up, *puta*," ordered Buitre, removing the belt that kept her wrists tightly bound. Blood surged into her freed arms and sent fire licking toward her fingertips. As he yanked her to her feet, pain knifed up one side of her back.

"Time for you to go," Buitre informed her. "Dress quickly," he commanded, thrusting her jacket at her.

Lucy weaved on her feet but refused to move. Gus couldn't be dead.

"Now, *puta!*" Buitre roared, startling her from her shock.

With awkward fingers and hampered by the pain in her hip, she buttoned her jacket mechanically, donned her mutilated boots, and tied them.

Cool, wet air roused her briefly as Buitre pulled her through the door. Only one other rebel stood outside—David, who glanced at her quickly, then averted his eyes.

Where had Captain Vargas gone? she wondered absently.

But then a thought—both terrible and wonderful—had her tripping over her own feet. The captain might have taken her microchip to lure her rescuers into a trap. That would explain why neither Gus nor his teammates had come for her. It wasn't that he was injured or dead. He simply had no way of knowing where she was. *Oh, God.* Without the microchip, she had vanished into the mountain mists, just like Howitz and Barnes before her.

CLOAKED IN A THICK MIST, with Haiku on point, the SEALs crept along the steeply ascending path with renewed stealth. The ruggedness of the terrain and the thin mountain air left them straining and out of breath. It came as a great relief when they consulted the laptop and realized the microchip, and therefore Lucy, had ceased to move.

At last the SEALs were closing in on a fixed location—

a remote crag standing twelve thousand feet above sea level.

Rather than feel relieved, Gus eyed the still, shadowy undergrowth with foreboding.

The jungle was too quiet. He had spent enough time in the rainforest to know that monkeys were the first to expose Special Forces trying to sneak unseen through the jungle. Perhaps it was the muggy humidity keeping them listless this morning. Rumbles of thunder portended an afternoon rain shower. High above the clouds, the fixed-wing Predator tracked their movements with the FLIR patches on their shoulders that distinguished them from the enemy. If worse came to worse, they could call upon the Predator to drop a missile or relay a request for reinforcements, even extraction.

Gus could not stop thinking that the enemy had questioned Lucy extensively by now. They would have had substantial time to beat her, rape her...

Another possibility made the hairs on his nape rise to stiff attention. He thumbed his mic. "Sir."

"Go ahead," panted the OIC, who tackled the rise several paces behind him.

"What if the hostiles don't have her?"

"Come again?"

"I don't know. I just have this feeling Lucy isn't here."

"Why wouldn't she be here?" countered the lieutenant. "We've been following tracks for hours now."

"No, sir. We've been following her microchip," Gus corrected him. "What if they took it from her body in order to lure us here?"

The sudden, thundering report of a dozen assault rifles cut his question short.

Startled, Gus dove behind an earthen wall carved by

rain-water and fired back, three rounds at a time, knowing he had thirty in his magazine.

Except he couldn't see what the hell he was shooting at. There was nothing but leaves and trees and bushes looming over him. But the hidden shooters were marksmen, no question. Bullets pelted the ground right behind him, pinning him in his tenuous location.

Haiku, who'd been on point, was in a similar quandary. Crouched behind a fallen tree, he sought to return fire while keeping himself covered.

"Shit!" Gus raged, cursing his instincts for warning him too late.

A flash of movement caught his eye. Two figures slipped through the undergrowth flanking their left side. He fired at them and missed.

"Sir, they're flanking left," he warned. At least they couldn't flank them on the right, where the earth dropped away into a steep ravine.

"Harley, head them off. Haiku, Atwater, can you fall back?"

"Negative, sir. They have us pinned," Gus shouted, ducking as a rock, knocked out of the dirt, whistled past his ear.

"Use your grenades," advised Luther. "Vinny, contact the Predator. Tell them 'Danger close.' We need support fire now, only don't hit us!"

"Yes, sir!" Vinny called.

"Hold them on the ridge!" the OIC commanded, shooting his weapon over Gus's head.

Easier said than done, Gus thought, using his teeth to tear the clip from the grenade he tossed. It was just a matter of time before he or Haiku got hit.

No sooner did that grim thought occur to him than

a bullet flung Haiku onto his back, in plain sight of the shooters. They would have made mincemeat of him, if Gus hadn't laid out a wall of fire, giving the point man time to drag himself to safety.

"Haiku took a hit, sir!" Gus informed his OIC.

"How bad is he?"

"I'll live," Haiku grated. Slamming a new magazine into his rifle, he glared uphill with the ferocity of a ninja and went back to firing.

"We can't hold 'em off much longer, sir," Gus warned.

"Predator estimates two minutes to strike," Vinny cut in. "Haiku, you need me, man?"

"Sorry, can't have company right now," Haiku gritted. "Forgot to clean house."

"I got some friends who'll clean your house," muttered Harley. In the next instant, cries of agony let them know he'd eliminated the left flank.

But then the Elite Guard retaliated, throwing grenades that made the ridge tremble and rained gobs of dirt on Gus's helmet. Artillery from the ridge escalated, cutting swaths through the vegetation. The SEALs had nowhere to go but down into the ravine.

"Sir, avoid the ravine!" Gus warned as the memory of Buitre's mine-laying flashed through his mind. "Mines! Mines!"

"Roger that, Gus. Missile incoming, ten seconds to impact. Fall back down the trail."

No sooner had Luther spat out those directives than a high-pitched whistle announced the imminent arrival of a hellfire missile. In the next instant, a thunderous explosion snuffed out the staccato of gunfire as the missile slammed into the ridge a hundred meters north of the SEALs' location.

With bits of bark and leaves and chunks of granite pattering his back, Gus dove into the alcove next to Haiku. "You good?" he asked, dismayed by the size of the stain on the scout's jacket.

"Sure," said the Japanese American, but his face was waxen, his eyes too bright.

"Fall back!" shouted the OIC.

Haiku pushed to his knees, then collapsed.

"I got you," Gus assured him. Holding him from behind, he backed swiftly down the trail.

Several hundred yards later, he caught up with the others, laying Haiku at Vinny's feet. "He's losing blood fast."

Vinny dropped to one knee to assess Haiku's injury. "Sir, we need to get him outta here," he corroborated, tearing open his medic's pack for supplies to help staunch the bleeding.

As Vinny worked to get Haiku hooked to an IV, Gus's hopes of finding Lucy plummeted. The team would look to their members' safety first.

With apology in his dark blue eyes, the OIC met his overwrought gaze. "We need to pull out," he said to Gus, gently.

"Sir," Gus pleaded. "What about Lucy? We can't just leave without her."

"We'll have to come back," the OIC replied. "We don't know if she was here or not."

Gus's frustrations bubbled over. "She's somewhere on this fucking mountain!" he raged. "We can't just leave her here!"

"We'll be back," the lieutenant repeated, his volume increasing just enough to get Gus's attention. "Now, let's move, in case the enemy recovers."

Gus nodded. He had no right to argue with the OIC when Haiku was fighting for his life.

Moving to a safer location, the SEALs waited for the rescue helicopter, a Longbow Apache, to lower a SPIE rig and extract them.

Twenty minutes later, the helicopter descended over their location. A thick rope dropped though the trees, and Harley ran to catch it.

Feeling nothing whatsoever, wishing he'd wake up from what had to be a nightmare, Gus clipped himself to the SPIE rig, as did the others. Luther checked their D-rings before hooking himself up. Within seconds, the rope whipped taut.

It lifted them one by one off their feet.

Gus clawed his way through layers of wet leaves, sticky spiderwebs, going up, up . . .

All at once he surfaced, rising over a carpet of green that undulated in all directions—east, west, north, south. Dangling in the air with wind whipping at his clothing, he searched for the camouflaged lookout tower that pinpointed the front commander's hideout.

But it remained elusive, swallowed up in the enormity of vegetation below him. Thanks to Gus and Lucy's endeavors, the JIC knew exactly where it was. But Lucy, without a microchip, could be anywhere on this mammoth-sized mountain.

They could search for a hundred years and never find her.

Showered and shaved and wearing a fresh battle dress uniform, Gus felt marginally more human, except that he hadn't slept since his and Lucy's last night strung up in hammocks in the *casita,* more than forty-eight hours ago.

His red-rimmed and watering eyes burned with the effort that it took to follow the debate raging in the JIC between the CIA staff and the Navy SEALs.

"I just spoke with the Colombian ambassador," John Whiteside informed them, pacing from one side of the room to the other. "He's outraged that we dropped a missile on the FARC."

"It wasn't the FARC, sir," Lieutenant Lindstrom calmly pointed out.

"He doesn't care who the hell it was," Whiteside interrupted. "The United States dropped a hellfire missile on Colombian soil, and if it happens again, he'll declare it an act of war. The Predator has been called away from that area. There will be no more attacks on the FARC—period—until the Colombian government resolves this issue with the UN."

Oh, Jesus. Gus raked his hand through his damp hair. Despite his testimony that the Elite Guard, dressed as Colombian soldiers, had only *pretended* to attack the FARC and jeopardize the UN team, there was still an inquiry underway. Colombia had frozen its military to keep from looking any more aggressive. Nor did they want their ally, the USA, taking any military action.

But they couldn't just leave Lucy on La Montaña and not go back. He sent Lieutenant Lindstrom a pleading look.

"Sir," said the OIC, putting his career on the line to argue with the station chief, "we're not asking for permission to fight the FARC. All we want is to return to rebel territory. We'll recon the target quietly. No one will even know we're on the mountain."

Gus's heart thudded painfully as he awaited Whiteside's reply.

"Son," the older man countered condescendingly, "that mountain covers more square miles than New York City. We had surveillance on it for ten months and never found Howitz and Barnes. How the hell do you think you're going to find Miss Donovan?"

"It could take a while," Luther conceded, "but we'll find her."

"We don't even know if she's alive," Whiteside shot back, snatching the air from Gus's lungs. "Her microchip stopped working when we hit the mountain. For all we know, she's dead already."

Gus found himself on his feet with his face on fire and his heart in his throat. "Lucy is not dead!" he insisted hoarsely. "She's up on that goddamn mountain with her hip cut open, subject to infection and God-knows-what-else. Do you want her to die like Mike Howitz, or are you going to let us do our fucking jobs?" he railed, his temple throbbing.

Luther put a hand on his shoulder, pushing him down into his chair.

Whiteside just looked at him. Hitching his trousers, he regarded the expectant SEALs with a thoughtful frown. "All right," he agreed irritably. "All right. I'll permit you to do a high-altitude low open, under the cover of nightfall. But no one, and I mean *no one* needs to know where you are. If you need to question a rebel, you kill 'em. And stay the hell away from the Venezuelans this time. I don't want this coming back to me in any way, shape, or form. You will be *invisible*. Is that understood?"

"Hooyah, sir!" chorused several Navy SEALs.

Gus sank weakly back into his seat. *Hang in there, Luce,* he thought. *I'm coming back to get you.*

*   *   *

THE HINGES AT THE GATE SQUEAKED, signaling another hour had passed. Roused from a fitful slumber, Lucy cracked an eye as Goliath, one of the two *jefes* who guarded Arriba, lumbered across the enclosure. The frosty vapor of his breath bespoke the chill that held Lucy in its cruel grip.

She had been warming herself with visions of a tropical beach, Gus's legs dusted with sand and tangled with hers as they lay on their towels soaking up the sun.

As Goliath's silhouette loomed over her, she braced herself for the glare of his flashlight. This was a nightly occurrence. Every hour on the hour, one of the *jefes* shone light into their captives' eyes. The action was purely psychological, a reminder that even in sleep, they were not free.

"You." He startled her by nudging her with his toe.

With a spiking of adrenaline, Lucy scrambled to a wary crouch. The wound on her hip protested. Steel links bit into her neck as she cringed against the plywood wall.

"Come," he commanded, unlocking her from the center beam. Fisting her chain, he gave it a jerk. "Hurry," he added.

"Where are we going?" she demanded. The other hostages, soldiers of the Colombian army who'd been held for many years, had awakened to watch with apathy.

This was an aberration. For the past three nights she'd been left in a feverish stupor. What if Goliath meant to drag her into the woods and rape her? If that happened, she might lose her will to live.

"No questions. Walk or I'll drag you," he said gruffly.

In a stiff-jointed walk, she trailed him to the gate.

Arriba was little more than a three-sided shed in a muddy pen encircled by barbed wire. A second guard, whom she'd dubbed Igor, opened the gate and locked it behind them.

Fear of the unknown kept her frigid. The scent of freedom tormented her. If she could just pull her chain from Goliath's grasp, perhaps she could make a run for it. But Igor would think nothing of shooting her in the back as she fled.

They tugged her, resisting, down a dark and twisting path. Her mind spawned visions of defilement. *This is it,* she thought. All at once, Goliath stopped and swung her before him. "Stand here," he instructed, his flashlight illumining the lip of a trench. "Don't move."

As the tip of his weapon gouged her ribs, her heart slammed against her breastbone. "What—what are you doing?" she breathed, glancing back. Suddenly, it was all too clear the trench was meant to be a shallow grave. Oh, no. Oh, God.

When is it going to end, Luce?
Not here, not now!

"I've told you," Goliath answered on a strangely gleeful note, "you have no value to us. Your country refuses negotiations. You are worthless." He released the safety on his pistol, and the sound of a round slipping into a well-oiled breech made her legs quake. "Any last words?" he sneeringly inquired.

Lucy's entire life flashed through her mind, freeze-framing on moments spent with Gus—the only moments that really seemed to matter.

With a vulgar crack, the pistol discharged, flinging her headlong into the wet pit, her senses smacked out of her, her thoughts scattered to oblivion.

Waiting for death to claim her, she overheard the mirthless chuckles of her keepers. Second by second, she realized her heart was still pumping. Painful little gasps inflated her collapsed lungs.

It was just a prank. She was still alive.

Alive! Oh, thank you! Thank you, God!

A sob of relief burst from her chest. She knew in that instant that *nothing*—neither starvation nor frigid temperatures nor unending incarceration, not even the cruelest violations—could prevent her from surviving.

Somehow, some way, she would reclaim her life to wring from it every drop of pleasure still left to her.

CHAPTER 17

The squeak of Buitre's screen door roused Gus from a light slumber. Snatching his head off his arm, he gazed uphill at the first sight of Buitre wandering from the camp to the tree line to relieve himself, unwitting of the fact that Navy SEALs lay waiting for him.

Following a high-altitude, low-open insertion three nights ago, they had questioned and killed half a dozen trail scouts, only to discover that Arriba's whereabouts was a closely guarded secret—hence the X on the map Gus had stolen. Only the highest-ranking FARC knew where it was.

Buitre was one of them, Gus was certain. He'd convinced Luther to snatch the deputy from Cecaot-Jicobo, which was crawling with Elite Guards. Once caught, they would bear him away for questioning. Gus had a suspicion the hardened rebel was a coward at the core.

Dark anticipation pooled in his gut. At last, at the break of dawn, after eighteen hours of endless waiting, Buitre descended through a thin mist into the jungle alone.

With a whistle that resembled a birdcall, Harley alerted

the others that action was imminent. He and Gus crept to their appointed positions near the area where the men relieved themselves.

Buitre had no idea he was being watched. He sauntered toward a tree, unzipping his trousers as he went. He was still wetting down the bark when Gus leapt up behind him, clapped a hand over his mouth, and injected him with a tranquilizer prepared in advance by Vinny.

Buitre struggled briefly, disturbing the loam under his feet. But then he collapsed, and Sean rounded the tree from the other side to help Gus shoulder his limp body. Together, they carried the rebel into the jungle, his fly still gaping.

Buitre's bleary and confused gaze rose from Gus's boots, to the knife clasped lightly in his hands, to his hard and merciless stare, illumined by a beam of morning sunlight. With dark satisfaction, Gus watched the blood drain from the deputy's swarthy face as he assessed his helplessness. Dangling from a tree by his wrists, he struggled in panic. His eyes widened further as four more SEALs, bristling with weapons, their faces savagely painted, stepped from the shadows.

"There's no escape," Gus informed him coldly. "Today is the day you die." A monkey screamed high overhead, echoing the fear etched on Buitre's now-pallid face.

"No!" he gasped, sweat beading on his forehead.

"Your Venezuelan comrades will never find you." They had carried him ten kilometers from Cecaot-Jicobo, covering their tracks as best they could.

"Your only concern," Gus added, twirling the blade in his hands, "is whether your soul will burn in hell for all of eternity."

Most guerrillas had been raised Catholic and were deeply superstitious. Buitre was clearly no exception, but he clung tenaciously to bravado. "I will tell you nothing!" he asserted, hacking a wad of spit at Gus's feet.

Gus stood up and reached for one of Buitre's fingers, intending to cut it off, when the deputy cried, "Wait! Wait!" He immediately began to blubber. "Have pity," he begged.

Gus ran the sharp edge of the blade he'd stolen over Buitre's good cheek. "Do you recognize this?" he asked, holding it up for him to see.

"My knife!"

"I sharpened it for you," he whispered, grappling with the urge to plunge it into Buitre's belly as images of Lucy, tortured and battered, clawed at his heart.

Tears began to gush from Buitre's eyes. "Please don't kill me," he whimpered.

"Were you the one who cut the microchip from Luna de Aguiler?" Gus asked, feeding on cold fury to keep rage from overcoming him.

"No, no. That was Captain Vargas. I didn't touch her. I swear it!"

"Is she alive?" Gus continued, not knowing what he'd do if Buitre said no.

"Yes, yes! Alive and well."

Relief left him faintly nauseated. "Where?" he asked, depressing the soft skin at Buitre's jugular with the point of the blade.

"Arriba. I will take you there, only let me live."

Gus stepped back, pretending to consider the offer. With a glance at Luther, who gave a subtle nod, he cut the captive free.

Now they could make some progress.

* * *

DAVID WAS BUSY INSPECTING his rag-tag army when Captain Vargas strode up to him. "Where is Buitre?" he demanded, a tin of hot coffee steaming in one hand.

David peered about the camp. Buitre's quarters stood quiet, though normally, by this time, the generator was purring. Premonition tightened his scalp. "I don't know," he admitted. "I saw him walk into the woods, that way, a while ago."

The captain's nostrils flared as he looked where David was pointing. "Come," he ordered. "Help me find his tracks. Ponce, Delgado, ¡vengan!" he added, and two commandos sprang up to follow them.

Uneasiness knotted David's insides as he led them down the hill, following Buitre's distinctive tracks with ease. He had heard the rumors, spreading like fingers of fear from other camps: Trail scouts had been disappearing. Rojas had warned everyone to keep their eyes peeled for intruders, agents of the CIA looking for Luna de Aguiler.

Wading cautiously into the jungle, David stopped where Buitre's tracks ended. His gaze slid from the stain at the base of a tree to the soil trampled under their feet. "There was a brief struggle here. One man came from this side. Another from here." He inspected the ground more carefully, pushing a frond out of his way. "Only two walked away, carrying the third," he decided. "They went that way." He pointed into the verdant shadows.

Captain Vargas whipped the radio off his hip, advising the remaining Elite Guard to arm themselves.

"You will lead us to these intruders," he then told David.

Reluctance strangled David's vocal cords. Peering into the silent, murky forest, he regretted not listening to his conscience. Now the blood would surely flow on La Montaña, but the end result would not be peace.

WITH SHADOWS THICKENING between the trees and monkeys swinging with abandon through the treetops, the captives endured the nightly humility of being secured to the shelter. As always, Lucy's chain was looped around a post and locked, the heavy padlock bruising her collarbone.

Adjusting it, she stilled, processing with astonishment what her fingers were telling her.

The lock had fallen open. Goliath hadn't secured it fully before turning the key!

For a stunned moment she just lay there, too shocked to conceive what this meant. But then the implications saturated her sluggish brain and turned her mouth cotton-dry.

She didn't have to wait for Gus to find her if she could free herself.

Only there was more to escaping than easing off the heavy chain. The shelter was surrounded by barbed wire. Beyond that, two armed guards performed their hourly vigil with the flashlights.

That was it! A plan took shape in her mind—a desperate and dangerous plan that required all the strength her frail body could muster, not to mention flawless timing.

Did she still possess either? Starvation and infection had weakened her considerably. But her courage was strong. Over the course of the past few days, she had discovered she could fight fire with fire.

With her thudding heart ticking off the seconds, she

eased the lock from the links and hid it beneath her. Draping the loose chain across her neck, she coiled it in either hand and waited for Igor, the second *jefe,* to make the first nightly inspection.

An hour had never seemed so interminably long. At last, the sound of metal scraping over metal signaled the opening of the gate.

Insects quieted as a lone guard approached the lean-to, preceded by a cone of light shining from his flashlight. It swung in a wide arc about the shelter, then settled on the hostages in the opposite corner. Shining light into their eyes, Igor checked their locks, then turned toward Lucy, chained on the opposite side.

Drawing a slow, tight breath, she summoned her resolve. *For Gus. For us,* she thought. Pink light shone through her closed eyelids. Unable to find her lock, Igor muttered an expletive. Through her lashes, she watched as he went down on one knee and leaned over her.

Now! Lunging, she looped the length of chain around his neck and yanked, cutting off his startled cry. As he fell on top of her, she reached for the pistol holstered to his belt, praying it was loaded. She flipped him over at the same time as she shot him, silencing his protests with a shot that went straight into his heart. *Bang!*

The other hostages came awake with shouts of fright.

"Qué es?"

"Díos mío!"

The body beneath her went slack. Igor was dead. *One down, one to go.*

Snatching up his keys, Lucy tossed them at the others. "Free yourselves," she urged, picking up the fallen flashlight. Briefly she considered joining forces with the former Colombian soldiers. But they had been kept apart from her, the only woman they had seen in years, for a reason.

Snapping off the light, she doused them all in darkness.

"*Jefe!*" Outside the pen, Goliath came flying from the shanty where the guards slept. "*Qué pasa?*" As he struggled to get into the gate, Lucy eased around the corner of the lean-to and hid behind it, her heart hammering.

Goliath had forgotten to bring a flashlight. As he bumbled into the pen, he ran headlong into the first Colombian to free himself. With a roar, he went to wrestle him down.

And Lucy darted to the gate, ecstatic to find it ajar.

Freedom!

With the barbed wire behind her, she sprinted past the guards' shanty, up the path they had trod each day to visit the natural spring. Along a dark tunnel of green, she flew as light as a feather, as fast as a doe.

Behind her, another pistol discharged, ringing out loudly. A cry of agony reached her ears, mingled with hysterical laughter as the captives overcame their captor and took off, fleeing into the night, crashing downhill. She figured their odds of escaping the FARC were at least as good as hers.

Wary of being followed, Lucy kept the flashlight off. She gripped the pistol hard, drawing courage from the hard metal against her slippery palm.

The trail, subtly illumined by moonlight, rose sharply. With every arduous step, the temperature seemed to plummet.

Delayed shock made Lucy tremble, made her legs wobble. Dear God, she'd done it! She'd escaped her captors! Now all she had to do was withstand the cold long enough to find the radio station perched somewhere at the top of this godforsaken mountain.

"ARRIBA IS CLOSE," Buitre panted as Gus hauled him in his wake along the dark, winding path.

Figuring the Elite Guard had noticed Buitre's absence by now, the SEALs hammered themselves to climb four thousand feet, staying as far ahead of trackers as possible, but they had only Buitre's word and his fear of dying to reassure them they were headed in the right direction.

"If we find out you've been lying to us, Deputy," Harley threatened in respectable Spanish, "the lieutenant here will cut out your tongue."

No sooner had Harley said this than a shot rang out, not too far away. Adrenaline flooded Gus's bloodstream. Fired at such close range, the shots sounded like mini-explosions. *Now what?* he wondered as they all crouched and froze, alert to imminent danger.

"Help!" Buitre shouted unexpectedly. "Over here!"

Gus silenced him, slamming the butt of his rifle into the man's thick skull. He crumpled where he'd stood, still and silent as the SEALs awaited the fallout of his cry for help.

Another shot splintered the night.

The sound of something crashing through the woods to their right had them raising their weapons in readiness. Only a human being—or several—blinded by the darkness and propelled by fear could make that much noise, Gus thought as the sound grew louder, then moved past them down the mountain.

As the beings floundered out of hearing, the SEALs

convened over Buitre's unconscious body. "What do you think that was?" Luther asked.

"People tryin' to get the hell away," drawled Teddy.

"Away from what? Arriba?" asked Vinny.

"What else?" Gus murmured.

"Why didn't they use the path?" Harley wanted to know.

"Let's just keep moving," Luther decided. "Maybe we'll find some answers."

All five men looked down at Buitre.

"Would you like Vinny to bring him back?" Luther asked Gus. Vinny carried smelling salts for just that purpose.

"No," said Gus. "Step back," he advised. As the men scattered, he pointed his silenced semi-automatic at Buitre's chest and fired a round at close range, killing him instantly, painlessly. With a bitter taste in his mouth, he turned and headed up the path, leaving the body as a warning to any who might be tracking them.

With a shared look, the others joined him.

A hundred yards later, they arrived at what had to be Arriba. To Gus's dismay, the hostage camp stood quiet, seemingly deserted. There was no sign of life or movement anywhere, only the sound of wire clattering in a breeze redolent with the scent of blood.

"The hostages ran right by us," Teddy realized, flicking a pitying glance at Gus.

No! He refused to believe Lucy was with them.

"There's a body at ten o'clock," Harley murmured.

Holding his weapon before him, Gus scurried toward the open gate. The crackle of a radio greeted him as he pushed inside, his gaze fixed on the body clasping it.

Seeing that the body was too large to be Lucy, he

blinked with relief, released the breath he was holding, and bent to free the radio from the man's lax grasp.

"*Jefe*," said a voice, startling him. "What's happening? We heard shots. Have you seen strangers?"

Ignoring the radio for the time being, Gus realized another figure lay prostrate within the shelter. Fear yanked his scalp tight as he ducked inside to investigate. A gaunt rebel lay at his feet with a bullet hole in his chest and a chain around his neck.

Not Lucy. But she had done this!

Of course, he couldn't be certain, but it was clean and professional, just the way she'd been trained to operate. He whirled around. "Lucy's not here," he murmured into his mouthpiece. Returning to the pen, he joined the others in studying the confusing montage of footprints.

"*Jefe!*" repeated the voice on the radio. "Are you there? We are headed your way."

Gus handed off the radio to Luther. "The Elite Guard are right behind us," he warned.

"Lucy must have fled with the others," Luther surmised.

"No, she wasn't with them," Gus insisted, knowing she would never run into the wilderness—not without him beside her.

"Then where is she?" the OIC demanded.

Gus pointed uphill. "Remember the E & E extraction point?" he asked with growing confidence.

"The summit," Luther recalled, looking sharply uphill.

"That's where she went," Gus answered with heart-swelling pride. "I bet if we look, we can find her tracks."

"Sirs, over here!" Vinny called.

The medic knelt some distance from the fence, shining his penlight at the ground. Gus and Luther hurried over.

The familiar impression of Lucy's boots made Gus'
heart thud with joy. "This was Lucy," he confirmed
They were so close now. "Sir?" he added, desperate to g
after her.

The OIC reflected for a moment. "Vinny, get on th
SATCOM and tell the JIC we need a helo capable of land
ing at a high altitude with plenty of cargo space and a sec
ond gunship for firepower support. The Venezuelans wil
be right behind us. I want us off this mountain in unde
an hour."

In spite of his certainty, desperation knotted Gus'
insides. The OIC had just put a timeline on finding Lucy.

Don't let me down, Luce, he thought. *This is my las
chance to save you.*

LUCY FOUND HERSELF STANDING on a windy slope wit
nothing but coarse, low-lying shrubs and spiny blades c
grass, all lit by a full moon.

Following an hour of arduous climbing, she ha
arrived at the mountain's alpine crest, where arctic con
ditions stunted the vegetation. It had been so long sinc
she'd seen the entire sky stretched from one horizon t
another that she halted with amazement, letting its vas
ness overwhelm her.

I'm free! she marveled, dazzled by the brightness c
the stars.

The sight of her breath crystallizing in the air jolte
her into action.

If she didn't find the radio station tonight, she woul
freeze to death. Setting her sights on the mountain's lumi
nous twin peaks, she climbed over thatch and thorny bri
ars, searching for the elusive station.

A glint of a solar panel drew her gaze to a radio antenna raking the night sky. Beneath the antenna, she made out a door, built into the face of walled cave. She stumbled toward it, conscious of an insidious weakness invading her limbs.

Not much longer, she assured herself. A pale line of light shone beneath the door, beckoning her with the promise of warmth and relief from the numbing wind. She prayed the SEALs' intel was accurate and that the station was minimally protected.

Checking the chamber in the pistol, she realized she had only three bullets left. Without the gun, she was as weak as a kitten and equally defenseless.

Putting her ear to the door, she willed her ragged breaths to subside, blew a warm breath on her frigid fingers, and listened.

The muted tones of meringue music struck a discordant note. Someone coughed. Stretching a hand to the sturdy latch, she was relieved to find it unlocked.

On the count of three, she told herself, clenching her jaw to keep her teeth from chattering.

One.

Two.

Three!

CHAPTER 18

Throwing her weight into the metal door, Lucy crashed into a room lit by the buttons from a soundboard display. "Freeze! No one move!" she barked as a lone silhouette lurched from blankets on the floor. "Put your hands in the air."

Spying a switch near the door, Lucy flipped it, flooding the cave with light, illumining a wide-eyed female who quaked with terror as she held her arms high above her head. A quick glance around assured her there were no more rebels. Lucy's luck was running high tonight.

Keeping her pistol trained on the girl, she kicked the door shut and bolted it. Searching the cave for weapons, she came up empty-handed. "One false move and I'll shoot," she warned, not putting it past the female rebel to try something. "I've killed one rebel tonight, and I don't mind killing another," she added fiercely.

"I am not with the FARC," insisted the young woman.

"Stand up," Lucy ordered, "Keep your hands where I can see them!" she added as the girl reached beneath the blanket.

"I need my crutch," the girl explained, showing the hand-carved stick to Lucy.

As the girl struggled to stand, Lucy realized one of her feet had been blown off, presumably by a landmine. "Have a seat," she offered, tempering her hostility with pity and waving her toward the only chair, positioned before the soundboard. "My name," she added, "is Luna de Aguiler. I'm with the United Nations."

"I am Maria," countered the young woman, her fear fading. "I was abducted by the FARC when they raided my village four years ago."

Lucy sent her a steady look. "Would you like to leave La Montaña, Maria?"

"Oh, yes!" she cried, suddenly luminous.

"Then I need to make an announcement on your radio."

The hope in Maria's face turned to fright. "Rebels will hear what you say. They will send soldiers to kill us!"

"How long will it take them to get here?" Lucy wanted to know.

The woman shrugged. "I don't know. An hour, maybe two?"

"We'll be gone by then," Lucy assured her with more certainty than she felt. "Please. Put me on the air. A helicopter will come for us in half an hour, I promise."

"But only the rebels listen to this station," the woman argued.

Despite herself, Lucy had to laugh. "Trust me," she said, stepping closer. "Others are listening." Like the National Security Agency, the eyes and ears of the CIA.

With reluctance, Maria nodded and reached for a knob, twisting it to silence the music. "You may speak

into the mike," she whispered, handing it to Lucy. "Pus[
the button."

Lucy depressed the button on the mike. "Mayday, may
day," she announced with crisp American consonant[
Picked up by an orbiting AWAC, it would take time fo[
her message to be forwarded to the NSA, then put throug[
filters to confirm her identity. "This is Luna de Aguile[
with the United Nations. Six-nine-seven-two-three-six,[
she added, throwing in her CIA identification number fo[
good measure. "Request immediate extraction from th[
summit of La Montaña, Colombia. Hostiles closing in.[
repeat..." She stated it a second time, intending to repli[
cate the process every five minutes.

Straightening, she nodded at Maria, who eyed her wit[
mixed terror and idolatry. "It'll be all right," she added[
bracing herself on the desk as sudden fatigue swep[
through her.

But then the doorknob gave a jiggle. With a gasp an[
an inner cry of despair, Lucy whirled to face it.

"¡Abre la puerta!" commanded a gruff voice on th[
other side. Open the door!

"Don't say anything," Lucy cautioned, her heart thud[
ding with terror and dismay.

How could the rebels have arrived so quickly? Ther[
had to be an outpost nearby. Oh, God. Oh, no. Thi[
couldn't be happening, not when she'd come so fa[
endured so much.

Boom! The imprint of a boot put an indentation in th[
metal door. Maria whimpered.

"Quick, hide under here," Lucy instructed, pushing th[
girl under the protection of the soundboard. "They won[
harm you," she added reassuringly.

As the door shuddered on its hinges, she darted across the room to stand behind it, gripping the pistol fiercely.

Great. Just fucking great. Here she was, headed into a fight for her life, and she had only three bullets left.

With a sob of regret, she thought of Gus, who'd had to live with his father's death and would now blame himself for hers.

I'm sorry, she cried silently, pressing her back to the rough wall. The intruders continued to pound on the door. Bits of cement crumbled to the stone floor, indications that the hinges would soon give away.

Her stiff fingers cramped around the pistol. Well-aimed shots to the center torso were the only thing that might save her now.

All at once the door lurched. With a loud groan it twisted inward, providing the intruders just enough space to wedge their way inside.

The dust cleared; still, she waited, guarding her precious bullets. *This is it,* she thought, praying for a speedy death—no more agonizing torture.

As a shoulder edged into the room, accompanied by a quick peek, she pulled the trigger. Her sluggish brain was still processing the pattern of the intruder's camouflage when her bullet whizzed by him and ricocheted off the opposite wall.

"Lucy!" exclaimed the voice she'd heard so often in her dreams this past week she was certain she'd imagined it. "It's us! For Christ's sake, don't shoot!"

"Gus!" she croaked. The pistol clattered to the stone floor as the strength drained out of her. He spun around the door in time to catch her wilting body.

"I've got you, Luce," he rasped, crushing her against him as they sank to their knees. Delicious heat leapt off him. His familiar scent enfolded her. Lucy tried to climb inside of him, so wildly relieved it was all she could do not to burst into sobs. "I've got you," he repeated as she squeezed her eyes shut and breathed, just breathed.

Hot tears seeped through her lashes to track her filthy cheeks. She was vaguely aware that four more SEALs had stepped inside the cave, calling words of reassurance to Maria, who crept from her hiding place. Opening her eyes, she took in the painted faces of her saviors—Luther, Harley, Vinny, Teddy, and Gus, her one and only partner. "I thought you were the rebels," she admitted hoarsely.

"They're right behind us," Gus informed her.

His words sent a shaft of fear through her heart. "But how? I just sent out a mayday."

"They've been tracking us all day," he explained, "since we captured and questioned Buitre this morning. He's dead, by the way."

She let the announcement sink into her consciousness, a balm to her fears. "Good," she said, quelling painful memories that threatened to unfocus her. "But how did you know I'd be here?"

"We got to Arriba right after you escaped. How'd you manage that?" he asked with amazement.

"It was a total fluke," she admitted wryly. "The lock around my neck fell open."

Horror flickered in Gus's eyes as they fell to her chafed neck. "And then what?"

"Then I shot the first guard paying his hourly visit. I tossed his keys at the other captives, who took out the second guard." And in hindsight, she could scarcely believe her own temerity.

"We heard the other captives heading downhill in the dark," said Gus, "but I knew you had more sense than to go with them. I knew you'd remember the E & E extraction point."

"I hate to break off the reunion," Luther interrupted gently, "but we've got a helo extract to prepare for."

Lucy's relief mounted. She wouldn't have to wait on pins and needles now for her mayday to be processed. She'd be flying out of here in a matter of minutes.

"Vinny, find out our helicopters' ETA," rapped out the OIC. "Tell them I want a read on the number of hostiles closing in."

The reminder of a lingering threat put a damper on Lucy's euphoria.

"Harley and Teddy, set up a perimeter outside," Luther added.

"Have some water," murmured Gus. Ignoring his leader's urgency, he pressed a canteen of reviving water to her lips. "How do you feel? How's the hip?"

"It's healing. I had a raging fever from the filthy knife they used, but I survived."

"My brave girl," he murmured, stroking her cheek with a gloved hand. His eyes glimmered wetly as he gazed down at her. "I'm so sorry for what happened, Luce," he added hoarsely.

"Don't. It wasn't your fault," she insisted. "You couldn't have known Buitre would dump you in the river. God, Gus, I don't know how you survived that, but I knew you would," she added, clutching him harder.

"We went after you that night," he told her quickly, "but we were too late. They'd already removed the microchip and used it to lure us away from you."

Lucy cringed at the memory of her torture.

"How's your hip now?" he pressed. "How badly did they hurt you, Luce?"

"I'm fine," she insisted. "They didn't break me, Gus. If anything, they taught me how much I want to live."

At her confession, his eyes blazed with love and words unspoken. Only this wasn't the time to talk about the future.

"Gus," interrupted the OIC. "Get Lucy dressed in cold-weather gear. We're moving out."

"Maria has to come with us," Lucy insisted, meeting the girl's hopeful gaze. "They'll kill her for allowing me to broadcast."

Luther and Gus both slid Maria an assessing look, taking in her missing foot.

"So be it," said the OIC, shaking off his rucksack. "Let's bundle you both up."

"MOTHER HAWK, THIS IS BABY BIRD," Vinny called on a note of desperation. "State your ETA, over."

With Lucy trembling in his arms, Gus prayed the rescue helicopter would arrive at any moment, preferably with a backup helo for fire support. The rebels were now keeping radio silence. The SEALs had no way of knowing how close they were.

Even with their backs to an escarpment, the icy wind pierced their protective clothing. The frozen pond between the mountain's twin peaks shone an iridescent blue under the starry sky. If they weren't rescued soon, they would freeze to death or fall under attack by the approaching rebels.

"Baby Bird, this is Mother Hawk and Hunter Hawk." The heartening reply sounded crystal clear. "We are within two miles and closing. Over."

Gus shared looks of relief with Vinny and Luther.

"Roger, Mother Hawk and Hunter Hawk," Vinny replied. "We are five in number with two civilians. We have a sniper and scout positioned on a ledge. Do you see our FLIR? Over."

"We see you, Baby Bird. Get FLIR patches on those civilians."

"Wilco, Mother Bird."

Luther was already grubbing in his pack for glint tape, sticking the Velcroed tabs on Maria's shoulders, then handing two to Gus to put on Lucy.

"Hunter One will approach forward of your position to defend the rescue," continued the pilot. "You may position infrared strobes on the LZ now. Keep your heads low and watch for rotor downdraft. Over."

"We copy, Mother Bird. Look for our strobes. Over."

"I'll do it," offered Luther as Vinny reached for the pack with the strobes. "Stay here and man the radio."

Gus watched Luther dart from their shelter and run in a low crouch toward the flat area that rimmed the lake. A whip-crack shot rode the edges of the wind, and Luther fell into a crouch, consulting Harley on his headset. In Gus's arms, Lucy flinched.

"That's Harley," he reassured her, not bothering to add that it was also Harley's signal that the rebels were closing to within firing distance. Damn it!

"Vinny," he said, trying to mask his urgency, "the second the helo lands, you grab Maria and go. We'll be right behind you."

"Hooyah, sir."

The whiz and bang of a sixty-six-millimeter rocket launcher, fired to retard the rebels' approach, made Gus's heart pound.

"Is that Harley, too?" Lucy asked between chattering teeth.

"Yes," he reassured her.

But then the rebels retaliated, filling the frigid silence with a thunderous barrage, and he could no longer deny that the bad guys had caught up to them.

Peering desperately up at the night sky, he was gratified to see the silhouette of a Pave Hawk helicopter detach itself from the inky sky.

"Here comes the rescue helo," warned Vinny, preparing to gather Maria in his arms.

The radio crackled. "All call signs, this is Hunter Hawk. Preparing to suppress enemy forces. Get your people on the rescue bird, now! Over."

Seeing Luther occupied, Gus summoned the sniper and scout. "Harley, Teddy, pull back now!" he ordered.

Twenty seconds later, the twosome skidded into the alcove, dropping down next to them. "Elite Guards," Harley shouted over the vibration of descending rotors. "Sneaky bastards slipped around from the east side."

Buffeted by a stiff wind, the rescue bird teetered, snatching their attention to the landing zone. Gus's heart almost stopped as the immense rotor came within inches of striking the escarpment. The slightest contact could send the helicopter crashing to the ground in a massive explosion.

The skilled pilots managed to bring it under control, easing Gus's fears. The bird touched down at last, whipping up flecks of granite as it waited for the SEALs' approach.

"Go, go!" he shouted, urging Vinny to precede him.

Lieutenant Lindstrom was the first to greet the crew, waving his teammates over as he took up a defensive position by the doors.

With Maria in his arms, Vinny lumbered out into the open. Bullets immediately ricocheted off the granite at his feet, driving him back into cover.

Son of a bitch. The Elite Guards had caught up to them, firing rounds that struck the helicopter with musical *pings.* Luther fired back, but the mounted gun, loath to put friendly forces in harm's way, did not.

Where the hell was Hunter Hawk? wondered Gus, breaking into a sweat under his cold-weather gear.

Then, with a *whop-whop-whop,* the second helicopter rose over the summit's lip, spewing fire from its Gatling gun, picking off the encircling Venezuelans.

"Run!" Gus urged, and Vinny tried again.

Banding an arm around Lucy's waist, Gus followed him, Harley and Teddy belting out a base line to cover their retreat.

This has got to work, thought Gus, speeding Lucy over the rubble. Heads tucked into their chests, they ran blindly into hands that pulled them into the helo's cabin. Track lighting revealed a team of four men, working furiously to speed them away.

"Go! Go! Go!" shouted the team leader to the pilots.

With whining rotors, the bird lurched off the ground, swaying like a cradle as the wind whipped around them. They swung so close to one of the jagged peaks, it seemed inevitable that they would strike it.

Gus felt Lucy tug at his jacket. "Gus!" she cried, capturing his attention.

He looked down at her, loving every curve of her beautiful, sculpted face.

"I want that date!" she demanded, her words scarcely discernable as both Hunter Hawk and Mother Hawk now pounded the enemy.

A sense of peace enfolded Gus abruptly, easing his tense muscles, compelling him to lower his mouth and touch his lips to Lucy's ice-cold ones. Suddenly he just knew, like he'd known she had fled to the summit, that they were going to survive this deadly night. And one day soon, they'd be enjoying their first date in eight long years.

"You've got it," he promised as the Pave Hawk soared straight up. Listing to one side, it bore them to safety as Hunter Hawk riddled the mountaintop, destroying the FARC's secret weapon once and for all.

CHAPTER 19

Escorted by her brother, Drake, Lucy crossed from the elevator to the door of her apartment outside Washington, D.C., with the sense that she was dreaming. The flight on a C-130 cargo plane from Ecuador to Andrews Air Force just north of D.C. had taken all day.

Prior to that, she had spent three days at Manta Air Base in Ecuador, enduring the FBI's Hostage Reintegration Program. She'd been fed, scrutinized by a physician, and allowed brief communication with her employer and with her family members before finally being sent home.

The only thing she hadn't done in those three days was talk to Gus. No sooner had the rescue helicopter delivered her to Manta Air Base than it had borne him and his teammates to a carrier in the Pacific.

Lucy had watched the helo disappear over the dark Andes hills and wondered how she would bear the wait to see him again.

"Uh, before we go in," her little brother cautioned, his hand on the doorknob, "I should probably warn you that Mom and Dad invited a few people over. So don't have a heart attack and try to look surprised," he added, smiling ruefully as he swung the door wide. Delicious aromas wafted from the dark interior. Drake reached for the light.

"Surprise!" Despite her brother's warning, Lucy was startled to see so many people crammed into her living room.

"Lucy!" Her mother and father rushed at her, sweeping her up into a joint embrace. In the circle of warmth, Lucy relaxed. Talking on the phone with them had been a healing experience, but their touch was what she really needed.

Over her mother's shoulder, she spied Gordon Banks, her supervisor, standing with a red plastic cup in one hand and tears in his eyes.

Her gaze strayed to the other faces, folks from the office—secretaries and analysts who had taken the time to welcome her back. Everyone was here but Gus, who had a job to do.

She couldn't blame him for that. Somehow, they'd work around the demands of their professions to see each other.

"Come on in, sugar," said her father, throwing a protective arm around her as he guided her around the room to greet each guest.

Her mother rescued her, passing her a plate of hors d'oeuvres and drawing her into the kitchen.

Seated on a bar stool consuming shrimp tempura, Lucy wondered if she would wake up tomorrow to find she was still chained on La Montaña. The panicky feeling was a familiar one.

Aware that her brother was hovering protectively, she sent him a reassuring wink. Her gaze went past him to the enormous potted plant gracing her glass dinette table. What on earth?

Her mother was the green thumb, but this looked nothing like the colorful flowers Karen Donovan favored.

Pushing off the stool, Lucy wandered over for a closer look. The plant's broad leaves brought back memories of the jungle.

Half cautious, half intrigued, she reached for the envelope and extracted the message inside, a tremor in her fingers.

To Lucy, my love. Keep it alive.

With a startled glance at the sturdy-looking plant, she recalled what she'd said to him on their last day at the *casita. People like us don't do relationships. I can't keep a houseplant alive.*

Stroking a dark leaf, she found it silky to the touch and oddly comforting. She'd do better than just keep it alive. A determined smile touched the edges of her mouth.

Glancing up, she caught Drake's thoughtful gaze and grinned at him.

Cell phones weren't allowed in the CIA's new headquarters building. While debriefing her boss and attending meetings that had anything to do with South America, Lucy stored her phone in the glove compartment of her new SUV, a Toyota Land Cruiser. Checking for missed calls was the first thing she did at the end of each day. Today, she eyed the number of her single missed call with a prick of hope.

A shiver of anticipation rippled through her as she accessed her voice mail. At the sound of Gus's velvety baritone, she closed her eyes in relief. *Finally!* He had kept his promise.

"So, Luce," he said, sounding hesitant and excited at the same time, "how about that date you promised me? Call me back," he said succinctly.

Good thing she wasn't expecting hearts and flowers. Hitting the TALK button, she started up her vehicle, prepared to drive whatever distance was required to see him.

"Is that you, Ethel?" he answered with a smile in his voice.

"Hey, Freddy," she replied, her heart leaping with joy. "You wanted to see me?"

"Hell, yes, I want to see you." His urgency was reassuring. "Can you make it to the Mellow Mushroom in Tyson's Corner in an hour?"

He was here in northern Virginia? Lucy glanced at her car clock. "I can make it in fifteen minutes," she told him, her heart pounding.

"I'll be waiting," he said, hanging up.

With a glance over her shoulder, Lucy peeled out of her parking place, laying rubber on the asphalt as she raced for the exit. Speeding along the George Washington Parkway, she glanced at her reflection and grinned.

Life was good. Two weeks in civilization had put some badly needed flesh on her bones. Her skin, once ravaged by insect bites, looked smooth and clear. Vitamin supplements had put the sheen back in her dark hair. She would have liked to have worn something sexier than this lavender linen suit, but it would do for a first date.

Twelve minutes later, she exited the Beltway at Tysons Corner. The Mellow Mushroom, a new restaurant, stood adjacent to the shooting gallery where she'd qualified as an expert markswoman seven years straight. With a minute to spare, she bounced into the parking lot, pulling her SUV into a spot near the back, close to a beat-up black Honda.

She'd bet her next paycheck the car belonged to Gus.

Looping her purse on her shoulder, she paused long enough to strap her Ruger onto her thigh—*Never leave home without it. Never again, anyway.* Then she marched toward the restaurant's entrance, projecting confidence.

They could do this. In spite of what they both did for a living, they could *make* a relationship work. Sparing a smile for the hostess, she brushed past her, searching the bohemian-style restaurant for Gus's dark head.

Across the room, their gazes collided, and Lucy's heart stopped, resuming its beat with a thud.

From a table topped with a dozen roses, Gus shot to his feet and grinned as she bore down on him. In lieu of jungle cammies, he wore a tan knit shirt and jeans. His jaw was clean-shaven, his hair shorn and combed. He looked so ordinary and domesticated that she had to laugh as she threw herself at him.

"What?" he said, grinning as he folded her into his embrace in front of the handful of spectators. He kissed her soundly on the lips. "You look beautiful," he murmured, pulling her close again.

"I was thinking the same thing," she purred, wishing they were alone somewhere. His scent, his touch notched her desire to dangerous levels.

He seemed suddenly conscious of the attention they were getting. "Have a seat," he said, pulling out a chair for her. "I've been sitting here a while waiting for your call."

Lucy eyed the spray of red roses with amazement. "Are these for me?"

"Of course."

"Wow," she exclaimed, inhaling their perfume as she sat. "I didn't know you had it in you," she admitted.

Dropping into the chair next to her, he caught up her

hand again, threading his fingers through hers. "I'd do anything for you, Luce," he added quietly. "Anything."

The implied commitment in his words took her breath away. "That's a good thing," she answered, "because seeing each other isn't going to be easy."

"Nothing worthwhile ever is," he insisted.

"That's true," she agreed.

"I love you, Luce," he added gruffly. "I always have."

She had to dab at a fat tear escaping the corner of her eye. "I love you too, Gus," she admitted, losing herself in the golden depths of his eyes. "I didn't always love myself," she added quietly, "which is why I cut you out of my life. But I always loved you."

He drew a breath that expanded his powerful chest. "Did you get my gift?" he asked with a searching look.

"Oh, you mean the plant? Yes, I did. Bella's alive and well," she reassured him, picking up her menu.

He sent her a quizzical smile. "You named it?"

"Of course. She's not just your average houseplant, you know. She's a *Calathia burlemarxii*. She makes these gorgeous blue flowers that grow right out of the stem. You should see them."

"I'd like to," he asserted, looking up as the waitress interrupted.

"What can I get for you?" the young girl asked brightly.

Gus glanced askance at Lucy, who shrugged. "Every thing tastes good these days," she drawled, leaving the decision up to him.

Without even glancing at the menu, Gus placed an order for spinach and vegetable deep dish.

"Nice flowers," said the waitress, flicking Lucy an envious look as she left.

"So..." said Gus when they were alone again.

"So," said Lucy, trying not to smile at his earnest fforts to be everything she could ever ask for and more. le would soon realize she loved him just the way he was.

"You changed your mind," he pointed out. It took her a econd to realize he was talking about their date, the one he'd refused their last day at the *casita*. That wasn't all he'd changed her mind about.

"I had a lot of time to think," she countered wryly.

His grip on her hand grew fierce. "God, Luce—" he egan, clearly about to berate himself.

"Don't," she cut him off. "I already told you, Gus. Vhat happened was no one's fault but the rebels' and the 'enezuelans', who paid for their mistake. Besides, like said when you found me at the radio station, I learned vhat it means to really live. You were right," she admited, her voice husky with emotion. "Ever since what hapened to my friends in Spain, I was afraid to get close to eople. I didn't think I had the right to enjoy my life."

With sympathy in his gaze, Gus stretched out a hand o stroke the side of her face.

"During captivity, I realized the best way to honor Amy, Melissa, and Dan would be to live life to its fullest— ou know? Not bury myself in my work or get swept away y terror's encroaching tide."

He sent her a heartbreaking smile. "I hate what hapened to you, Luce, but it makes me so happy to hear you ay that. I understand survivor's guilt. I dealt with it when ny father died."

"It's taken a long time to come to terms with what I aw in Spain," she admitted, recalling with a private hiver how detached, how fearless she had felt for years fterward. "But that's behind me now," she added. "I don't want to shut you out anymore. We can do this, Gus," sh added, laying her hands over his. "I know we can."

The pleasure shining in his eyes slowly dimmed "Lucy, I'm only in town for five more hours," he admitte quietly.

The confession dropped like a bomb on her conten ment. She tried to speak, but disappointment put a choke hold on her vocal cords. She nodded instead. No big dea she told herself, drawing in a tight breath. At least she' gotten to see him, to tell him how she felt.

"That's why I've been sitting here," he added sadly, " make the most of my time."

She didn't bother asking him where he was headed. H couldn't tell her anyway. She wasn't sure she even wante to know.

But if the FARC couldn't break her spirit, then she' be damned if she would let the scarcity of her time wit Gus get her down. "Excuse me, Jackie," she called, sum moning the waitress by name. "We're going to need tha pizza to go," she informed her with a grimace of apology

Glancing at Gus, she found a crooked smile on hi face. "Good thinking," he murmured.

"Yeah? You want to hear something else?" she asked a wicked smile kicking up the corners of her mouth.

"Sure."

She leaned toward him, a sultry invitation in her eye "The windows of my SUV are tinted," she whispered i his ear. "We don't even have to go anywhere."

"Hot damn," he murmured, his eyes darkening wit desire.

But then Lucy glanced at the dozen roses and her gri faded. "Oh, we can't do that, the roses will wilt."

"To hell with the roses," said Gus, folding up his napkin. "I'll buy you more next time."

Because there would be a next time, Lucy swore. And then a next time after that. After everything they had been through, *nothing* could get in the way of their happy ever after.

EPILOGUE ===========

Six months later

Lucy entered her boss's third-floor office suite with a drag in her step. She knew she was ready for a new assignment. Her PTSD, reawakened by the trauma in Colombia, was on the wane, and there was only so much paper pushing a girl like her could stand. But finding time to spend with Gus was her priority these days, and that was about to get much harder with her job sending her overseas.

Rhonda, Gordon's secretary, glanced up as she eased into the doorway. "Oh, honey," she sympathized, whipping off her glasses, "it's not going to be that bad, I promise."

"Right," said Lucy forcing her chin up. God, was she that transparent?

"He said for you just to go right in," Rhonda added with a reassuring smile.

Behind the closed door, Lucy could hear Gordon either talking on the phone or in person with a third party. For no reason whatsoever, except that he was always on her mind, Lucy thought of Gus, who'd been training for the last two months in the Mediterranean. She pictured him tan and vibrant, surrounded by way too many girls wearing bikinis. Wrenching the latch on Gordon's door, she thrust her way into his office and drew up short.

Her sour mood fled as she beheld the object of her obsession rising from his seat with a shy smile on his face. Two months in the Mediterranean had put copper highlights in his hair. He looked so healthy and vibrant that Lucy had to lean on the door to steady her weak knees.

"Gus," she breathed. "What are you doing here?"

He glanced at Gordon. "I'll let the boss answer that question, since he's the one who wanted to surprise you."

Spearing Gordon with a sharply curious look, Lucy managed to cross toward Gus with outward poise, brushing a kiss across his cheek while resisting the impulse to lean against his solid, suit-clad body. "You look good," she added faintly.

His whisky-brown eyes raked her with a look that sent her heart pounding. "Likewise," he replied.

She sank weakly into the seat beside him. "So, what's up?" she asked, her curiosity thoroughly piqued.

Gordon's dark eyes danced with amusement. "Well, Lucy, I have a new assignment for you," he announced.

She nodded. "I figured as much. That doesn't explain why Gus is here."

"I think you should be the one to tell her," Gordon said to Gus.

Lucy's gaze swung back and forth between them. "Tell me what?" she demanded, her anticipation rising. She could sense positive vibes coming from both men.

Gus drew himself up straighter and announced definitively, "I resigned my commission."

Stunned, certain she'd misheard him, Lucy just looked at him. "What commission?" she asked.

"My officer's commission. I'm no longer in the Navy."

Aware that her mouth was hanging open, Lucy snapped it shut. "But why? You worked so hard to make it."

"I did it for my father, Luce," he explained, holding her gaze with a steady look. "At the time, it was the right thing to do. But today I'd be honoring his memory more by spending time with you."

Lucy shot a guilty glance at Gordon, who grinned. "It's okay," he reassured her. "Your passion for Gus isn't exactly a secret. Nor is your closeness surprising, given all you've been through."

She turned her attention back to Gus. "Are you sure it's what you want?" she asked, even as her heart expanded in relief. It would be so much easier to get together now that he wasn't a Navy SEAL.

"Positive," he said, grinning at her happily.

"Gus has decided to join us full-time," Gordon announced, adding to her incredulity, "working on the paramilitary side. As a matter of fact, I've assigned you two to work together on another assignment."

A quiver of excitement shot through Lucy. "Where?" she asked, sharing a look of anticipation with Gus.

"You're about to be sent to Phuket, Thailand, allegedly to enjoy your honeymoon..."

The word *honeymoon* caused Lucy's heart to stop on a downstroke, then take off at a trot. She'd been dreaming about that honeymoon Gus had described at the *casita* ever since he'd mentioned it. To think that it was about to become a reality! Only...they weren't married.

"...and then to remain when Gus gets a cover job at a local shipping port," Gordon continued, oblivious to her racing thoughts. "Lucy, you'll be a freelance photographer. Your objective will be to monitor an Islamic insurgency group suspected of planning attacks on westerners at any one of the resorts in Phuket. Terrorism has been a rising concern in the area. Lucy, I assume you're willing to partner with Gus on this assignment?"

Even with her extremities tingling and her heart racing, Lucy managed a cool, "Of course. He is my partner," she replied.

She ruined it by grinning at Gus as she envisioned the glorious months to come—white beaches, shockingly blue water, sun, and just a dash of danger to keep life interesting.

An hour later, with a date set for an in-depth briefing, Gus and Lucy were dismissed for the day. With their relationship out of the bag, he deliberately held her hand. Recalling how upset he'd been the last time they'd walked out of a briefing together, Lucy had to smile at how far they'd come.

As Gus pushed the button for the elevator, his sidelong look warned her of his intent to kiss her silly as soon as they found themselves alone.

The elevator slid open, and he drew her sedately into the cubicle, waiting with deceptive patience for the door to close again. In the next instant, he jerked her into his embrace, crushed her mouth under his, and kissed her like a man starved of affection.

Lucy moaned. If there were just some way to keep the elevator from opening again.

His taste, his intensity was everything she needed to

be happy, except…using all the strength in her arms, she freed her lips. "Marry me," she demanded on a breathless note.

He gave a startled, incredulous laugh. "What?"

Lucy's confidence faltered. "We're going to Phuket," she reminded him, worried that the stunned look on his face meant he never intended for them to exchange vows of any kind. "You told Bellini and the others you wanted to take me on a honeymoon," she reminded him.

He laughed again, releasing her to rake his fingers through his hair in his signature gesture of discomfiture.

The thought occurred to Lucy that his talk about a honeymoon hadn't been sincere. He might have just been making up words to reinforce their roles.

With a self-conscious step backward, she pulled away. "I'm sorry," she said as the elevator touched down. "I thought that was where our relationship was headed. My mistake." The door slid open, and she dove for the exit, intending to retreat with her dignity intact.

With a groan, Gus caught her elbow and swung her back into his arms. Two quick jabs of his finger, and they were isolated in the soundproof space again, headed to the uppermost floor.

"There's no mistake, Luce," he reassured her, stroking her defiantly lifted chin with his fingertips. "It's just that you took the words out of my mouth before I could say them, and I've been practicing," he admitted ruefully.

Lucy's stiff posture relaxed. "You've been practicing proposing to me?" she asked with incredulity and relief.

"I should have guessed you'd beat me to it," he added without rancor.

"Well, go ahead," she urged. "Let's hear what you've got."

Seriousness vied with humor in his golden-brown eyes. "Nah, I never got it right. I think you should do it," he decided. "You're the one who took the initiative."

He surprised her further by reaching in the lining of his jacket and producing a velvet pouch. "Go ahead," he urged, placing it in the center of her palm. "Ask me."

Lucy swallowed hard. With a wide-eyed glance at him, she pulled the ring out of the pouch and gasped in delight. The glittering tier of diamonds on the platinum band reminded her of the stars viewed from the top of La Montaña. "Oh, Gus. It's beautiful!"

The elevator slowed to a stop and the door slid open. A distracted glance revealed the director of the CIA himself about to join them. Taking in the vignette before him, he hesitated, then, to Lucy's dismay, stepped right inside and pushed a button. "Don't let me interrupt," he told them with an indulgent smile.

Gus cocked an eyebrow at Lucy, who wavered with uncharacteristic cowardice.

"We can do this later," she assured him, trying to give the ring back.

"No, you started it. You finish," he insisted, humor edging out seriousness for the time being. "Besides, it should be spontaneous, not practiced."

The elevator began its agonizing descent. "Okay," she agreed, drawing a breath to clear her head. Ignoring the director as best she could, Lucy focused exclusively on the man she loved. Her thoughts went back eight years ago to the carefree days of college, then fast-forwarded through their harrowing experience on La Montaña, to the last bittersweet weeks of mixed pleasure and yearning. "I wish I'd never shut you out of my life," she admitted, pushing her confession through a tightening throat. "Please marry me, Gus. Stay with me forever and never, *never* leave."

A slow, tender smile lifted the corners of Gus's mouth as he pulled her into his arms. "That was beautiful," he praised. "What do you think, sir?" he added, surprising Lucy, who had almost forgotten the director was still there, playing witness. "Should I accept?"

"Lucy Donovan, is it?" the man asked, running an assessing gaze over her. "Your reputation precedes you. I'd say you're in good hands with her, young man," he decided, clapping Gus on the back.

"Then I accept," said Gus, relieving Lucy's trace fears. Taking the pouch from her hands, he slipped the ring onto her fourth finger, a perfect fit. "I've had this since the end of my senior year," he surprised her by admitting. "I was planning to give it to you when you got back from Spain."

"Oh, Gus," she whispered, regret stitching through her at how terrorism had torn them apart. Ironically, it had also brought them back together.

"I've never stopped loving you, Luce. You're the only woman I've ever wanted to share my life with," he added gruffly.

The elevator gave a bump as they touched down for a second time. With a handshake for Gus and a kiss for Lucy, the director stepped out ahead of them. "Now, that's a story for the grandkids," he added, wagging a finger at them before walking away.

"Wait," said Lucy, drawing Gus back in the elevator. "I want to savor the moment," she added, pressing the button for the uppermost floor again. "Besides, my mother's still in my apartment."

Gus groaned as he encircled her in his arms. "Maybe

we should get a hotel room," he suggested in advance of a blistering kiss.

Desire rose in conjunction with the ascending elevator.

"I don't suppose you know how to jam the door?" suggested Lucy breathlessly.

He slanted the door in question a considering glance. "I bet I can figure something out."

Lucy's blood thrummed with anticipation as he forced open a panel under the buttons and eyed the display. "We could lose our jobs over this," she added with a nervous laugh.

"I won't do anything that can't be undone," he promised, flicking a switch. Immediately, the lights in the cubicle dimmed as the elevator slowed to a halt.

They met in a clash of silk and wool, lips and tongues. Within seconds, Lucy's back was against the wall, Gus's hands bunching the slippery material of her skirt. Encountering bare skin beneath, he growled with appreciation. "I'm so glad you hate pantyhose," he muttered thickly.

Lucy hummed her agreement. This was one story the grandkids probably shouldn't overhear.

Dear Readers,

As you probably already know, SHOW NO FEAR is the most recent addition to my Navy SEAL series, all centered around the absolutely irresistible heroes of Navy SEAL Team Twelve. My joy in writing this series came from bringing seven very distinct but equally captivating men to life. I hope you'll indulge me as I tell you a little about each one of them.

From FORGET ME NOT, the decisive Lieutenant Gabe Renault.

Gabe had ample time in a North Korean prison to consider what really matters to him—winning back the love of his estranged wife, Helen, and stepdaughter. A daring escape makes his dreams a reality. But hampered with PTSD and a spotty memory, Gabe struggles to make good on his intentions. Can he convince his women that he's a changed man before a mysterious traitor seeks to betray him yet again?

From IN THE DARK, the contemplative Lieutenant Luther Lindstrom.

Without a doubt, Luther is six feet and six inches of all-American integrity. Squared away and humble, this former professional football player turned down millions to serve his country. All he wants is a sweet, uncomplicated woman to keep the home fires burning. Too bad he can't get the sassy redheaded DIA agent Hannah Geary out of his head!

From TIME TO RUN,
the tough guy, Chief "Westy" McCaffrey.

Sniper Westy McCaffrey thinks he turned off his heart when he buried his family twenty years ago. While helping Sara Garret flee from her abusive husband, Westy returns to his childhood ranch to face his demons. Sara's loving touch brings his shattered heart back to life. Only how can he continue to be a ruthless sniper with his feelings getting in the way?

From NEXT TO DIE,
the hunky Lieutenant Commander Joe Montgomery.

Newly appointed commander of Team Twelve, the once charmed golden boy is back from Afghanistan, scarred and wounded. While Joe nurses survivor's guilt in secret, his neighbor and physical therapist, Penny Price, vows to return him to his former glory. Even as Penny slowly heals Joe's brokenness, she is haunted by a killer who threatens their unexpected bond.

From DON'T LET GO,
the powerful Master Chief Solomon McGuire.

Solomon has distrusted women ever since his first wife ran off with his infant son. On a mission to pluck an American woman from war-torn Venezuela, he forcibly separates Jordan Bliss from the orphan she is trying to adopt. Jordan's devastation strikes a chord of remorse that is compounded by Solomon's sudden, powerful desire for her. Now he will do anything to reunite Jordan with the orphan Miguel, earning the right to her love and the chance to find a new family.

**From TOO FAR GONE,
the irresistible Chief Sean Harlan.**

Sean can get any woman he wants. It's too bad the only woman he thinks of is Ellie Stuart, the single mother of three boys who's off limits to him. But when Ellie's boys are violently kidnapped, Sean is the first to come to her aid and lose his heart. When the police begin to suspect Ellie, Sean will stop at nothing to reunite Ellie with her boys.

**And last but not least, you've already met
Lieutenant Gus Atwater.**

He may have been a geek in college, but dedication and determination have made him one of the deadliest men on the planet. No wonder Lucy can't resist him.

If you haven't fallen in love at least seven times with this series, you probably missed a book!

Enjoy,

Marlie Melton

THE DISH

Where authors give you the inside scoop!

From the desk of Susan Kearney

Dear Reader,

I came up with my idea for LUCAN (on sale now), the first book in the Pendragon Legacy Trilogy, in the usual way. A time machine landed in my backyard early one morning, and I forgot all about sleeping in—especially after a hunky alien sauntered right up to my back porch and knocked.

Scrambling from bed, I yanked on a cami and jeans, stashed a tape recorder in my back pocket and ran my fingers through my hair. Like any working writer worth her publisher's advance, I was willing to forego sleep for the sake of research.

I yanked open the back door.

Did I mention the guy was hot? No way would I have guessed he was an archeologist back from a mission to a planet named Pendragon. But I'm getting ahead of myself. From his squared jaw to the intelligent gleam in his eyes to his ripped chest, Lucan was all macho male.

And for the next few hours he was all mine.

"I understand you're interested in love storie
written in the future," Lucan said, his lips widening
into a charming grin.

"I am." Heart pounding with excitement, I joined
him on the porch. We each took a chair.

Lucan steepled his hands under his chin. "In the
future, global pollution will cause worldwide ste
rility."

Uh-oh. "Humanity is going to die?" I asked.

"Our best hope will be a star map I found in King
Arthur's castle."

"A star map . . ." Oh, that sounded exciting. "You
followed the map to the stars?"

"To find the Holy Grail."

"Because the Holy Grail will cure Earth's infer
tility problem?"

He nodded and I was pleased. I was a writer for a
reason. I could put clues together. But I wanted
more. "You mentioned a love story?"

Lucan's face softened. "Lady Cael, High Priestes
of Avalon."

"She helped you?"

His full lips twisted into a handsome grin. "First
she almost killed me."

"But you're still alive," I prodded, settling back in
my chair. There was nothing I liked better than a
good adventure story about saving the world, espe
cially when it involved romance and love.

If you'd like to read the story Lucan told me, th

book is in stores now. And if you'd like to contact me, you can do so at www.susankearney.com.

Enjoy!

Susan Kearney

♥ ♥ ♥ ♥ ♥ ♥ ♥ ♥ ♥ ♥ ♥ ♥ ♥ ♥ ♥ ♥

From the desk of Marliss Melton

Dear Readers,

"What inspires your stories?" my readers ask. I tell them *everything*—news stories, movies, dreams, but most especially personal experience. "Write what you know" is wise advice, especially when it comes to painting a vivid setting. Though I've never visited the jungles of Colombia the way my characters do in my latest book SHOW NO FEAR (on sale now), I did get to experience the jungle as a child living in Thailand. During my family's three-year tour there, we often vacationed at a game reserve called Kao Yai.

Children are wonderfully impressionable. I will

never forget the moist coolness of the jungle air or the ruckus of the gibbons, swinging in the canopy at dawn and again at sunset. And the birds! There was a great white hornbill named Sam, hand-raised by the park rangers, that liked to frighten unsuspecting tourists by dive-bombing them! One morning, I fed her Fruit Loops off my bungalow deck. By day, my parents would drag all five of us kids on mile-long hikes, an experience stamped indelibly into my mind, providing inspiration for Gus and Lucy's perilous hikes. Our labors were always rewarded by a swim in the basin of a thirty-foot waterfall. Behind the waterfall, I discovered a secret cave, just like Gus and Lucy's. On one hike in particular, we stumbled into a set of huge tiger tracks. Who knew how close a tiger was lurking? Luckily, it left us alone.

Without a doubt, my childhood adventures have provided me with tons of material for my writing. I hope you enjoyed Gus and Lucy's adventures in SHOW NO FEAR. To read more about my adventurous childhood and what inspires my writing, visit my Web site at www.marlissmelton.com.

Sincerely,

Marliss Melton

From the desk of Michelle Rowen

Dear Reader,

In my *Immortality Bites* series, I've put fledgling vampire Sarah Dearly through a great many trials and tribulations, and she's weathered them all with her trademark sarcasm (her greatest weapon against nasty vampire hunters), grace, and charm (although this is usually mixed with a whole lot of anxiety and paranoia).

In TALL, DARK & FANGSOME (on sale now), the fifth and final book in the series, Sarah finds all of her vampire-related issues coming to a head. Her nightwalker curse seems likely to turn her permanently into an evil, bloodsucking vamp; she's being blackmailed into helping Gideon Chase, the leader of the vampire hunters, become the strongest vamp ever created; and her romance with master vamp Thierry seems destined to break both of their hearts.

Life sure ain't easy for a vamp.

How will it all work out? Will Sarah get the happily ever after she's been hoping for?

I wish I knew!

(Ha. I *do* know. I wrote it! But I can't just give away the ending so easily, can I?)

What I know for sure is that writing these crazy characters for the past five-plus years has been a pleasure and I'm going to miss them very much! I hope you've enjoyed the journey and that you're as pleased as I am with the ending to Sarah's story . . .

Happy Reading!

Michelle Rowen

www.michellerowen.com

*Want to know more about romances at
Grand Central Publishing and Forever?
Get the scoop online!*

GRAND CENTRAL PUBLISHING'S
ROMANCE HOMEPAGE

Visit us at www.hachettebookgroup.com/romance
for all the latest news, reviews, and chapter excerpts!

NEW AND UPCOMING TITLES

Each month we feature our new titles
and reader favorites.

CONTESTS AND GIVEAWAYS

We give away galleys, autographed copies,
and all kinds of fun stuff.

AUTHOR INFO

You'll find bios, articles, and links to personal
websites for all your favorite authors—and
so much more!

THE BUZZ

Sign up for our monthly romance newsletter,
and be the first to read all about it!